CONVOY SOUTH

BY THE SAME AUTHOR:

CONVOY SOUTH

Philip McCutchan

St. Martin's Press
New York

Library of Congress Cataloging-in-Publication Data

McCutchan, Philip.
      Convoy south / Philip McCutchan.
          p.   cm.
      ISBN 0-312-02178-X
       1. World War, 1939-1945—Fiction.   I. Title.
    PR6063.A167C66 1988
    823'.914—dc19   88-14782
                                              CIP

First published in Great Britain by George Weidenfeld & Nicolson Limited.

First U.S. Edition

10 9 8 7 6 5 4 3 2 1

890283

One

By now the convoy was well to the westward of Cape Leeuwin, having taken its departure some days before from that so often stormy promontory to the east of which lay the Great Australian Bight, where the waters of the Southern Ocean ran clear from the Antarctic wastes. The ships had made a little northing so as to come free so far as possible of the westerlies that blew without cease around the bottom of the world, blustering past Cape Horn and the Cape of Good Hope, below Australia and New Zealand, to fetch up once again off the pitch of the Horn. On the early part of this voyage the ships had met exceptionally bad weather – though not entirely unexpected in the Australian mid-winter of July, when the Bight became a grim waste of mountainous waves and flung spume that lay like heavy mist over the waters; a time of damp cold and an atmosphere of gloom, depressing in the extreme.

But now, clear of Australian waters, the weather was moderating.

Commodore John Mason Kemp, on the bridge of the Royal Fleet Auxiliary oiler *Coverdale*, chosen as the Commodore's ship on account of her reserve speed and manoeuvrability, lifted his binoculars to the horizons all around. It was a blue morning, with white horses curling from the wave crests, the ships still steaming into the fringe of a strong westerly but with the rain gone and the feel of better weather ahead. Kemp studied the escorts: ahead of the convoy, one on either bow, were two destroyers of the Royal Australian Navy, *Timor* and *Ayers*; away astern was one more destroyer, HMAS *Bass*, acting as rearguard and ready to chivvy

1

any stragglers. Leading the whole convoy, ahead of the Commodore's ship, was the senior officer of the escort in the cruiser *Rhondda*.

Kemp paced the bridge, then came to rest beside his assistant, a young sub-lieutenant of the Royal Canadian Naval Volunteer Reserve. 'Fresh, Cutler. Fresh but no more than that. It'll warm up soon.'

'Yes, sir, Com –' Cutler, a United States citizen, in fact, who had been anxious to join in the War in advance of the rest of his countrymen, bit off the rest of the form of address. Kemp didn't like being addressed as both sir and Commodore, but Cutler had found the habit hard to drop. 'Sooner the better, I guess.'

'You may change your mind once we're into the South Atlantic and coming up to the tropics.'

Kemp felt unusually tired: the long-drawn war at sea had become a strain in itself when you had reached middle age . . . and now that wasn't all. For many days and nights Kemp had had the extra worry, the personal anxiety as a result of news that had reached him in Sydney of a sinking, a convoy escort in the Mediterranean. Until he was given further news the anxiety would continue; but he was doing his best to thrust it down and not let it show.

The sun was up now and Kemp was grateful for the touch of physical comfort. Warmth stole slowly into his bones, penetrating the oilskin that he hadn't yet discarded. Probably it wouldn't be long now before the dress-of-the-day signal was made from the *Rhondda*: time soon to shift into lighter clothing, Number Thirteens – white shirts and shorts – for the underlying temperature was tending high if until now overlaid by the filthy weather, the wet and the wind: the deadly cold of the Bight was far behind them.

But when the signal came it was not concerned with anything so mundane as dress: it was the signal that had been half expected ever since the convoy had cleared away from the Australian coast. The big signalling projector sprang into life from the *Rhondda*'s flag deck; Kemp's convoy signalman, Leading Signalman Good-enough, was beaten to the acknowledgement by the *Coverdale*'s own signalman, Gannock, ex-yeoman of signals RN and anxious to let wartime ratings know he hadn't lost his speed in his old age. He reported to the master, Captain Dempsey.

'From senior officer, sir, addressed escort repeated Commodore. *"Radar indicates vessels twelve miles bearing 315 degrees. No identification, am investigating. Remainder of escort will maintain course and speed."* '

'Thank you, Gannock.' Dempsey caught Kemp's eye. 'This is it, Commodore.'

Kemp gave a tight grin and rubbed the weariness from his eyes with a sunburned hand. 'An open mind for now, Captain, but I'll ask you to go to first degree of readiness. Cutler?'

'Sir?'

'Make to all ships in convoy, assume first degree, maintain course and speed but stand by for immediate orders.'

As the messge was passed by light from the *Coverdale*, the officers on the bridge saw the cruiser alter to starboard and increase her own speed, coming up to her maximum, butting her stem into the sea so that an immense white bow wave curled back to mingle with her streaming wake. Within the next ten minutes the further signal had come, read off this time by Leading Signalman Goodenough.

'Commerce raider, sir, believed to be *Kormoran*. *Rhondda*'s engaging.' Goodenough added, 'Senior officer's hoisting battle ensigns, sir.'

A moment later the *Rhondda*'s 6-inch turrets opened in flashes of distant flame and heavy belches of smoke. Kemp turned to Dempsey. 'The bag, Captain. That's the first priority.'

'Taken care of,' Dempsey said. 'Ready for ditching the moment you give the word.' As he finished speaking a bright flash was seen below the *Rhondda*'s bridge superstructure, then another higher up, and the cruiser's foremast crashed down on the searchlight platform aft. *Kormoran*, it seemed, could have got the first blow in.

ii

Just three weeks earlier, Commodore Mason Kemp had brought another convoy into Sydney, loaded chiefly with heavy machinery and war material – armoured military vehicles, artillery, ammunition – to aid Australia's defence against a possible invasion by the Japanese armies. After the devastation of Pearl Harbor, which to Thomas B. Cutler's guilty relief had brought the United States into the War, it was thought possible that the Japanese were ready for an all-out assault against what was left of the British Empire. As he brought his ship in past Sydney Heads, Commodore Kemp was not yet aware of extraordinary decisions already being formulated in the minds of the Chiefs of Staff on both sides of the North Atlantic far, far away that were to send him to sea again within so short a time taking a division of troops away from Australia's defence to be landed across the world in USA and thence UK; neither that weird quirk of the high command's mind, nor its ultimate purpose, had interfered with Kemp's simple pleasure in once again taking a ship into Port Jackson harbour to secure alongside at Circular Quay as he had done countless times in the happy days of peacetime sailoring. Kemp was Royal Naval Reserve, one of the professional naval reservists who had earned their qualifications in the Merchant Service and in time of war put them at the disposal of the Admiralty to serve in HM ships and shore establishments or, as in his case, as commodores of convoys.

Kemp had served the Mediterranean-Australia Line for most of his career to date, from junior fourth officer to master; and for all that time Sydney had been his turn-round port at the Australian end of the run. Tilbury and Sydney, each as familiar to him as his cottage in Meopham in Kent – Tilbury and Sydney, and in between Gibraltar, Malta, Port Said, Suez, Aden, Colombo, Fremantle, Adelaide, Melbourne, all as regular as clockwork. The Australian arrival in Gage Roads, Fremantle after the fancy dress ball customarily held the night before . . . the Australian port forms, the P2s, customs, sales tax, prices going up in the bars and ship's shop, Australian accents as the coastal passengers embarked, the start of the break-up of shipboard friendships and romances . . . it had been a way of life utterly unknown to shoresiders and it had all ended abruptly with the outbreak of the War in September 1939 when Kemp had brought the Mediterranean-Australia Line's *Ardara* into Tilbury to find himself bidden to attend the Admiralty for appointment to the naval service. From then on it had been unending convoy duty, across the North Atlantic time and again, or northward bound to Russian ports with vital cargoes to be used against Hitler's invading armies, Nazi legions as ruthless as the hordes of Attila the Hun; or eastwards through the Gibraltar Strait to bring succour to

4

beseiged Malta, and on again to Alexandria or Port Said to take reinforcements to the British Army ready to extend across North Africa from Egypt.

It was a very different story from the glitter of liner life, from the bugles that called the first-class passengers to the saloon in their evening dress, from hot, balmy days when crossing the Indian Ocean, sultry moonlit nights, port arrivals in the haze of early dawn . . . passengers, some of them very wealthy, many of them good company for a master at his table in the first-class saloon, some of them odious, but all of them suitably impressed by the brassbound autonomy of a shipmaster aboard his own command.

That day of entry three weeks before, Kemp had watched the familiar landmarks slide past as he had come inward of Sydney Heads: North Harbour away to starboard, running down to Manly Beach where sun-bronzed Australians had swum under the care of the lifeguards and the shark barrier; past Obelisk Bay and the Military Reserve, into the West Channel for Port Jackson, Watson's Bay coming up on his port side . . . Bradley Head, Rose Bay and Shark Island . . . Darling Point and then Garden Island, the naval base where now there were lean grey warships in greater quantity than the last time Kemp had seen Sydney. Dead ahead the great harbour bridge, with streams of traffic crossing; before the bridge, the turn to port to come alongside Circular Quay, the busy harbour tugs pushing the ship in.

Then, as the ship's master rang down Finished with Engines and the shore gangway was put in place, an act of courtesy: Commodore Kemp found a visitor waiting when he went below to his cabin a few minutes later: Hugh MacAndrew, Mediterranean-Australia Lines' General Manager in Australia.

'Well, John. I got the word you were bringing this convoy in. Welcome home! It's nice to see you . . . been a long while. Notice any changes, do you?'

Kemp grinned as they shook hands. 'Not so many small boats cluttering up the entry channel. Not so many gawpers on the quay. All the company colours gone. More warships.'

'Don't you know there's a war on?' MacAndrew winked. 'Go on, say it: do we have that bloody idiotic phrase out here as well? Answer: yes, we do. Excuse for every bloody balls-up, every shortage, not that we have that many shortages.' The General

Manager's expression altered. 'What sort of a war have you had, John?'

'So-so,' Kemp answered non-committally. 'Care for a gin?'

'Not got any Vickers yet, have you?'

'Yes,' Kemp said. 'I brought a bottle ashore from the *Ardara* in Tilbury . . . back in '39. Sheer nostalgia. I promised myself I'd open it the first time I came back to Sydney.'

'Well, good on you, John! I'll have a case sent aboard your homeward ship. How's the missus, and the children?'

'All well – or I hope they are. The boys . . . they're both at sea now themselves.'

'You don't say? Well, I reckon time passes.' As Kemp rang for his steward and the Vickers' gin, MacAndrew went on, 'You had a grandmother, right? Pretty old by now, eh?'

'Not so far off a hundred. A bit of a strain on Mary. When they get to that age, they tend to complain.' Kemp, stretched out now in an easy chair, found home thoughts crowding. What he would give to have his family around him again, to have the boys as they were as children, with no anxieties for their safety to disturb the mind of a convoy commodore at sea. His thoughts drifted back: families were never allowed to travel in the same ship, but a couple of years before the war Kemp had booked passages for them aboard another of the company's ships at a time when his own ship would be cruising out of Sydney and he would have time to see a good deal of them between cruises. That was when MacAndrew had met them; it had been a very happy time, a wonderful holiday to look back on. It could never come again now the boys were grown up.

Kemp's steward poured the gin: both men took it with plain water. There wasn't time even for a toast before the Commodore had another visitor: a lieutenant of the RANVR. Commodore Kemp was requested to attend at Naval HQ immediately.

iii

A staff car had been waiting: Kemp was driven from Circular Quay, along Macquarie Street and down towards the Domain and Woolloomooloo, parts he had known well as a junior officer in the Line. You always took precautions in that part of Sydney, in fact, if you were wise, you used taxis to and from any ship berthed at Woolloomooloo. Along the roofs of the houses bordering the street, the sandbaggers lurked. A swing of a bag on the end of a rope had put many a seaman out for the count, and when he recovered, if indeed he did, he found his money gone. Sydney Town, as the old-time square-rigged seamen had known it, could still be a place of danger; but now the peacetime dangers had been overlaid by the larger dangers of the War. At Woolloomooloo a picquet-boat had been waiting, and Kemp was transferred to this, together with the young lieutenant, and taken across the water to Garden Island where once again he saw the many warships at the berths, cruisers and destroyers and some small craft. Some of them were from the British Navy, others were Australian or from New Zealand. Kemp was taken into Naval HQ, where a Rear-Admiral of the Australian Navy was awaiting him. There were no delays: Kemp sensed urgency, and the welcome was brief.

'Ah, Kemp. You're known out here, of course. Glad to have you. Sorry it's not going to be for long. All right, Glover.' The Rear-Admiral waved a hand at the lieutenant, who came to attention and left the room. 'No peace for convoy commodores, Kemp.'

'You mean another convoy's forming up, sir?'

'Correct, but it won't be sailing immediately. That's all I can say for now, except that something big is in the air and there's a very heavy security shield. I was told to give you your orders personally – your immediate orders, that is.' The Rear-Admiral paused, looked for a moment out of a large window, across Port Jackson harbour towards Kurraba Point. Kemp followed his gaze: the sun was high and the water was sparkling as he remembered it over so many years. A couple of large tankers were lying at anchor off Kurraba Point itself, one of them wearing the Blue Ensign with the fouled anchor in the fly, the ensign of the Royal Fleet Auxiliaries. The Rear-Admiral began speaking again. 'You're for Canberra, Kemp.'

'Canberra? A far cry from the sea and convoys!'

'You won't be there long. You'll pick up orders, that's all. You'll go incognito. Plain clothes. Got any with you?'

'No, sir, I –'

'Didn't think you would have. I've made arrangements – you'll

7

have to make do whether or not they fit. I'll see to it that your gear's removed from your present ship and taken aboard your next. You'll leave for Canberra the moment you're shifted into plain clothes. There's a train in . . .' The Rear-Admiral looked at his wrist watch. '. . . one hour and ten minutes precisely.' He added, 'On arrival you'll report to the offices of the Military Board.' He banged at a bell on his desk and at once the lieutenant reappeared. 'Commodore Kemp's ready to change his identity,' he said. He held out a hand to Kemp as he got to his feet. 'The best of luck, Commodore, and I'm sorry to be delivering you to the bloody pongoes, my word! Thank God we've got a navy.'

Two

It hadn't been difficult to guess that the next convoy was to be a troop lift; and movements of troops always had a high security classification. But where to? There were already Australian and New Zealand armies in the field in North Africa. Tobruk, Derna, Benghazi, Mersa Matruh, in and out and in again as the fortunes of the war swayed this way and that, and Kemp believed that an Australian brigade had in fact recently been withdrawn on replacement by Polish and British units. Lieutenant-General Sir Leslie Morshead had commanded in the Tobruk area – a territorial soldier of distinction and until called up for the War, Hugh MacAndrew's opposite number in a rival shipping company. Morshead had been the Orient Line's General Manager in Australia, one up for the sea services. Kemp, as he was driven across Sydney in a plain car, recalled the Rear-Admiral's comment about pongoes, and grinned to himself. With exceptions, the pongo mind tended towards rigidity, or so seamen liked to make out.

Kemp shifted uncomfortably in an ill-fitting suit, tight under the arms and across the chest. Kemp was a big man and his very size was now causing him to feel conspicuous in lurid light blue of execrable taste, a colour not unlike the 'hospital blues' worn by ambulant other-rank patients in military medical establishments. He wore his own white uniform shirt but the black tie had been replaced by a red one with yellow spots; and Kemp had been provided with a brown pork-pie hat with a small feather in the band. He felt like a greengrocer on a bank holiday.

Deposited at the railway station complete with return ticket,

9

Kemp settled into the train for Canberra, around a hundred and fifty miles south from Sydney. His appointment with the Military Board was for four p.m. which gave him time in hand. The staff lieutenant had provided him with reading matter: the *Sydney Morning Herald*, and the *Sydney Sun*. Just as the train started to pull out, two soldiers came aboard with what looked like a bum's rush. Both were drunk; Kemp used the *Sydney Morning Herald* as a shield. There was heavy belching and a strong brewery smell: Australians liked their beer.

'Got the time, mate?'

The remark was addressed to Kemp; he glanced at his watch and gave it.

'Bloody pom.'

Kemp continued to read his newspaper.

'I said, bloody pom.'

'Yes. I heard you.'

The drunken soldier lurched to his feet and stood over Kemp. 'Want to make something of it, eh?'

'Not particularly.'

'Not partic'ly,' the soldier repeated in a mincing voice. 'Bloody pom scum, ought to be in bloody uniform, letting real men fight the bloody war for you!'

Kemp put down his newspaper. 'Shut your mouth,' he said. He didn't raise his voice.

'Eh?'

'You heard me.' Kemp got to his feet, towered over the soldier. 'One more word out of you, soldier, and I'll heave you off the train.'

The drunk swayed backwards, looked towards his mate but without result: the other man had passed out cold. Kemp resumed his seat. He had no further trouble. The soldier revenged himself in safety by keeping up, nearly all the way to Canberra, a low monologue about the iniquities of bloody poms. To Kemp, the man hadn't the look of belonging to a fighting unit; he was probably a clerk in some military headquarters in the capital. Such were frequently more aggressive than the men who did the fighting.

Kemp was shown into the office of a staff brigadier, a bulbous-faced man whose red tabs clashed with his nose.

'Good of you to come along, Commodore.'

Kemp grinned. 'Not much option.'

'I suppose not. Well, I'll not keep you here longer than it takes to tell.' The brigadier extended a hand towards a chair. 'As you say at sea, I believe – bring your arse to an anchor.'

Kemp sat, relieved that the brigadier appeared to be human. As if to give the lie to his nose, the soldier offered tea, which Kemp accepted. A bell-push was activated and an orderly came in. Whilst awaiting the tea, the brigadier started.

'Name's Hennessy, by the way. Irish stock. All you poms like to think we in Australia are descended from convicts. A lot of us are but I'm not. My ancestors didn't get found out. Me own great-granddad was a foot soldier in the British Army, sent out to guard the other buggers. Married an Aussie girl and settled. Right, now.' The brigadier pushed papers about on his desk, which looked like a filing system gone mad. 'Your convoy. Troops. A whole Aussie division to be lifted in four liners. *Asian Star*, *Asturias*, *Southern Cross*, *Carlisle Castle*. They'll all be bloody packed out with men and equipment. This is to be a military convoy, right? You'll have three armament carriers, all in ballast . . . plus three grain ships tagged on to break off for UK somewhere around the Azores. Right so far, Commodore?'

Kemp nodded. 'And the troops, and the armament ships? Mediterranean – North Africa, Egypt?'

'No, reckon not. Norfolk, Virginia.'

Kemp was astonished. 'The US? What in heaven's name for?'

'You may well ask. Look, I'm as bloody flabbergasted as you are. Don't tell me you've just brought out a war materials convoy from home – I know that – to give us the wherewithal to fight off any Jap invasion in the north and now we're under orders to strip ourselves of a fighting division –'

'May I,' Kemp interrupted, 'ask whose orders?'

'Your war cabinet. I wouldn't be positive, but I believe it's Churchill's personal idea. It's fairly common knowledge that one day there's to be a second front opened up and –' Hennessy broke off as the tea-tray was brought in and the orderly poured and handed the cups round. When the man had gone Hennessy went

11

on, 'We reckon Churchill's already starting the troop build-up in the UK. God knows when it'll come, but it can't surely be yet. The Allies . . . we've got our hands full in North Africa, dealing with bloody Rommel. But the orders from the high command are that we strip ourselves as I just said – us down under, that is. Let bloody Australia sink, just so long as UK stays afloat.' The nose, under the stress of obviously strong emotion and disapproval, grew deeper in colour. 'Well, that's poms for you. I'm not being personal, of course.'

'I know that, Brigadier. And I understand how you feel.' Kemp paused, thinking ahead. It wasn't going to be a happy convoy, at any rate aboard the liners acting as troop transports, not with a whole division probably feeling as disgruntled as Hennessy, every man knowing that he was depleting his homeland's defence. Kemp knew that the anxieties about a possible Japanese invasion were real enough. Someone in Whitehall, he believed, had really pulled a boner this time.

He asked a further question. 'You spoke of a build-up in UK. Do I take it your troops will be going on across the Atlantic straight away?'

Hennessy shook his head. 'No, you don't. They're to be held in the States. Further training's the given reason. Well, it may be so, but I have other thoughts. They're being held there because it's safer. Out of the way of the Nazi bombers, right up to the time Churchill feels he's ready to go. And –'

'And that,' Kemp said heavily, 'could be years yet.'

'Exactly – too bloody right! A whole Aussie division, kicking their heels. If you as a seaman like to say the military mind's a madhouse, well, I'm not going to disagree, sorry as I am to have to say it.'

Kemp blew out his cheeks: any comment would be superfluous: Hennessy had said it all. But he said, 'All this isn't the reason I was ordered to report here. Is it?'

'Partly, yes. I wanted you to know, you personally, as the convoy Commodore – to know how we feel. I think that's your due – anyone in command of anything has to know the pulse, so to say. The Navy in Sydney, they wouldn't put it across the same. Anyway, that's how I looked at it. Maybe I'm just getting old, gathering bees in me bonnet. But of course there is something else. It's this.'

Hennessy pushed his chair back a little way and reached into the middle drawer of his desk. He brought out a canvas bag and laid it on the desk. It was around nine inches square and was pierced by a number of holes with brass eyelets. When Hennessy had laid the bag on his desk there had been a noticeable thud: it was lead-weighted so that when thrown overboard in an emergency it would sink fast.

'Vital,' Hennessy said. 'Most Secret classification. By Hand Of Officer throughout. Right now, By Hand Of Commodore.'

'For Sydney?'

'Wrong again. For Washington – the Pentagon. It'll be collected from you at the US Navy Operating Base in Norfolk.'

'I see.' Kemp paused. 'Am I to know its contents, in a broad sense, that is?'

'In a broad sense, yes. That bag contains detailed information, garnered by our intelligence boys, as to the Jap intentions to saturate New Guinea and Papua. When they do that, they'll be as far as the Torres Strait and the Arafura Sea. . . . Reckon I don't need to tell you, just the hundred miles of the Torres Strait'll separate us from the Jap armies.' Hennessy grinned suddenly. 'Reckon that brings me full circle, eh? Back to a moan about taking our troops off us. . . .'

iii

Kemp left the offices of the Military Board with Hennessy's parting words loading his mind: if ever that bag fell into enemy hands it would be dynamite, for if the contents became known the Japanese high command would surely move before Australia was fully ready – and Hennessy had said that they were in fact far from ready. Any invasion of Australia by way of the Torres Strait and the Cape York Peninsula would bring the Japanese hordes quickly down into Queensland and that departing division would be badly needed; but it had been impossible to shift the top brass in Canberra who considered the intelligence reports to be hysterical, considered that the threat if and when it came could be met and held without too much strain. Hennessy had disagreed violently with his own superiors: as it happened he had been in Singapore with the British troops when the Japs had come in

strength and the great naval and military base had been sur-
rendered; Hennessy had got out by the skin of his teeth and a
dangerous sea voyage in a fishing boat. He knew the Jap potential
at first hand. Though he didn't in fact say as much, Kemp was left
with the strong impression that the despatch of the vital bag was
a case of Hennessy acting on his own initiative and without the
knowledge of the brass. Also that in basis the bag's contents were
a plea for United States assistance and a hint that the Australian
division might yet be recalled in defiance of the wishes of the
British war cabinet. When Kemp had asked why the information
couldn't be sent by cyphered signal Hennessy had shrugged and
said any cypher was liable to be cracked. True enough: but – again
a guess – Kemp figured that a brigadier acting behind the back of
the brass would be unlikely to find the radio waves open to him.

In the meantime the security appeared crazy: the canvas bag
was wrapped in a brown paper parcel and given a sticker with
Happy Birthday on it and some pink ribbon binding. A present
for the kids, Hennessy said. No car was provided to take Kemp to
the railway station – that could make him conspicuous, he was
told, since cars were not provided for all and sundry – there was a
severe petrol shortage just as there was back in UK. Off Kemp
went with the parcel under his arm. He felt like a good strong
drink but wasn't going to take the risk so long as he had the bag in
his charge. Australia was now approaching its drunkest hour, the
daily ritual when all drinking Aussies got well and truly tanked
up before the bars shut for the night at six p.m. Kemp recalled
past days in Sydney, the Long Bar of the Hotel Australia – said to
be the world's longest – packed like the Queen's Hall on the last
night of the proms, all male, each man fighting for his pints of
beer, one after another, an endless glug until the point of near
paralysis was reached when the drunks seethed blindly out into
the streets as the shutters came down.

The train journey back was uneventful if somewhat fraught
with anxiety: Kemp didn't care for the close proximity of military
secrets. On arrival he took a cab to Woolloomooloo, checked in at
the naval picquet-house and got a message sent across to Garden
Island for a boat. At the island he found that the Rear-Admiral
had, in naval parlance, gone ashore – in other words, home. The
staff lieutenant took temporary charge of the brown-paper
parcel, locking it in a safe without asking any questions. He

confirmed that Kemp's gear had been shifted from the Commodore's ship and a room booked for him in the Hotel Australia.

He had a fragment of news: the sailing date of the convoy had not yet been fixed but the name of the Commodore's ship had been notified.

'One of the liners?' Kemp asked.

'No, sir. RFA *Coverdale*. You'll be pretty comfortable, sir.'

Kemp nodded but didn't comment: he had guessed the likely reason – the greater speed and manoeuvrability. But tankers were always liable to blow up a sight faster than anything else short of an ammunition ship. Kemp, in his time of war service, had seen them go up like roaring bonfires spouting out streams of burning oil fuel, or simply disintegrating in one big flash if they had been carrying aviation spirit. He had always hoped he would never be put aboard a tanker; but he would never say so.

All he did was to ask, 'Where's my assistant – Cutler?'

'Supervising your gear in the Hotel Australia, sir.'

'Right. I'll be joining him directly. You'll know where I am if I'm wanted. I'll not be going out again.'

He saw, or maybe he just fancied he saw, a glint of suppressed humour in the lieutenant's eye, almost a smirk. Well, let him think the Commodore was an old fuddy-duddy. The young were mostly predictable: when that lieutenant had a free night on the town he would make the most of it, and why not? Drink and women, the easy lay. Kemp had been young once. But at fifty-three you looked at things differently, or anyway he did. Kemp's family was always much on his mind: Mary, facing rationing and other shortages at home, Nazi bombing, constant alerts day or night – Meopham in Kent was in one of Britain's most dangerous corners – cold in winter because of power shortages or often total failures if the Nazi bomb aimers had hit their targets. And always worrying about her three menfolk out at sea. It wouldn't be fair to do anything but have a drink and a meal and go to bed.

iv

A couple of hours before Kemp had got back from Canberra, a hand message had gone across by boat from Garden Island to Kurraba Point, being put aboard RFA *Coverdale* addressed to the

15

master, Captain Giles Dempsey. When the envelope was brought to his cabin, Dempsey was having a gin with his chief officer.

He read the message and said, 'God damn!'

'What is it, sir?'

'We're to be Commodore's ship, a doubtful honour sure enough.'

'A bit of variety,' Harlow said vaguely.

Dempsey glared. 'I can do without that, thank you! The Commodore's ship – always a special target at the best of times, and no tanker needs to be singled out.'

'Nothing we can do about it, sir.'

'I know that. You're full of helpful suggestions, Harlow, like a dog is of fleas. Better have another gin to keep your mouth full.'

'Thank you, sir.' Harlow, as his glass was refilled, looked covertly at the master. Old Dempsey wasn't all that worried about being singled out as Commodore's ship. He had sailed the seas in peace and war aboard fleet oilers too long for that; the risks had always been there and would remain just as long as they all stayed at sea. The presence of the Commodore wouldn't make all that much difference to the Germans or the Japs and Harlow, who along with Dempsey knew the composition of the forth-coming convoy though not as yet its destination, believed that Commodore or no Commodore the first target would be the troop transports currently lying beyond the harbour bridge at Pyrmont. There was something else eating deeply into Dempsey, and Harlow knew very well what it was, for he'd sailed with Dempsey ever since the outbreak of war. Dempsey would dislike having nanny looking over his shoulder. This Commodore could, for all they knew, be a pernickety old bugger, might even be an ancient, retired admiral crammed to the gills with memories of days when he had commanded battle fleets and bowled captains down like ninepins. Dempsey wouldn't go much on that for like all the officers and men of the RFA, he was basically of the Merchant Service. All the officers had masters' or chief engineers' certificates gained before they had entered Admiralty service; their uniforms were those of the Merchant Service except for the cap badge, which was basically RN but with the silver anchor encircled by a blue lifebuoy bearing the letters RFA. In a sense they fell between two stools, a part of each service. But Dempsey, an Irishman, from the wild country of Connemara, still saw himself as a master mariner first and foremost and was inclined to act independently of the RN.

Much was going to depend on the Commodore of the convoy.

v

In the ratings' accommodation aboard the Commodore's ship Petty Officer Rattray, a recalled Fleet Reservist with the non-substantive rating of gunner's mate, was writing a letter home, home being a two up, two down in a road off Arundel Street in Portsmouth. Rattray wrote slowly with an indelible pencil, the writing purple from a sucked tip. Ratty, as he'd been known to his equals in pre-war days, was no scholar and had surprised even himself when he'd completed the gunner's mates' course at Whale Island. Hence his letter home was stilted, short, and contained a lie: he wrote that he hoped the wife's mother was keeping well. This was expected of him. If he left it out the next letter from Pompey would contain a rebuke. Rattray's mother-in-law was accorded the respect due to great age, and in his absence she ruled the home. Rattray had gone out on pension back in 1932 and got himself a job as handyman in a gunsmith's shop, which seemed suitable enough for an ex-gunner's mate, and he had enjoyed it at first.

Until Ma Bates had been left a widow and come and plonked herself on him and his wife, after which life had gone very sour. . . .

Petty Officer Rattray finished his letter, licked the envelope and stuck it down, giving a long-suffering sigh. He'd been overjoyed to be recalled to active service in 1939; it had seemed like a kindly act of God, or even of Herr Hitler who could almost have started the war specially to free Rattray of his mother-in-law. The first thing he'd done had been to have a good old booze-up with a lot of his old mates who'd also turned up in the petty officers' mess in Pompey barracks. Life had been great, the more so when he did a course for defensively equipped merchant ships and got a draft to sea in charge of a gun's crew aboard, first, a cargo ship and then the *Coverdale*, which he preferred because she was within the ambit of the Admiralty and carried a

17

signalman who'd once been a yeoman of signals and had served aboard the old *Iron Duke* with Rattray.

The joy hadn't entirely lasted: his mother-in-law was with him still, at any rate on paper. Every letter from Doris contained news of her in detail: how she felt, what she said, the state of her bowels, her rheumatics, her teeth, corns, bunged-up ears, indigestion, heart, lungs, the lot. What her opinion was of the War, Churchill, Anthony Eden, Hitler, Mussolini and the Japs, the latter added only recently, after Pearl Harbor, like the Americans. And the Royal Family. Even though the old biddy was a socialist she had a lot of time for the King, and this was the one and only point on which they saw eye to eye.

As Petty Officer Rattray finished sealing down the mendacious hope for his mother-in-law's well-being there was a tap at his cabin door.

Rattray called out, 'Yer?'

A full-stomached leading seaman with a lurid purple birthmark disfiguring his face appeared in the doorway: Stripey Sinker, Rattray's Number Two. He said, 'Just going to nip ashore, PO.'

'Oh? Who says so, might I ask?'

Sinker gave a cough. 'Asking permission, like.'

'That's better. Piss off, do.' Rattray chuckled. 'Don't take that as an invite. Remember there's a war on. So don't overdo the muck they call beer out here.'

'As if I would,' Sinker said virtuously. 'You know me, PO.'

'Which is why I issued the warning. Here.' Rattray chucked the letter across to the leading seaman. 'Post this for me, eh? Fleet mail box.'

'Right, PO.' Leading Seaman Sinker waddled off, making for the gangway to await the routine call of the harbour boat detailed to attend on the ships at anchor off Kurraba Point. He wore a look of keen anticipation, but it wasn't for the Aussie beer, which he agreed was gnat's piss compared with what they brewed in the UK. It tasted like straw and looked like it too, a nasty unappetising yellow. Sinker had found himself an 'up homers' in Sydney. It had been fast work, since the *Coverdale* had been in port only a week. Sinker's 'up homers' was down by Kings Cross – the Cross, the Aussies called it – which was a kind of Soho, night life, prozzies, the lot. Dinah Deeling wasn't a prozzy, of course, but she was willing enough and Sinker suffered from continuous desires that had to be satisfied. His birthmark was no help at all; some women fled from it. Dinah, whose old man was somewhere in North Africa fighting Rommel, had a job in a shoe shop down the Cross, both of which circumstances left her free in the evenings. Stripey Sinker's interest had first been aroused when he'd entered a bar a little ahead of closing time and had been squashed against her. At that time he hadn't known enough of Australia to be surprised at seeing a woman in a bar, and anyway she'd been obviously accepted by the men. What had tickled his interest had been a huge Australian wearing a bush hat and a sort of lumber jacket against the winter chills and looking as though he'd come in from the outback who had addressed the woman in a carrying shout – Australians, Stripey found, always shouted.

'And 'ow's Feeling Deeling tonight, eh?'

She'd given him a cheeky answer and had turned round virtually into Stripey's arms, where she had remained since the crush forced his arms tightly about her. Feeling Deeling; it held possibilities and Stripey, never slow when it came to trying it on with women even if he hadn't always succeeded, had made the most of it. He would buy her a meal, he said.

'Expensive, mate.'

Stripey made up his mind to be generous. 'Sod the expense, buy the cat a goldfish.'

He'd gone ashore each night thereafter; he had to work watch and watch with the PO, but Rattray didn't seem interested in going ashore, so that wasn't a problem. That first night, after the meal, they'd gone to the girl's flat over a butcher's shop and he'd stayed till morning. Feeling Deeling was very experienced but she definitely wasn't on the game – she was selective, she said, and never did it for money, not in a direct sense anyway. That was a relief: women who did it for cash on the nail could have nasty diseases, and Stripey Sinker, who'd once caught a dose in Hong Kong, tended to be careful. Feeling Deeling didn't do it for love exactly, though she did do it because she liked it, and liked the British Navy and what the British Navy was prepared to spend on her. Stripey Sinker was relieved that there were no Yanks around yet.

Tonight he walked from the landing stage at Woolloomooloo,

across the edge of the Domain towards the Cross, whistling to himself. *There'll always be an England . . . wherever there's a bit in bed. . . .* The words, as they ran through his head, being mostly his own. Dinah was very attractive: slim, petite, dark with big eyes and long lashes and a seductive scent that had over-ridden the smell of beer and sweat in the bar. Big breasts and all, like the heavy fenders they put out when a ship went alongside in the dockyard. Stripey knew the saying: every man was either a tit man or a bottom man. Stripey was both, which he felt ought to be unusual. Dinah was pretty good down there as well. Feeling Deeling, eh! And at a guess she wasn't much more than say twenty-four or five. That did his ego a lot of good: he wasn't going to see forty again. Of course, his rate might have helped: that first night, Dinah had taken an interest in his badges, gold ones since he'd worn his Number One uniform. He'd explained.

'The anchor, see, that means I'm a leading 'and.'

'And the three chevrons, like a sergeant?'

'Good Conduct badges. Thirteen years exemplary service. Stripes . . . that why they call me Stripey.'

'An important man. . . .'

'Well, you might say so. Aboard a ship.'

'And the crossed guns?'

'Gunnery rate. The star, like, above them guns . . . means I'm a gunlayer. What lays the guns on the bleeding Jerries.'

'You are so . . . interesting.' The voice was sultry and when she was undressed she was darkish all over, almost like someone from a South Sea island. 'Men who go to sea . . . you are going to sea again soon?'

'Could be for all I know. Ships do.'

'So interesting. . . .'

'Yes, well, it's all routine, like, far as I'm concerned, nothing to it.' Stripey's hand moved; he didn't want to talk about the bleeding Andrew or about the *Coverdale*; that wasn't what he'd come ashore for. She didn't either and the questions stopped. His hand roved again. It was somewhat calloused from a working lifetime spent hauling on ropes and handling heavy steel gun parts, but women always liked real men and certainly Dinah didn't seem to mind.

20

Kemp turned in early, after spending a while looking from his window at the lights of Sydney. You didn't see city lights so often in these dark days of war. The whole of England, under the stringency of the blackout, seemed to have stepped into the dark ages. London's streets, though Kemp in fact avoided the place whenever he could, were as dark as the night itself. Air raid wardens, officious men wearing steel helmets and armbands and carrying gas masks saw to that. Sydney in that sense was a blessed relief and quite a striking sight. From the window Kemp looked down on the New York-like pattern of straight streets crossed by other straight streets, well delineated in the lights.

There was plenty of life down there, plenty of crowds even though the bars were shut. Libertymen from the warships drifted, looking for women no doubt. Raucous song came up: a crowd of Australian soldiers on the rampage, seeking excitement. Perhaps they were some of those detailed for the troop lift to the United States. Kemp wished them all the luck in the world for their last few days in Australia but hoped there wouldn't be trouble between them and the British seamen. Fights so soon developed and didn't do anyone's image any good. Kemp's thoughts drifted homeward: once he'd got the convoy safely into Chesapeake Bay in Virginia he might, with luck, get orders for a homeward convoy across the North Atlantic – never a picnic but at least pointed in the right direction. Kemp had unpacked an overnight bag and brought out a silver-framed photograph of his wife. That photograph, taken just before the war, was always beside him, remindingly – as if he needed reminding.

He had drifted off to sleep when a knock came at his door and it opened.

'Who's that?' Kemp reached out for the light switch.

'It's me, sir.'

'Oh – Cutler. For God's sake . . . what is it?' Kemp sat up, ran a hand through tousled, greying hair. 'For a moment I thought I was back at sea. What's the panic?'

'No panic, sir, Commodore.' Cutler was looking awkward, standing unnecessarily at attention but fiddling with a brass button on his uniform jacket: he seemed almost in a state of embarrassment. He went on, 'I just took a phone call from Naval HQ, sir.'

'Well, go on, what was it?' Kemp was testy: he'd had the sort of day he didn't much care for, attending on shoreside bigwigs and travelling incognito in railway trains.

'Ship losses, sir.'

Suddenly Kemp felt a constriction in his throat, for no real reason. Many ships were lost in time of war; but there was a premonitive feeling because of Cutler's manner. Kemp said harshly, 'Let's have it, laddie.'

'Yes, sir. *Burnside*'s gone down. I'm very sorry, sir. But –'

'Survivors?'

'Not known yet, sir.'

'How did it happen?'

'Convoy through the Med, sir. Eyetie torpedo-bombers.' Cutler hesitated, fiddling again with his button. 'I'll let you know, of course, as soon as there's more news.'

'Thank you, Cutler.'

'I'm very sorry, sir.'

'I know, Cutler. Thank you. That's all.'

'Will you . . . be all right, sir?'

'Yes, Cutler, I'll be all right.'

'I guess a shot of Scotch –'

'If I feel in need, I'll call room service. Off you go, and turn in.'

Kemp's assistant left the room. Kemp got up, walked around in something of a daze. Two sons at sea, and one of them an RNVR sub-lieutenant in the destroyer *Burnside*. A little over twenty-one, was Harry. There had been a letter from him on the convoy's arrival in Sydney: he'd been enjoying life and was hoping he might get accelerated promotion to lieutenant, always assuming the Admiralty accepted his captain's recommendation.

Always assuming: there were so many potential slips. Kemp was a realist: that convoy through the Mediterranean – it would never stop to pick up survivors, not in the middle of an attack. The ships and their cargoes were the primary concern of the Commodore and the senior officer of the escort – in action, the only concern. And of course there would have been a lot of casualties before the *Burnside* had gone down. Kemp wished he could be with Mary now.

Three

'Boat, sir, coming across from Garden Island, a naval picquet-boat. It'll be the Commodore.'

'Thank you, Harlow.' Captain Dempsey, followed by the chief officer, left his day cabin and went down two decks to the accommodation ladder, pulling at starched shirt-cuffs as he went: starched cuffs were not easily laundered in wartime, but Dempsey felt that the first arrival of the Convoy Commodore merited their use. Dempsey believed in smartness: he had set a standard in the RFA that was recognized throughout the fleet. Ratings in the RFA ships were not provided with uniforms, at least not at the Admiralty's expense. Dempsey had always seen to it that each man in any ships he served in was provided with a seaman's cap and cap ribbon, and working overalls, all out of his own pocket, and he insisted they be worn at all times when aboard. He believed it paid dividends.

Standing just inboard of the platform at the head of the ladder, Dempsey and Harlow saluted as the Commodore ascended. Dempsey, like Cutler a few nights earlier, felt some embarrassment. News travelled fast between ships and shore establishments and the sinking of the *Burnside* had in any case been announced. Word of Commodore Mason Kemp's personal anxiety had reached the *Coverdale* along with the news, and so far as Dempsey was aware there had been no information about survivors, which didn't look too good. Other news had filtered through that Dempsey and Harlow were both pleased to hear: the Commodore was no dugout admiral. He was genuine RNR, a merchant service man like themselves. . . .

23

Kemp, at the head of the ladder, returned the officers' salutes.

'Good morning, Captain.'

'Good morning, Commodore. Welcome aboard.'

Kemp smiled, a rather drawn smile, and held out his hand, which Dempsey shook. 'You have a smart ship, Captain.'

'Thank you. The work of my chief officer, Mr Harlow.'

Kemp nodded; he seemed abstracted, as well he might Dempsey thought. 'I take it you're ready for sea, Captain Dempsey?'

'All ready.'

Behind the Commodore came Sub-Lieutenant Cutler followed by two ratings bringing up his and Kemp's personal gear. Dempsey turned and led the way to his quarters below the bridge, hands clasped behind a broad back, the four gold rings of a master riding above the starch. He offered drinks when they reached his day cabin.

'Thank you, whisky. Just a small one.' Kemp looked around the day cabin as Dempsey's steward brought glasses. 'You have comfortable quarters, Captain.'

Dempsey laughed. 'We need them! In peacetime we used to spend a good deal of time up the Persian Gulf at Abadan – a dump like that calls for some sort of compensation!'

Dempsey had the feeling they were both talking trivialities in order to avoid another topic of conversation, a mutual embarrassment. He coughed and uttered another superfluous remark. 'As I understand it, the troop transports leave first and we follow. Right?'

'Yes, quite right. The escort will precede the transports. Once we're outside the Heads, *Coverdale* takes up station ahead of the transports. Have you been in many convoys, Captain?'

'One or two. We work largely with the fleet, of course . . . and even when in convoy we're to some extent a part of the escort.'

Kemp nodded. 'Yes. With but not of! You fellows have a similarity with the Marines – what Kipling called "giddy hermaphrodites" if I remember correctly. Anyway – you'll know all about station keeping.' He paused, looking from the master's ports across the harbour towards Circular Quay: the Manly ferry was embarking passengers and there were a number of yachts about – not so many as in peacetime, as Kemp had remarked to Hugh MacAndrew, but it took more than a world war to keep the

Australians away from the water entirely. He hoped that they would keep well clear when the convoy left but doubted if they would: there would be plenty of people who'd want to wave a last farewell to the America-bound troops.

He spoke again to Dempsey. 'I'd appreciate a look around your bridge before we leave, and a run-down on how she handles.'

Dempsey led the way up the ladder to the bridge and wheelhouse, where the *Coverdale*'s second and third officers were making a last-minute check. Dempsey gave brief information: twin screws which made for good handling, plenty of speed in reserve over the convoy's advance – twenty-two knots if need be. The ship would be sailing with water ballast except for three of the cargo tanks. Apart from the facility to refuel the escort, you didn't take fuel oil from Australia to the United States. After Chesapeake Bay the *Coverdale* was under orders to proceed to Galveston, Texas to load for UK. As for the convoy, Kemp's orders were that they would enter Simonstown at the Cape for bunkers as necessary before making the long haul up the South Atlantic. Kemp looked fore and aft, towards the ship's arma-ment. Two 3-inch guns behind open gun shields, both on reinforced platforms, plus close-range weapons, Oerlikons, Lewis guns at each bridge-wing and on monkey's island above the wheelhouse and chart room, a single pom-pom mounted aft of the bridge, more small stuff on the deck above the engineers' accommodation in the stern and on each side of the fo'c'sle. There was the question of the naval guns' crews and Kemp decided to broach it with the ship's master right away.

'They're your permanent gunners, Captain, of course. You'll know I'm not bringing gunnery rates aboard with my own staff on this voyage.'

Dempsey nodded; Harlow, guessing what was coming, watched covertly for Dempsey to get his dander up. Kemp went on, 'It's up to you, naturally. But I'd appreciate it if my assistant and I could deal directly with them when necessary?'

Dempsey spread his hands wide. Harlow relaxed: these two were going to get on, they were in fact chips from the same block – no bull and blimpery from a man like Kemp. Dempsey said, 'Sure thing. They're RN, you're RNR. I've no objection.' He paused. 'Is there anything else you'd like to see?'

'That's all for now,' Kemp said. He stared again across the

harbour, an inward look in his eyes. The Manly ferry was coming out now. That family visit to Sydney, years ago . . . he'd taken Mary and the boys across to Manly and Harry had been much intrigued by the sharks that were displayed in a vast tank not far from where the ferry berthed at Manly beach. People used to throw coins down to them, for luck. There had been a notice indicating that copper was bad for the sharks and Harry had made a joke, asking his father which sharks copper was bad for, the actual sharks or the business sharks who ran the show.

Dempsey sensed the atmosphere and made a guess; then he took the plunge. It had to be uttered sometime or other. He said, 'I'm very sorry, Commodore, very sorry. I take it there's been no news yet?'

'No,' Kemp said. 'There hasn't.'

ii

The troop embarkation had taken place the day before, men having been entrained from all the military commands of the Commonwealth of Australia – from Darwin in the Northern Territory, Queensland, Victoria, South Australia, Western Australia, as well as New South Wales and Australian Capital Territory in which Canberra lay. It was a constant procession of marching men from the railway station to the docks at Pyrmont, bands playing them to the troopships. Bush hats and khaki greatcoats, rifles and packs and singing from both the troops and the farewell crowds, *Waltzing Matilda* predominating. The Sydneysiders had been there in their thousands to cheer the big contingent away. Kemp had been among the crowd, having decided to walk across to Woolloomooloo to take the picquet-boat to Garden Island and regain possession of that vital bag. It had been a cold day and a wet one, but it failed to dampen the send-off. Kemp, having in mind what Brigadier Hennessy had said, was surprised; he would have expected some note of dismay that Australia was being bereft of her fighting men . . . on the other hand, of course, they would want to give the troops a proper farewell and then the doubts and worries could come out later. Certainly the soldiers themselves didn't appear worried as they marched along the packed streets; there was an air of anticipation, or it could have been no more than a reaction to the ballyhoo, the bands and the cheers and the somewhat pathetic streamers damp and limp with rain. Those streamers brought more memories back, of the great liners of the Mediterranean-Australia Line, the Orient Line and P&O just before leaving the berth at Circular Quay or Woolloomooloo, seemingly unable to move off for the thousands of colourful paper links attaching them to the shore, the shore ends being held as a last remembrance by the godspeeders. But of course they had parted one by one as the big hulls had drawn away, hanging sadly down the ships' sides as the emotional singing started from the quay-bound friends and families, the singing of the haunting words of 'The Maori Farewell' imported from New Zealand. *Soon you'll be sailing, Far across the sea. . . .*

Kemp had still believed there would be a good deal of brooding once the convoy was away in limey ships, pommie ships taking them out of Australia's immediate defence. . . .

He had gone on to Garden Island and collected the canvas bag still in its brown-paper parcel. The Rear-Admiral had had a word with him, personally. *Burnside* was, strictly, no concern of Australia, being a British ship manned from the home ports, but Naval HQ in Sydney, on Kemp's account, had asked for details to be signalled. It appeared there was still no complete list of survivors . . . the Rear-Admiral hadn't said much, but Kemp could read between the lines well enough: there could have been severe burns cases, even some of the survivors unrecognizable, and identity discs often became detached: held by string around men's necks, they were not all that secure in fire and explosion. In any case it was often a long job to sort out the facts and the Admiralty liked to be sure before informing the next-of-kin.

iii

In *Coverdale*'s chart room Kemp laid his parcel on the chart table. He was alone with Dempsey. Dempsey asked, 'A present for home?'

'Not exactly.' Kemp stripped away the brown paper, balling it in his fist. The canvas bag emerged.

'Despatches?'

'Yes. Highest classification.'

'My safe –'

Kemp shook his head. 'No, Captain. They have to go overboard in certain circumstances. Such as – capture and a boarding party. The safe could be unavailable, say after being shelled. I want them immediately handy. Any suggestions?'

Dempsey said at once, 'Surely. I keep my revolver handy – similar sort of reason! You might not be able to get to your cabin. There's a locked drawer in here. I have the key.'

'Good. May I suggest, then, that we share the key? Whichever of us is on the bridge?'

'By all means,' Dempsey said. He produced a bunch of keys and opened the drawer. Kemp put the canvas bag in and the drawer was locked again. Dempsey glanced at the bulkhead-mounted clock. 'Half an hour to go. If you'll excuse me, Commodore.' He went into the wheelhouse and Kemp heard the orders passed to the chief officer who had now come to the bridge: stand by in the eyes of the ship to weigh anchor and meanwhile shorten-in to two cables. Kemp left the chart room to stand in the starboard bridge wing. Now the escorts were coming off the berths in Garden Island, *Rhondda* followed by the destroyers. In the distance, up beyond the harbour bridge, the first of the transports was manoeuvring off Pyrmont. A couple of minutes later there was a rattle from for'ard as the links of the *Coverdale*'s cable started coming home across the chafing plate, drawn in by the windlass below the break of the fo'c'sle. Now there was a feeling of expectancy, a sense of departure, of being away across the seas, away from the constrictions of the land. It was always like that at the start of any voyage, even to some extent in peacetime a probing into the unknown since no one could foretell what joys and difficulties each voyage would bring.

Kemp knew there wouldn't be any joy this time.

He watched as the senior officer aboard the cruiser turned to starboard for the outward passage, the destroyers following in formation Line Ahead. The minutes to departure ticked away. The leading transport was now coming up to the harbour bridge: the RMS *Asturias*, once of the Royal Mail Line, a smart ship and a popular one with passengers in pre-war days, now in her camouflage paint; behind her the *Carlisle Castle* of the Union Castle Line, a ship launched immediately before the outbreak of war so that she had never known the peacetime run from Southampton to the Cape. Now the *Coverdale* was at stations for leaving harbour, Dempsey standing in the bridge wing with Kemp. As the last of the troop transports came past from beneath the harbour bridge, Captain Dempsey passed the order to weigh; and then, with the anchor held underfoot until the ship was through the Heads, the *Coverdale* moved out into the main stream to be followed after an interval by the remainder of the convoy, the armament carriers and the grain ships, all of them seemingly surrounded by the well-wishers, the godspeeders in their various sailing boats. Hands waved and shouts were exchanged.

'Good on yer, cobber! Sod bloody Hitler, eh?'

'Up the poms!' That could be taken either way at choice; Stripey Sinker, watching from the after three-inch, made his own choice and lifted two fingers in a jerking motion.

'Cut it out, Stripey.' This was Petty Officer Rattray, being officious.

'Winnie does it, PO.'

'With a flippin' difference. The Aussies, they're touchy when it comes to poms.'

Stripey nodded agreement; they were. Even Dinah Deeling could get very Australian when she wanted to. He believed it had underlain their whole brief relationship; at times he had felt she'd been waiting for an opening to make slighting remarks about poms and their ways and in fact, the night before, or rather that early morning, they hadn't parted on quite the best of terms. Stripey was suffering a touch of unease because of what had led up to it: that evening he'd got a little tight, not unusually of course, but he believed he'd been indiscreet. During the day he'd been checking around the close-range weapons, stripping down and greasing the bridge Lewis guns; and he'd happened to see what he shouldn't have seen, and that was a hand message from Naval HQ. Naturally, he'd read from the corner of his eye: the convoy would leave for Simonstown at 1030 hours next day, and the order of leaving had been given. Troop transports . . . well, you couldn't ever hide a troop embarkation and all Sydney knew. Nevertheless, Stripey had had no business at all to let the Aussie beer prize it out of him for the benefit of Feeling Deeling and never mind that she would be able to see, with all the rest of Sydney, the convoy's very open departure. Careless Talk Costs

Lives. Very true, was that. But of course he'd had to say goodbye properly, which meant reaping the benefit of sadness at his going out across the seas, all heroic. There were not all that many highlights in the life of a middle-aged leading seaman and you had to make the most of the drama of distant waters filled with lurking enemies. And really it wasn't likely that Feeling Deeling had a personal hot line from the Cross to wherever Adolf Hitler might be, Berchtesgaden probably, or Berlin. All the same, the nagging thought that he hadn't Been Like Dad Keep Mum had made Stripey a little short and withdrawn at their farewell and he'd tried to walk back on what he'd said the night before.

'Don't know for sure, like. I could be back this evening for all I know.'

'Make yer bloody mind up fer God's sake.'

Something in her tone, a sharpness, made him ask, 'Why, eh?'

She pushed at her hair. 'Oh . . . nothing, I reckon.'

Another man; it would scarcely be surprising. Even though not on the game, she wasn't made for celibacy. But Stripey had been stung into making a remark about tarts and she hadn't taken it well. He could have wrecked a lovely friendship, destroyed an up homers the next time he came back to Sydney. If ever he did. In wartime, you never knew the next move. . . .

'Look at that,' Rattray said in tones of astonishment. 'Just bleedin' *look*!'

Stripey looked where bid: the cockpit of one of the closer yachts. There was a girl standing up, straight and tall and slim, waving the Australian flag. She was wearing a pair of khaki shorts and that was all, never mind the cold. No bra. Twin tanned hillocks, with sharp peaks. A cheer went up from the *Coverdale*'s decks and a storm of acclaim was heard from the transport next ahead as the yacht winged on the wind faster than the outward convoy's progress in confined waters.

'No bloody modesty,' Rattray growled sourly. 'Besides which, it ain't fair – not when we're outward bloody bound!'

On the bridge, Kemp caught Dempsey's eye and they both grinned. 'A refreshing lack of inhibitions out here,' Kemp said. 'I must say she's very well equipped.'

'It's an Australian attribute,' Dempsey said, and added solemnly, 'so I'm told. It's all the fresh air and sun, I expect.'

'And plenty of steak.'

Dempsey moved to the azimuth circle on the gyro repeater. 'Bradley's Head abeam, Commodore.'

He spoke to the helmsman. 'Port ten.'

'Port ten, sir.' A pause, then: 'Ten o' port wheel on, sir.'

'Midships . . . steady!'

'Steady, sir. Course, oh-four-five, sir.'

'Steer oh-four-seven.' Dempsey straightened. The outward convoy was now on course for the Inner North Head and the next alteration would come when Middle Head was abeam to port. In the van of the escort HMS *Rhondda* was already turning for the passage between the North and South Heads and the harbour launches were already preparing to take off the pilots once the ships had moved out into the Pacific.

iv

As usual there was a deep-sea swell outside the Heads, but that was all. As yet, little wind. The pilots were transferred and the signals began from the senior officer of the escort, bringing the convoy onto its southerly course for Cape Howe and then Wilson's Promontory to the north of the Bass Strait between the mainland and Tasmania. Weather reports followed: a blow was now expected in the Bight, but this was normal for the southland's winter season. There was time yet before they moved into the Bight.

Kemp had a word with the Captain; and Dempsey spoke down the engine-room voice-pipe: 'Chief. . . . '

'Yes, sir?'

Dempsey said, 'The Commodore would like a look around the engine spaces, Chief. All right?'

Chief Engineer Warrington's initial response was loud. 'Good God!' It was seldom enough any deck officer even recognized the existence of the engine-room, except on the occasions something went wrong when it was a different story. Warrington added, 'Of course. At his convenience.'

'Now,' Dempsey said, and clipped down the voice-pipe cover. 'All yours,' he added to the Commodore. 'Any orders for the convoy while you're below?'

'No, thank you, Captain. Just my usual standing orders: I'm

always to be called to the bridge immediately if required, if you'll be so good to let all your watch-keeping officers know that.'

Kemp went below, taking, at Dempsey's suggestion, the third officer as guide: he was not familiar with the layout of tankers. Down three ladders from the bridge, past the master's accommodation – and his own, for he was being accommodated in Dempsey's spare cabin – past the deck officers' cabins and onto the starboard after flying bridge, one of the long, narrow walkways that ran over the tank tops on the cargo deck, the covers well clipped down against sea and fresh air. He spoke to Third Officer Peel whose single gold stripe was very new.

'Did you do your apprenticeship with the RFA?'

'No, sir, British Tanker Company –'

'Persian Gulf?'

'Largely, yes, sir.'

Kemp grinned. 'I believe it's a bloody awful place. It didn't put you off seagoing?'

'No, sir, only off the Gulf itself!'

Kemp grinned again. 'Hence the RFA – more variety?'

'Yes, sir, though there's still been time up the Gulf since.'

'Of course.'

They moved on aft, making for the engineers' accommodation at the end of the flying bridge. Young Peel had reminded Kemp of things he would prefer not to think about – the third officer was about Harry's age and there were other similarities, a youthful keenness, perhaps a youthful lack of imagination, no bad thing when you served in tankers with their immense explosive potential. Peel didn't seem concerned with the dangers. The boredom of Abadan and the Persian Gulf loomed far larger, as no doubt did the terrible enervating heat and the airlessness that would hang about the cabins and all below-decks spaces throughout the ship. It would be nothing short of hell in the engine-room and boiler-room.

Reaching the after deckhouse Kemp followed the third officer down many decks to the air-lock leading to the engine-room and its criss-cross of shining steel ladders, the spider's-web that led down to the starting platform with its many dials and gauges and the indicator from the engine-room telegraph in the wheelhouse, the pointers currently showing half ahead. As Kemp reached the platform bells rang stridently and the order from the bridge was seen in the shifting pointers: full ahead. A moment later there was an eerie howl from the sound-powered telephone, answered by Warrington.

'Full away,' he repeated, speaking to his second engineer. This was the signal for the engine-room to stand down from stations for leaving harbour: the *Coverdale* was away on passage for the Cape, no more messing about with alterations of speed for a while.

'Mr Warrington?' Kemp asked, having to shout.

'That's me, sir.'

They shook hands. There was clamour all around, a controlled clamour, a smell of oil and of hot metal inseparable from any engine-room. Ratings moved about with long-necked oil cans, the second engineer felt around bearings. There was an air of efficiency and the place was clean, shining. Kemp passed a complimentary remark; Warrington was clearly pleased at his interest and put into words the thought that had come to him earlier. 'The deck people don't always appreciate us. But you'll know that, I dare say!'

Kemp nodded. 'I've been as guilty as any, Mr Warrington. I'll try to improve! I've some appreciation of what you have to put up with down here. My first convoy . . . two years ago and more now . . .' He didn't go on: all too clearly he could see the shattered bulkhead aboard the old *Ardara*, could see the mess that he had inspected during the final hours of that Atlantic convoy as the *Ardara*, in the care of ocean-going rescue tugs, had inched homewards for the safety of the Clyde. From the air-lock he'd looked down at the water-filled engine spaces, where the pulped body of the liner's chief engineer lay submerged, trapped as the damaged bulkhead finally went, the end result of torpedoes from the Nazi U-boats. The worst job in any ship, Kemp often thought, helpless down below when things went awry.

'I'd appreciate being taken round, Chief. It's helpful to know just what I've got down here, what power's available – you know what I mean?'

'I do, sir, and it'll be a pleasure. If you'll follow me?'

Kemp took an interest in everything. The *Coverdale*'s propulsion was by steam turbines and she had a normal cruising speed of sixteen knots; the extra six knots could be produced when required in an emergency. Warrington, a tall, spare man with receding hair, somewhat grey, was a good instructor, a man of plenty of patience with deck officers when they showed an interest. His own dedication to his engines was obvious to Kemp: he spoke of them as he might of his children. Kemp was not to know that in a sense that was what they were now. Warrington had had a son, killed at the age of fourteen a few years before the war, knocked off his bicycle by a speeding car when on his way to school. His job filled a blank, and he himself reckoned he was better off than Jean, his wife, sitting at home in Southsea and thinking. Sitting because there was nothing else she could do: war work, for instance, was out for her. A bad case of multiple sclerosis; she was virtually helpless and dependent on Warrington's sister. Warrington tried not to think at all if he could help it. Just sail the seas, tend his engines and do what he could to flatten Hitler before Hitler, or Goering, flattened any more of Portsmouth and Southsea. Last time at home, he'd seen that Palmerston Road had gone, just ceased to exist, along with King's Road and most of the little streets between there and the Guildhall. By some quirk of fate, Brickwood's brewery had survived to continue to bring some sort of cheer to the shoregoing sailors of the fleet. Perhaps there was a kind of justice, but not too much: Warrington's old mother had bought it during one of the raids. She was probably better off out of it all, though. . . .

'Thank you, Chief.'

'No bother. You can rely on us down here, sir.'

'I'm sure I can.' Kemp turned away and went back up the ladders. He felt a sense of relief as he made his way from the airlock into the engineers' alleyway. The *Ardara* was a little too much on his mind: he must watch that. He'd done plenty of convoy runs since then. So why? He gave a sudden shiver; there was almost an element of foreboding.

Four

Now well past Wilson's Promontory, the convoy was in the grip of the winds roaring along the Great Australian Bight that ran below Melbourne and Adelaide to Cape Leeuwin at the western end, an area of almost constant storm at this time of the year. The ships rose and fell, plunging into mountainous seas that washed them from end to end, swilling, in the case of the *Coverdale*, over the tank tops to rush aft and discharge themselves through the washports or straight over the side. Semi-laden and in partial ballast, the ship was not down deep to her marks and she rode like the old County Class cruisers of which *Rhondda* was one: roll and pitch, the roll being the worst, a constant motion that made life uncomfortable in the extreme as men moved about the decks trying to keep some sort of balance.

Porter, the Captain's steward, was something of a wizard with a tray. Mugs of steaming cocoa reached the bridge, miraculously unspilt after the climb from the pantry.

'Kye up, sir.'

Four mugs – Commodore, Captain, Officer of the Watch and Sub-Lieutenant Cutler, Commodore's assistant.

'Good on yer, Porter,' Cutler said.

'I thought you was a Y – American, sir?'

Cutler grinned. 'Sure, that's right. Only I try to accommodate to the natives wherever I am.'

'Very wise I'm sure, sir. You'd best start practising Afrikaans, sir. Whoops!' Porter reached out for a stanchion as the *Coverdale* fell away to starboard and pitched at the same time, a nasty corkscrew motion.

'Ever work in a circus?' Cutler asked.

'Me, sir?' Porter's eyebrows went up. 'No, sir. Why, sir?'

'Acrobatic. Tightrope expert?'

'Not with my figure, sir.' Porter was short and fat, almost round, with a cheery face that carried a perpetual smile. 'Me, I've been at sea all me working life, sir. Last five years with Captain Dempsey, ever since 'e got command like. Relies on me, 'e does.'

'Not in vain, I guess.'

'Never let it be said, sir.' Porter, the officers having been served, retreated below with his tray. In the pantry, he fared better than the bridge personnel: he opened a cupboard and brought out a bottle of Dewar's whisky and poured a slug into a cup of tea. It was good stuff, gave a glow in filthy weather and at other times too. Took the mind away from its nagging worries, and by worries Porter didn't mean the war, he meant a young woman in Rothesay, Isle of Bute. Last time on the Clyde he'd gone and put a bun in her oven. That was four months ago; he was now worried sick, though he never let it show. He had no wish to get married, and if he ever did it wouldn't by choice be to Beryl, the one with the lodged bun; but on the other hand he wouldn't let her down. That wasn't his style at all. Fostering? But then Beryl would still be basically an unmarried mum with all that that entailed, especially in Scotland though presumably Scotsmen did it the same as Sassenachs – or maybe not since they drank so much whisky. Porter started whistling to himself. Without especially realizing it, he whistled a Scots tune, a catchy one that he'd picked up in Glasgow one Saturday night: 'We're no awa' tae bide awa'.'

Still whistling, Porter emerged from the pantry, making for the Captain's day cabin, just as Captain Dempsey came in through the lee door from the bridge ladder. Seeing Dempsey, Porter stopped whistling.

'So I should damn well think,' Dempsey said sourly. 'As if we haven't enough wind!'

'Sorry, sir, I'm sure.' It wasn't done, to whistle at sea. Something of a superstition, though tending to die out among the younger seafarers. Captain Dempsey, he'd done his apprenticeship in sail, aboard the old Cape Horners, where you never whistled other than when you wanted a wind to carry you on across the world's waters. A lot of whistling used to be done, so

Porter had heard, in the Doldrums. Dempsey vanished in the direction of his bathroom; Porter stared after him, speculatively. They knew one another well, and though the Old Man could be short-tempered and pernickety, he was human. A word of advice in his predicament? It always helped, so they said, to talk things over and the Old Man just might come up with something. He would have to choose his moment, though, and it wasn't now. Wait till the convoy had cleared the Bight, maybe. Captain Dempsey, he could be caught on his wrong side and God knew he had enough to occupy his thoughts, at sea in wartime and in command.

In the meantime, after Dempsey had gone back to the bridge, Porter sat in his pantry with a pad of notepaper and wrote a line to Beryl, for posting at the Cape. Just to let her know he was thinking of her.

ii

Spray whipped across the open bridge-wings, brought salt to Kemp's weather-beaten face. He shivered beneath his duffel coat: the spray was icy, so was the wind. Despite the weather the convoy was keeping good station. Kemp thought with sympathy about the troops aboard the transports, packed tight. As sick as dogs, very likely. The peace-time passengers from home had never liked the haul through the Bight; quite a few of them used to disembark at Fremantle and go overland to Melbourne or Sydney rather than face it when it was in one of its moods, like now. It was always incredible what a difference came to a liner in the Bight in winter: the air of gaiety gone, the ship rolling and pitching, the air dank, the sky grey when you could see it at all through the flinging spume, the public rooms largely deserted, even the bars not doing their usual trade. Today Kemp was feeling that same old depression, brought not only by the weather but also by his anxieties: Harry, and that confounded bag locked in the chart room drawer. He mustn't think about Harry: he must concentrate on that bag. It was quite a responsibility to have in one's personal charge. Presumably its loss to the enemy could affect the course of the war, but that was not going to happen. It would be easy enough to recognize the moment, if

37

and when it came, for jettisoning overboard; but even that could no doubt cause consternation in high place, at any rate in Australian Army circles. Or that brigadier's anyway.

Not too late, and not too soon either; and with luck he would never have to make the decision which, in spite of his thoughts as to the ease of recognition of that moment, would have to be finely balanced.

He paced the bridge-wing, uphill and then downhill with a controlled rush as the *Coverdale* did its horrible roll: he could almost believe he could hear the surge and gurgle of the cargo tanks beneath the main deck. He looked for'ard along the flying bridges, at times half submerged by the tons of swilling water, along the mostly invisible tank tops with their heavy covers and clips and all the clutter of a tanker's working deck, the valves and pipes and the access ladders from the flying bridges. With all that water, it was akin to looking down from a submarine's conning tower to a hull not fully surfaced.

Submarines, U-boats: this was far from the North Atlantic and it was highly unlikely Admiral Doenitz would have any of his hunting packs in far southern waters – hence the current paucity of the escort, which would be strengthened at the Cape for the much more dangerous run from there to the Virginia Capes outside Chesapeake Bay.

Kemp felt a presence at his side. He glanced round.

'Well, Cutler. Looking forward to home?'

'I guess so, sir.' Cutler hesitated. 'Any chances of leave, are there?'

Kemp shrugged. 'Don't be premature, laddie! Who knows, in war?'

'No, sir. . . .'

'I'll do my best for you, you can reckon on that. Your parents –' He broke off, things that he was doing his best to suppress coming back to him.

'They'll be glad, sir. I guess they worry.'

'Yes. Well, when you see them, you can assure them of one thing: you've been a credit to the United States all the times we've sailed together.'

Cutler seemed surprised. He said, 'Why, thank you, sir, Commodore, I guess I don't deserve that. I –' Then he too broke off. 'Signal from the senior officer.' He turned. 'Signalman!'

'Seen it, sir.' Ordinary Signalman Lashman had taken over the watch from his leading hand and was screwing up his eyes towards the flashing lamp from *Rhondda*'s flag deck. A Hostilities Only rating not long qualified as a convoy signalman, he wasn't as fast as *Coverdale*'s own signalman, ex-Yeoman of Signals Gannock.

It was Gannock who reported to the Commodore.

'From senior officer, sir, addressed escort and Commodore, repeated all ships . . . cypher from Commander-in-Chief Ceylon indicates German surface raider operating in Indian Ocean believed to have moved south-west towards Madagascar.' Gannock looked up from his clipboard. 'Message ends, sir.'

That, Kemp knew instinctively, was to be the start of it. That raider could have other quarry, of course; but she could have had intelligence of the convoy's movement out from Sydney, and if she had she would know, or guess, its course for the Cape. At Kemp's side Cutler, as if sensing the Commodore's thoughts, said, 'Could be just searching on the off-chance, sir. Not us in particular.'

'Perhaps. But I don't go much on coincidence, Cutler. I'm going to assume she's got the word.'

'We have a strongish escort, sir.'

Kemp laughed, a bitter sound. 'Strong my backside. Just one old County Class cruiser and a handful of destroyers! I'll tell you one thing: if that raider's presence had been known earlier, I'll bet the Admiralty would have held the convoy back in Sydney – either that, or strengthened the escort.'

'I guess it depends on the raider's identity, sir. If it's a battle-cruiser or a pocket-battleship, why then it's not going to be so good. But it doesn't have to anything that heavy.'

'True. If only they'd identified . . . I can only assume they're going by the bush telegraph!'

Cutler grinned. 'A bunch of native fishermen off the Mada-gascan coast?'

'Something of that sort,' Kemp said savagely. 'In the meantime there's damn-all we can do about it – except carry on and await further information.'

'Yes, sir. Any special orders for the convoy?'

'No. All the masters have had the signal, Cutler. They'll be on the top line without a prod from me.'

Cutler nodded; there was, in any case, no immediate emergency. There were still a couple of days to go to Cape Leeuwin and the southern extremity of the Indian Ocean.

iii

Ordinary Signalman Lashman had what Leading Signalman Goodenough called a big yap; even if he hadn't, the word about the senior officer having made a signal would have spread throughout the ship in no time and would have led to that peculiarity of shipboard life, especially in wartime: the buzz. The lower deck lived on buzzes, they brought variety to dull routine. The buzz all hands always hoped to hear was that they were going home, but they heard that one all too seldom on the galley wireless. And certainly they didn't this time as the *Coverdale* rolled uncomfortably on across the Bight. From Lashman they heard the truth: there was a Nazi commerce raider at large ahead of their track and the Commodore had expressed the wish that the convoy hadn't left Sydney. That meant he was apprehensive, not to say scared. The buzz grew and extended into a possibility that the convoy might be ordered into Gage Roads off Fremantle, to wait there until naval forces had been moved in from the Eastern Fleet or somewhere to despatch the Nazi. Since nice buzzes seldom came about in fact, the more experienced of the men didn't give that one much credit.

Petty Officer Rattray was one of these: he made the rounds of his guns, anticipating the order that would come down from the bridge before the day was out. Plenty of gun-drill, plenty of maintenance of moving parts of the guns before they rounded the Leeuwin. All they had were popguns but they would have to do their stuff if they met the Jerries. Rattray was a chivier, and he chivied hard in the tradition of what he was – a gunner's mate trained at Whale Island, the navy's principal gunnery school, the place that *inter alia* produced the Portsmouth Port Division's entry for the gun contest at Olympia each year in peace. One year, Rattray himself had been for a few performances the PO of the gun team, standing in for the chief gunner's mate gone sick when some cack-handed rating had dropped the gun barrel on his foot. Even now, Rattray could hear the language.

40

Aboard a battleship or cruiser the pipe would have been Hands to Quarters Clean Guns. Today, Rattray passed the equivalent order himself, moving from one gun position to another accompanied by Leading Seaman Sinker. In point of fact there wasn't a lot in it; Rattray always saw to it that his guns were in tip-top condition; he wasn't going to have it be said that he was past his best just because he was an RFR man who'd taken his pension. Fuddy-duddies they were regarded as, out-of-date and out of condition. True, many of them had lost their bark and bite; not Rattray. For one thing, he was always smartly turned out whatever the weather. Look beneath Rattray's oilskin or duffel coat and you'd find his Number Three uniform complete with badges, plus a collar and tie. Not for him the jerseys and scarves and clutter worn by such as hadn't the advantage of being trained as gunner's mates, the elite – in Rattray's view – of the whole navy.

Today, moving with difficulty along the starboard after flying bridge with Sinker, he looked sour.

'You don't have to,' he said.

Stripey Sinker looked blank. 'Don't have to what, PO?'

'Look like a bloody scran bag. Just because you're a fleet reservist.'

'Well, I'm buggered!' Stripey looked offended. He glanced down at his oilskin, held together around his stomach by means of a length of codline. That oilskin had seen better days it was true, but it sufficed, as did the scuffed leather seaboots. 'There's a war on,' he said huffily.

'Don't you answer me back, Leading Seaman Sinker, or else.'

Stripey stifled a groan: it was to be one of those days. Rattray, he knew, suffered from indigestion and when he had a bout, which mostly came after he'd had a letter from home, he was like a monkey with a sore arse. Other times he was all right, so when he was in a mood you did best to endure it and keep your trap shut. This time Rattray had something nagging at him and he wasn't going to let up.

'On'y time you smarten up is when you go ashore, right? On the prowl for women. Ought to know better, a bloke of your age.'

'I'm not that old, PO.'

'Bloody pity you aren't *too* old.' Rattray's face looked like Punch, a long nose reaching down to a long chin, with a slit of a mouth in between. 'If I had my way, I'd confine all hands to the bloody ship except in home ports.'

Stripey failed to see the connection between his age and proclivities when ashore, and any need to curb shore leave. He said as much. Rattray spoke vehemently if tongue-in-cheek: 'That commerce raider. A suggestion came down from the bridge – she could know our movements. There's plenty of sodding careless talk around. We all know that. I s'pose, Leading Seaman Sinker, you didn't drop anything else when you last dropped your trousers?'

Stripey gave a jerk and his face flushed: it was as though the PO had been reading his mind as they left Sydney. Feeling Deeling . . . Rattray didn't know anything about her and Stripey knew there was no serious intent behind his last utterance, it was his idea of a joke. Also, Stripey knew that his own thoughts had been sheer melodrama or even maybe a sort of self-punishment for acting as an old goat. All the same, what Rattray had said rankled. Take the thing to its extreme, however unlikely . . . it wouldn't be nice to have on one's conscience for the rest of one's life, that one had a responsibility for maybe thousands of deaths.

Stripey managed to laugh it off. 'You know me, PO, soul of discretion.' Rattray didn't comment and they left the flying bridge to climb up to monkey's island for a check on the Lewis guns. From way up top Stripey Sinker looked out at the convoy and its escort, the plunging little destroyers out on the bow acting as the screen ahead of the old cruiser, which was taking the weather badly, climbing the seas and rushing down the other side, rolling like a bathtub. Stripey felt glum: it was well known that the old three-stackers, with their very high freeboard, were terrible gun platforms, never still for a second in anything of a sea, never a chance to get their sights on. Stripey had served in the old *Cornwall* of the pre-war China Squadron. Half the time on practise shoots the 6-inch batteries had fired down into the hogwash or up at the sky. And now the *Rhondda* was just about their only defence. The destroyers were all right against U-boats, but they were not built to fight heavy surface ships. The convoy could become a sitting duck; the consequences were best not even thought about. But perhaps the buzz was right after all, and they would be ordered into Gage Roads. Troops were valuable; you might chuck away poor old matloes, but not troops. The public back home were accustomed by now to ship losses as such, but there would be a God Almighty fuss if four troop transports got it, all in a bunch.

Two days later, with no amendment of its orders, the BT convoy left Cape Leeuwin on its starboard quarter and headed out through the Roaring Forties for Simonstown.

Five

With the Western Australian coast now well behind, another report reached the senior officer of the escort and was passed to all ships: the German raider, whose identity was still not known, had become lost in the wide waters. After the first report a search had been mounted but without success. As a precaution, two cruisers had been detached from the Eastern Fleet with orders to steam towards Madagascar and on down to the convoy's track; but these would take time to arrive, perhaps too much time in Kemp's view. Nevertheless, the fact that they were on their way was some comfort.

'Means we're not being left to it,' the Commodore remarked to Dempsey. 'They care after all!'

Before Dempsey could utter, a lamp began flashing again from the *Rhondda*. Leading Signalman Goodenough made the acknowledgement and then reported to the Commodore. 'From senior officer, sir: "Estimate raider to be well north of our track as yet. Speed of arrival Simonstown considered paramount. Convoy will accordingly alter north to come into calmer waters. Course to be 315 degrees until further orders then west. Executive will follow."'

Kemp stared in concern. Dempsey put his thoughts into words: 'He must be crazy! Taking us closer –'

'Yes. I tend to agree, Captain. However, I can follow his reasoning . . . calmer waters, better speed. You know these westerlies, they just don't come to an end – remember?'

Dempsey laughed: he remembered all right – the days, sometimes weeks, spent trying to beat round Cape Horn from the

44

South Atlantic into the teeth of the storm, those never-ending westerlies. And never mind steam propulsion: it was only too true that the gales had cut the convoy's speed quite considerably and would continue to do so unless they got out of their track. Like Stripey Sinker earlier, he looked all around the closer waters: the ships were wallowing, the laden grain ships making heavy weather of it as they butted into the wind and waves. The destroyers were largely invisible behind the crests, reappearing at intervals as they climbed the sheer-looking sides of watery mountains.

The executive came and the orders were passed to the convoy from the Commodore. Captain Dempsey brought the *Coverdale* round onto her new course and the ships re-formed behind the senior officer of the escort, the destroyers shifting fast to take up their screening positions, rolling heavily as they cut across the wind and sea.

By the time the order was passed that night to darken ship, the convoy was already moving into somewhat easier waters. Below in his cabin, the *Coverdale*'s chief steward was pouring himself a whisky and checking through some stores requisitions for Simonstown: there had been certain items unobtainable in Sydney that the Cape might provide. One of the things he hoped to persuade the Old Man to sanction was a case or two of South African brandy – Van der Humm. The chief steward knew that HM ships calling in at the Cape usually took a stock aboard, and the Old Man, used to visiting the wardrooms of the warships, would probably approve though he wouldn't overdo it in case there were queries from the Naval Stores Department of the Admiralty. And normally the Old Man preferred ordering through Saccone and Speed: that excellent firm was generous when the orders went in, in Portsmouth, Chatham or Devonport, or Malta or Gibraltar, for the usual stock of whisky, gin, port, sherry and cigarettes by the hundred thousand. It was the Old Man that got the benefit of the free gifts – gold watches, canteens of cutlery and so on, but if he was a decent bloke he usually passed some of it on to his officers who were the consumers, and to his chief steward who did the donkey work. Chief Steward Lugg had garnered plenty before the war, when he'd served in the Mediterranean Fleet oiler *Brambleleaf*. . . .

There was a knock at his door.

'Come in.' Lugg looked up. 'You, Porter.'

'As ever was, chief. Captain'll do rounds of the accommodation and storerooms, tomorrow, eleven hundred hours.'

'All right.' Lugg was unworried: he ran an efficient department. 'I'm on the top line whenever he says.' One of Dempsey's foibles was to make rounds at different times, nothing routine about them, with fairly minimal notice. It had largely to do with the exigencies of war, of course, but it wasn't just the War, it was Dempsey. And he could be pernickety, real RN, white gloves and all, the gloves showing every trace of dust concealed, until his probing hand met it, on the tops of steam pipes and so on. As Porter stood there the chief steward looked at him closely. There were worry lines visible and he'd noticed an absent-mindedness at times, nothing much, but it was there and Porter wasn't quite the first-rate steward he'd been a few months ago, not that the Old Man had ever complained. But it was the chief steward's job to keep an eye on that sort of thing; he would watch out.

'That Commodore,' he said. Porter attended also, this voyage, on the unexpected addition. 'What's he like, eh?'

'No bother. Decent bloke.'

'From the liners.'

'Yes.'

'Still no word about his son.' The news had reached everyone aboard, by galley wireless. 'Rotten, that. Not the only one, of course.' The chief steward looked Porter in the eye when he went on, 'We all have our worries, right?'

Porter nodded, shifted his feet, looked away and rearranged the cloth which he always carried over his left arm. 'Yes, that's right.'

Lugg waited a few moments but nothing emerged and he said, 'All right, Porter, tell the skipper I'll be ready.'

The steward went off. Lugg shook his head and poured another whisky, a small one. You had to watch that in wartime – you might have to act fast at any moment of the twenty-four hours, see to your department, your men and your boat station if needs be, and there was that commerce raider at large somewhere to the north. Lugg looked up at his life-jacket, hanging from the hook on his cabin door, carried with him at all times when at sea like the gas-mask that was supposed to accompany you at all times when ashore, though no one had seemed to bother in Australia. Australia was remote from the War, except up around the Cape York peninsula which was pretty close to the Japs by all accounts.

Lugg's thoughts went ahead to Simonstown where he hoped to get some news of a grandchild, to be his first, offspring of his only daughter. Susan was just twenty-one and the last news was that it might be a difficult birth. They were all keeping their fingers crossed back home in Devonport. Lugg's wife, Janet, had gone into details in her last letter, quite explicit: Janet was never the sort to keep worries to herself, had always to spill them out to a husband and father away at sea and unable to do anything about them except worry himself sick.

As he'd suggested to Porter, no one was exempt . . . no one who had given hostages to fortune. Often enough since the War had started Lugg had envied the bachelors.

Porter was a bachelor. Something up with his parents? They counted too, bachelors weren't entirely alone. But then Lugg remembered Porter's parents were both dead, carried off by the 'flu epidemic, the Spanish 'flu back in 1917 when Porter had been a small child. Thereafter he'd been brought up by Dr Barnado's. Might be a girl . . . Lugg sucked in his cheeks and tut-tutted. To Lugg – coming spot on though he didn't realize it – girl trouble, if that was what it was, meant only pregnancy and Lugg was old-fashioned in that way. He simply didn't care to think about it and he switched his mind back to Van der Humm.

ii

Next morning Captain's Rounds had just been satisfactorily completed and Dempsey was back on the bridge with Kemp when the urgent signal came from the *Rhondda*. The order went down for first degree of readiness and the closing of all watertight doors and hatches. Petty Officer Rattray reported at the double to the bridge.

'Commodore, sir –'

'Ah, Rattray. All guns' crews ready?'

'All closed up, sir, yes. For what they're worth, sir.'

'They'll do their best, Rattray.'

'That they will, sir.' The PO hesitated. 'Do we know who it is, sir? The raider?'

Kemp nodded. 'She's believed to be the *Kormoran*.'

Rattray's lips moved into position for a whistle that never came: he hung onto it in time. But the *Kormoran* was worth a whistle and to hell with it. She was one of the big jobs, successor to an earlier *Kormoran*, sunk by HMAS *Sydney* off Shark Bay in Western Australia on 19 November the year before while the new *Kormoran*, immediately renamed as such in honour of her predecessor, had only just completed her fitting-out. Petty Officer Rattray went down to talk to his guns' crews about the *Kormoran* mark II.

He said, 'More or less standard armament for the commerce raiders, plus a little: eight 5.9-inch main armament, six torpedo tubes. Believed to have sunk upwards of 30,000 tons of Allied shipping in the South Atlantic and Indian Ocean already. Diesel electric engines with a cruising range of 70,000 miles at ten knots, and capable of twenty knots, which is more than the first bloody *Kormoran*. You, Leading Seaman Sinker.'

'Yes, PO?'

'Know anything else about the first *Kormoran*, do you?'

Stripey Sinker nodded. 'She and the *Sydney* . . . they sank each other.'

'Right! Remember that, you lot. She sank a County Class cruiser, like the *Rhondda*. So watch it, all right?' Rattray turned away and marched for'ard along the flying bridge towards the other of his two main guns, left-right-left, smart as ever and bugger Hitler. This, he knew, was going to be a day to remember, to tell any grandchildren about in his dotage, how granddad fought the *Kormoran*. That was, of course, if he didn't find his name inscribed on one of the Jerry projectiles.

He continued firmly for'ard, fixing his mind on Whale Island and past glories at Olympia, and of his time as gunner's mate aboard the old battleship *Emperor of India*. As he reached the 3-inch the battle ensigns were going up aboard the *Rhondda* and on the heels of this the cruiser was heard to engage the enemy.

On *Coverdale*'s bridge Captain Dempsey took a report from his W/T office: a transmission had been intercepted from the *Kormoran*, a transmission in the German naval cypher. Once engaged, there remained no point in maintaining wireless silence. A moment later Sub-Lieutenant Cutler emerged from the wheelhouse carrying Kemp's perforated canvas bag. Then the

Rhondda was seen to be hit below and abaft her bridge superstructure and her foremast carried away. Two minutes later there was a dull glow from her after section and a monumental explosion came across the water, a roar of sound followed by a blaze of light. Debris was seen, as the officers on *Coverdale*'s bridge brought up their binoculars, flung high into the air.

Kemp said, 'After 6-inch turret by the look of it.'

Below Petty Officer Rattray was shaking a fist in the direction of the not-yet-visible *Kormoran*. 'Buggers!' he yelled at the top of his voice. 'Dirty buggers!' He had a fair idea of what the inferno inside a turret would be like when it took a direct hit. Searing flame, molten metal, strips of flesh, a whole turret's crew fried. There would have been a gunner's mate in that turret . . . and almost certainly it wouldn't be just the turret: the flash would probably have gone downwards through the decks to the shell-handling room and there would be nothing left of the handling parties, the men who sent the big ammo up in the hoists to the guns. And the magazines would be in danger, the order very likely being passed from *Rhondda*'s compass platform to open the flooding valves as a precaution, drowning men in the process, men shut beneath the clipped-down hatches who would have to be sacrificed for the greater good of a whole ship's company. A nasty moment for the skipper faced with giving that order.

When the next explosion came, to be followed by a series of similar explosions, Rattray knew that at least one of the magazines had gone. And only a matter of seconds later, with her remaining guns firing to the last, the *Rhondda* blew up, an immense and sickening cataclasm, her decks erupting in flame and thick black smoke all along her hull from stem to stern. On *Coverdale*'s bridge Leading Signalman Goodenough read off a signal from Captain(D) in the destroyer leader.

'From Captain(D), sir. "Intend to engage the enemy." '

'Thank you, Goodenough.' As the destroyers, moving under maximum power, raced across to starboard with their battle ensigns streaming along the wind, Kemp gave what he knew to be the inevitable, last-hope order.

'Cutler?'

'Sir?'

'Pass to all ships from Commodore, convoy is to scatter.'

'Aye, aye, sir –'

'And give me that bloody bag.'

Cutler handed it over: it was the Commodore's personal responsibility and would go down with him if it came to that.

iii

Kemp was thinking of Harry as he watched all the ships making off in their different directions so as to spread the target for the German raider. Harry would have faced something like this, aboard his convoy escort in the Mediterranean, would perhaps have been blown up unrecognizably, or gone over the side to drown in a hail of gunfire or dive bombing. Or he might yet be safe: there was always the hope, though it was growing fainter as no news came through. It didn't fade entirely: there could be word at the Cape, probably would be, they probably wouldn't clutter up the air with personal messages to a convoy's Commodore. . . .

Moving now under the direct orders of Kemp, the *Coverdale* was coming up to her maximum speed. Below in the engine-room Chief Engineer Warrington had given her all he'd got and the oiler moved like a cruiser, very manoeuvrable, very fast, as Kemp moved in and out between the scattering ships while the signal lamps passed the final order for them to proceed independently to Simonstown. After that it would be up to each master where he took his ship to be as safe as possible from the *Kormoran*'s guns: Kemp expected that mostly they would choose to head down again into the Roaring Forties, accept their inevitably slower speed of advance and hide in the immensity of the seas and the spume-blown rollers of the westerlies. As they watched the ships moving apart – the four big troop transports, the ammunition carriers and the unwieldy grain ships – Dempsey remarked on the wisdom or otherwise of the senior officer's original order to move the convoy up into better weather.

He said, 'We'd have remained safer if we'd kept farther south, in my opinion.'

'Being wise after the event, Captain?'

Dempsey shook his head. He stood four square in his belief and reinforced it. 'Those seas would have thrown off the German gunners. As it is, we've steamed right into her.'

Kemp said nothing: Dempsey was at least half right. It so often happened that way: you tried to assess the odds and strike a balance and you stood only a fifty percent chance of being right. If things went the other way, then you were wrong and took the consequences, death or court martial for making a mistake. Well, the Captain of the *Rhondda* would face no court martial now for a possibly wrong assessment: almost certainly he would be dead. If he'd survived those explosions that had wracked his ship . . . the *Kormoran* would certainly not be standing by to pick up any survivors. And that wrong assessment: it would have been open to Kemp at least to disagree and put a different point of view to the senior officer of the escort, but he hadn't, because he'd believed it was the right decision, or anyway the best gamble. So he was also to blame, if anyone was.

'*Kormoran* in sight, sir, bearing –'

'All right, Cutler. I've got her.' Kemp was looking through his binoculars. A long, lean ship, not unlike a cruiser, with puffs of smoke coming from her gun-batteries. Shells fell among the retreating merchant ships. Kemp called out, 'Zigzag, Captain. Take the ship, please.'

Dempsey ordered the helm over at precisely the right moment: a projectile took the sea off his port bow and spray came up like a waterfall in reverse. The *Coverdale* moved on, shuddering to another near miss, shuddered further as a small-calibre shell exploded on the port waterline for'ard.

Kemp swung round.

'Hit?'

'Near miss. Not serious, I think.' Dempsey leaned over the bridge screen and called down through a megaphone to the fo'c'sle. 'Bosun!'

'Aye, sir?'

'Get the carpenter. Sound round below, port side.'

Bosun Pedley lifted a hand in acknowledgement of the order, left the fo'c'sle and vanished into the accommodation beneath. Kemp said, 'The destroyers are moving in.'

'Good luck to them,' Dempsey said. 'They've got guts, all right.'

Now the *Kormoran* was being engaged: but she was still firing towards the convoy, and as Dempsey finished speaking there was a hit on the stern of one of the grain ships and she began

51

circling: rudder gone, most likely, to bring a lame duck to the convoy and one that Kemp would wish to stand by. But the bite had gone out of the gunfire as the German turned his attention to the destroyers, now worrying him like a pack of terriers, each with all her guns in action, blasting away at the *Kormoran's* decks. As Captain(D) in the leader handled his ship so as to come between the German and the other destroyers, Kemp latched on to what was being attempted.

He said, 'Captain(D)'s getting in close –'

'Inside the German's ability to bear?'

Kemp nodded. 'He's risking the smaller stuff but if he can make it, it'll be worth while. He'll be making a torpedo run, for my money!'

'It looks like it,' Dempsey said, his voice tense. Down by the after 3-inch Petty Officer Rattray was also tense. He, like Kemp, had recognized the manoeuvring for what it was. Rattray hadn't much opinion of torpedoes nor of torpedo-gunners' mates, who were of a different stamp from the gunnery branch – sloppier and not so bright, didn't ever have ceremonial duties to perform: who wanted a tin fish at Olympia for instance? And who manned the Commodore's guard at the home depots? Not the torpedomen. But, of course, they had their uses, and this just could be one of their times of glory.

Rattray found that he was gripping a stanchion as though strangling it; also that he was praying for the torpedomen's success, and sweating like a pig with excitement and hope. He knew he was standing on a time bomb himself – oilers were always that way inclined. Then the unexpected happened and a groan went up from the *Coverdale's* decks: HMAS *Timor*, carrying Captain(D) close to the port side of the *Kormoran* with the latter's heavy guns helpless, came under withering fire from the secondary armament and from rifles and close-range weapons aimed down on them from all along the high side. From the *Coverdale's* bridge Kemp, through his binoculars, saw it all in greater detail than Rattray: men fell in heaps and swathes, scattered from the torpedo-tubes like ninepins, the bridge left with apparently not a man alive, the destroyer swinging out of control and heading away once more from the *Kormoran* to cause confusion to her consorts.

But not for very long.

Kemp believed something from the German had set off a vital part of one of the *Timor*'s torpedoes. The destroyer blew up with terrifying suddenness and began to settle fast; for a while her blazing hull drifted across the other destroyers of the flotilla and then as she went down further, almost on an even keel, and started to roll over to starboard, she vanished beneath the sea and the blazing fires were doused into clouds of steam. A few heads bobbed in the water, a handful of men trying to swim to the succour of the destroyers' nets that were being put over the sides as fast as possible.

Then, as Kemp watched in increasing anxiety, one of the other destroyers, HMAS *Ayers*, altered course parallel with the *Kormoran* and Kemp saw the splash through his binoculars as what looked like four torpedoes hit the water and sped on their set courses, point blank, for the high, sheer sides of the *Kormoran*. It seemed to Kemp impossible that they could miss. But the Nazis reacted quickly, the helm went hard over and the *Kormoran* swung to present her bows to the destroyer, giving a smaller target as she steadied on a ramming course.

iv

The word went down to Chief Engineer Warrington from the bridge: there was alarm in his face as he took the message and turned to his second engineer.

'Bridge reports apparent damage, strained plates maybe. Number One summer tank, port. Smell of vapour. . . .'

Evans sucked in his breath sharply. 'Can't be, sir! Summer tanks, they've been cleaned –'

'Bloody is, according to the carpenter. And some people are cack-handed enough when it comes to doing a job properly.' Warrington wiped a handful of cotton-waste across his streaming face. It was the empty tanks that were potentially the most dangerous in certain circumstances, like now, and they were always cleaned as soon as possible after discharge, gas freed by steam cleaning and swilling out with water. Empty tanks, improperly cleaned tanks anyway, could hold explosive gases and poisonous fumes, and if breached in the smallest degree could spread those gases and fumes throughout the hull between the cofferdams fore and aft, could get into the double bottoms, anywhere within the confines of the cofferdams, and form a kind of bomb.

Evans asked, 'Any water coming in, sir?'

'Not a lot. Pumps are coping easily.' As a precaution the pumps had been started the moment the bridge had felt the reaction from the near miss against the outer plating. Warrington went on, 'Take over on the starting platform, Evans. I'm going to take a look for myself.'

He climbed up through the maze of steel ladders to the air-lock and emerged from the engineers' alleyway through the door giving access to the flying bridge aft. He looked up towards the bridge, saw Dempsey and the Commodore in the starboard wing; they were staring astern through their binoculars. As he went for'ard he glanced astern himself, just in time to see a big explosion against the port bow of the *Kormoran*. He gave a grim smile and turned for'ard again: the Nazi raider wasn't having it all his own way.

Dempsey called down from the bridge: 'That tank, Chief –'

'Just going to have a look, sir, before I give a diagnosis. I'll need to open up Number One summer –'

'Dangerous!'

'Necessary,' Warrington called up.

Dempsey waved an arm. 'All right, Chief. Take care. Report as soon as you can.'

Warrington lifted a hand in salute to the peak of his oil-stained uniform cap; in the other he carried a very long, very powerful battery torch encased in rubber against any possibility of striking a spark off metal: one spark, if there was vapour around, and the *Coverdale* would be away as finally as the *Rhondda* and the *Timor*. He doubled along towards the for'ard tank deck to join Pedley and the ship's carpenter by the hatch leading down into Number One summer tank. With them was the third engineer, who had not yet opened up pending permission from the bridge and the arrival of the chief engineer.

'Right,' Warrington said tersely. 'Clips off.' He found a slight shake in his fingers as they lifted the torch like a baton: Dempsey had said there was danger. He hadn't needed to remind Warrington of that. For no real reason Warrington thought suddenly of his wife, Jean, and her terrible incapacity. . . . The clips came off and he stopped thinking of anything but the ship when the hatch was lifted and a taint of vapour came up.

'God Almighty,' Warrington said, stepping backwards involuntarily. Then he moved forward again: in truth it was not a hell of a lot of vapour – but any at all was bad, was highly dangerous. He flicked on his torch, beaming it down into the tank's deep darkness, stared down along the beam as it struck off the sides and brought a pool of light to the bottom some fifty feet below. There was something there, some obstruction.

'Well, sir?'

This was the third engineer. Warrington said, 'Not well at all.'

'What is it, sir?'

'I don't quite know. Have a look yourself.' Warrington stepped aside and the third engineer, using his own torch, peered down for some while, then came upright looking puzzled.

'I can't see any damage, sir. There's something there that shouldn't –'

'Yes. But what?'

'Looks like some sort of deposit. Sludge from the last cargo.'

'Which was fuel oil, the heavy stuff. It shouldn't happen, but I'll not go into that now. Later, somebody's guts are going to be had for garters. Point is, it's obscuring the damage as you've seen, and we have to know the score.'

The third engineer said, 'There's not a lot of gas there, sir. I'll go down –'

'No. Not you, laddie. It's my responsibility. And I'll not involve the Captain either – he's got enough on his plate.' Warrington waved towards the Nazi raider, firing still though quite badly down by the head. 'As for the gas, well, I'll have to improvise.' He reached around inside his overalls, turning his back, a handkerchief in his hand. One day someone might get around to providing anti-vapour helmets or some such but that day hadn't come yet. A urine-soaked handkerchief, like the troops had used against poison gas in the trenches in the last war, was at least some sort of protection and Warrington didn't intend to take long over his dangerous job. As soon as the handkerchief was soaked through he swung a leg over the hatch coaming and groped with his rubber-soled shoes for the steel ladder that would take him to the bottom. He went down fast, the handkerchief knotted over nose and mouth. Down, down . . . the vapour was largely held at bay by Warrington's simple precaution, but not entirely. His head began to swim: he went on doggedly. His thoughts proliferated: maybe he was getting light-headed. He saw Jean, saw his sister, almost heard them telling him to take care, that he was needed in Portsmouth as well as aboard the *Coverdale*.

vii

Away astern of the oiler, the *Kormoran* had continued on her ramming course; and although there had been that one torpedo hit for'ard it had come too late to take off her speed sufficiently. She hit the destroyer fair and square with all her 15,000 tons flinging fast through the water. The little *Ayers*, her back broken by the huge impact, was sent broadside through the water, her fore part wrapped around the *Kormoran*'s port side, her after part swinging off along the starboard side. From the Nazi's deck the close-range weapons and rifles were brought to bear, to sweep what was left of the destroyer before her two parts broke away and plummeted down beneath the surface. The firing was continued on the survivors and the *Kormoran* swung to carry on the action against the remaining destroyer. The Nazi's bows were down in the water but apparently she was seaworthy still, as Kemp remarked.

'She can stay afloat, I think. And carry on firing. It's up to the *Bass* now. The last one left! If she gets her, then God help us!'

As Kemp spoke, the gunfire was resumed against the convoy, now mostly dispersed and moving out of range. The *Kormoran* seemed to be concentrating her fire on the *Coverdale*, proclaimed Commodore's ship by Kemp's broad pennant flying out from the starboard fore yard, and a valuable ship in herself, a blow to the fleet if she went. But by now the *Kormoran*'s firing was erratic: she was being harried by the Australian destroyer, and was constantly altering her course – from the look of the action, Kemp thought, she was taking avoiding action against torpedoes.

That was when the *Coverdale*'s masthead lookout made an urgent report to the bridge: 'Torpedoes, sir – two trails bearing green one-three-five, distant four cables!'

So now the Nazi was using his own tubes: *Coverdale* wasn't yet quite out of torpedo range, but Kemp believed those tin fish must be almost at the end of their run. Dempsey gave the helm order before Kemp spoke.

'*Wheel hard-a-port!*'

The big oiler turned under her full port helm to run before the torpedo trails, presenting her counter to the attack, a smaller target than her long broadside would give. She heeled over in response to her rudder, was then steadied by the Captain who ordered the wheel amidships. With Dempsey Kemp watched the twin trails closely.

'We have the legs of them,' he said. 'Thank God for your speed, Dempsey! I think all's well now.'

Dempsey was about to make some response when there was an urgent shout from the port side forward, from the bosun standing by Number One summer tank. Dempsey went fast into the port bridge wing. 'What is it, Pedley?'

'Chief engineer, sir, gone down into the tank –'

'No permission was given, Pedley.'

'No, sir. Chief hasn't come up . . . he's at the foot of the ladder, sir, and I don't reckon he's moving.'

'I'll come down immediately,' Dempsey called.

Six

It had started with that swimming in the head, the odd sensation that had produced jumbled thoughts of home leading Warrington back into the past, something akin to a drowning man in his last moments of life. Deeper into the tank the residue of gas that was no doubt coming from the sludge at the bottom had grown quite strong and Warrington had begun breathing it through the handkerchief, the effect of the soaking wearing off fast. Small things came to him, Portsmouth and Southsea as they had been before the war, Commercial Road and Queen Street filled in the evenings with seamen from the ships in the dockyard or from the barracks, all of them in uniform – no plain clothes allowed to ratings on short liberty – many of them the worse for drink as the evening rolled on. The old Coliseum in Edinburgh Road near the Unicorn Gate into the dockyard, the Hippodrome opposite the Theatre Royal, the clanging trams running from South Parade Pier to the Hard and the dockyard's main gate, the urchins known as the mudlarks who paddled about in the slimy ooze inshore of the harbour station, catching pennies thrown to them by the passing crowds. Often he'd taken Jean to the Isle of Wight before her affliction, catching the paddle ferry from the harbour station or Clarence Pier, happy days walking along the sea shore at Ryde and looking across the waters of Spithead towards Southsea common and the castle, and the naval war memorial. That, or a trip in the steamy old train that ran from Ryde pierhead to Ventnor; sometimes a trip around the island in a charabanc and climbing down to see the many-coloured sands of Alum Bay in the lee of the Needles.

Johnny, mown down by a motorist at the age of fourteen . . .
how he'd enjoyed those and other trips! A fair-haired, blue-eyed,
happy lad who'd wanted to go to sea one day, following his
father's footsteps around the world. Warrington had served in
RFA ships in Hong Kong, the Persian Gulf, Malta and Gibraltar,
the West Indies, Australia.

It had all come back in extraordinarily vivid flashes until it had
faded into a blankness at the bottom of the ladder, where he had
hooked an arm over one of the steel treads, his body sagging
against the uprights.

ii

'I'm going down,' Dempsey said at the tank top. He'd had words
with Kemp, a brief statement of his intent. He knew Kemp had
wanted to demur: the Captain's place was on the bridge and he
shouldn't risk his life elsewhere. But Kemp had said none of this,
had just nodded. He had understood, and, as ever, the Captain
commanded the ship. Dempsey had gone down at the double,
almost sliding down the ladders to the tank deck. Once again the
third engineer had volunteered but Dempsey had cut him short.
As master of the ship he wouldn't send any other man down,
volunteer or not. Dempsey felt his own responsibilities keenly,
knew that as top of the pyramid of command he was finally to
blame for an improperly cleaned tank even though it was entirely
normal to take the word of one's chief engineer, the man most
immediately responsible together with the chief officer.

'Pedley . . . the chief should have gone down on a line.'
Dempsey was angry, as much with the bosun as with Warrington: Pedley should have seen to it that the chief didn't go down
untended. Dempsey looked down into the tank behind the third
engineer's torch: Warrington was slumped against the ladder.
Now there was no time to wait while a line was fetched:
Dempsey, hardly aware now of the action going on away astern
of the oiler, nor of the fact that there was no more gunfire, went
over the hatch, felt as Warrington had done for the treads of the
ladder, and went down very fast, holding a deeply-indrawn
breath.

With no time wasted he pulled Warrington from the ladder and

59

got him across his shoulders. Another valid reason for not letting the third engineer go down: Dempsey was twice his size, twice his strength. As soon as Warrington was in place, Dempsey started to climb back, sweating like a pig, still just about holding onto his breath. It went out with a gasp as he neared the hatch. The bosun and third engineer leaned over and between them took Warrington's weight.

They laid him on the deck, between the tank tops. Dempsey knelt beside him, pulling away the overalls and feeling for heartbeats.

He looked up. 'Dead, I think. Get some hands along – he's to be taken to his cabin. I'm no doctor – there'll be tests we can make, just to be sure.'

Mirrors held before the mouth, an incision in a vein – or should it be an artery? *The Ship Captain's Medical Guide* would settle that one, perhaps. The *Coverdale* carried no doctor and treatment of the crew, with the assistance of the chief steward, was another of the master's responsibilities – a case of diagnosis by guess and by God. As soon as Warrington had been taken aft to his cabin above the engine-room, Dempsey made his researches into the fact of death. He left the cabin heavy hearted and went back to the bridge after a word with Evans, now acting chief engineer.

iii

Petty Officer Rattray gave a shout. 'She's going! She's bloody well going!'

The *Kormoran*, well down now by the bow, was beginning to slide, the water reaching up along her fo'c'sle and lapping round the for'ard 5.9-inch guns. The after armament was firing still, but with no effect; the remaining destroyer, HMAS *Bass*, was answering the stricken Nazi's fire. More explosions appeared on the raider's upper deck and then within the next few minutes she started to go with a rush, her stern came up sharply as the weight of water in her fore part increased, and suddenly she took a very fast dive and was gone, leaving the sea's surface dotted with wreckage of boats and rafts and other moveables and with swimming men making for the safety of the destroyer, now standing by to pick up survivors. From the after superstructure of the *Coverdale*, Rattray watched, and despite his loathing for the Nazis watched with mixed feelings, because he knew what it was like to have to swim for it, as he started to remark to Leading Seaman Sinker.

'Poor sods, swimming through spilt fuel oil, and likely enough wounded. I remember –' He checked himself: he didn't want to get the reputation of labouring his own part in the last war, and he'd told Stripey Sinker before now how he'd been tin fished as a young AB aboard a destroyer of the old Dover Patrol and had been hauled from the drink by a collier coming down from the Tyne to Frazer and White's coal wharf in the Camber off the entry to Pompey dockyard. Feeling the heel of the deck beneath his feet, he looked at the wake. 'Skipper's altering, going in to help the destroyer.'

'Looks like it.' Stripey paused. 'Heard about the chief, have you, PO?'

Rattray nodded. 'Saw him being carried aft.' He spoke without much feeling: he'd never exchanged a word with the chief engineer, never been in contact, not his department. He glanced at Stripey Sinker and said with a touch of sardonic malice, 'Best search your conscience, eh?'

'What d'you mean, PO?'

'What I said earlier. Careless talk. Look what you've been and gone and done, eh!'

Stripey flushed behind his lurid birthmark, though he knew Rattray was once again only indulging in his idea of a joke. It wasn't seemly, to joke. Besides, Stripey was already feeling that sense of guilt. Daft, but there it was. You couldn't help yourself. They always used women as spies: Stripey remembered some bit of stuff called Mata Hari who wormed all sorts of secrets out of the brass whilst in bed, not that Feeling Deeling was Mata Hari any more than he was the brass. He moved for'ard along the flying bridge, Rattray's number two checking round the guns after action. Looking down at the tank deck he saw some of the ship's crew gathered around the top of Number One summer tank. They all looked up as he passed along above their heads. Maybe it was his imagination but he didn't like the way they looked at him. He gave himself a mental shake: he was seeing trouble where none could possibly lie. It was just that perishing sod Rattray. . . .

61

On the bridge there was an exchange of signals in progress, lamps flashing in all directions as the convoy was ordered by the Commodore to reform and resume course for the Cape. A signal from the *Bass* had indicated she could take all survivors aboard without assistance.

When that signal had come Kemp had felt relief: he had that weighted canvas bag in mind and he didn't much want any Nazis aboard if he could avoid it – just in case. When the *Kormoran* had gone down, the bag had been returned to its locked stowage in the chart room. Kemp walked up and down the starboard wing with Captain Dempsey and raised the question of the dead chief engineer.

'Committal, you mean?' Dempsey asked. 'Sooner the better.'

'Yes. In case of further alarms.' Right now, it should be safe enough to stop engines, Kemp considered.

'That and other considerations. You know merchant seamen, Commodore.'

Kemp nodded. Corpses were not popular aboard ships, they were a bad-luck symbol. 'I know it's not my business, Captain, but what's your acting chief like?'

'Evans? Oh, he's reliable – if relatively inexperienced. This is his first voyage as second, let alone chief.'

'A big responsibility. What about that tank?'

Dempsey said, 'I'll wait for my chief officer's report. We'll probably steam clean the tank, then the hole can be plugged until such time as we reach Simonstown –'

'A dockyard job?'

'I expect so. I'm not risking welding or riveting at sea with a partly loaded ship.'

'You mean you'll have to discharge first?'

Dempsey said, 'Certainly! And then clean all tanks.'

'What sort of delay is that going to mean?'

'That depends on the dockyard mateys. The convoy's scheduled to remain three days in Simonstown, isn't it? That ought to give us time, but I repeat, it's up to the dockyard.' Dempsey grinned. 'I don't suppose you've had much experience of HM dockyards, Commodore! Sometimes they're pretty good. Other times, it's a case of dead slow and stop and when you complain you're met with a brick wall.'

Kemp said, 'We shall see about that.'

Dempsey grinned again. 'I wish you all the luck in the world!'
He turned away into the wheelhouse, and passed word down
that the chief engineer's body would be despatched overboard as
soon as the Commodore had shepherded the convoy together
again for onward passage behind their now solitary destroyer
escort. Dempsey would read the service and the body would go
over from the tank deck, port side aft, whilst engines were
temporarily stopped, something that probably wouldn't have
happened in the areas liable to U-boat attack.

Alone now, Kemp watched the ships of the convoy come
together again and resume their formation. Through his binoculars he saw the crowded decks aboard the transports, the
Australian soldiers who had now had their first taste of war and
would have something to think about as they queued for grub
along the messdecks. As he watched he pondered on what
Dempsey had referred to: his lack of experience of Royal
dockyards, a lack shared with any liner officer. Like all permanent Royal Naval Reserve officers, Kemp had done his periodic
time with the fleet, just short appointments aboard a cruiser or
battleship at sea when he had been supernumerary to the
complement and was never involved in dockyard refits or
repairs. Kemp pondered on the great diversity of life in the
merchant service: cargo-ships, liners, tankers of the British
Tanker Company or Shell for instance, down to coasters and
ferries and even the steam yachts belonging to a handful of
millionaires. Separate from all stood the Royal Fleet Auxiliaries
with their fleet oilers and replenishment tankers, their dry cargo
ships and their armament supply vessels, ships that hadn't the
advantage – as some would see it – of a regular run with regular
sailings and always the same ports at each end, where dockers
and repair firms were attuned to the ways of the particular
company and were employed for the express purpose of keeping
that company's ships ready for the next embarkation of
passengers. The RFA ships went anywhere according to the
dictates of the Admiralty and the various Commanders-in-Chief
of overseas stations, and presumably were subject to the same
frustrations of dockyards as were the warships of the fleet.

Dempsey rejoined Kemp half an hour later. 'Ready when you
are, Commodore.'

'The committal?'

'Yes. D'you want to come along?'

'I'd very much appreciate that, Captain. Mr Warrington was very helpful, very patient when I joined you in Sydney.'

They went down aft together, the chief officer in charge on the bridge with Sub-Lieutenant Cutler standing in for the Commodore and ready to report any signals to his lord and master. The ship's second officer and third engineer, the latter now acting second, were standing by the plank bearing the body beneath the Blue Ensign of the RFA provided by ex-Yeoman of Signals Gannock from his flag locker. As Dempsey read the sombre words of the committal service the plank was tilted and the canvas-shrouded body slid down into the water, lead-weighted at the feet, vanishing fast. A final salute and the small party broke up, officers and men going back to their various duties about the ship. As Kemp and Dempsey reached the bridge, the telegraph handles were pulled over for full away, and the *Coverdale* began once again to vibrate to the thrust of her screws and to move through the re-formed troop convoy to the Commodore's station.

From the master's deck outside Dempsey's accommodation, Steward Porter, his tea-cloth over his arm, looked around at the ships and the clearing weather. The grey skies had gone now, had been left to the south and the antics of the Roaring Forties. The sea, like the sky, was blue, dappled with white horses from a wind that was still fairly strong. Porter breathed deep: the air was good. So far as was ever possible aboard a ship at sea in wartime, there was a relaxed feeling. The *Kormoran* had gone; so far as Porter knew, and like any Captain's steward he always made it his business to keep a flapping ear, there was no other known enemy around and they should have a nice, clear run to the Cape.

After that – well, the South Atlantic wasn't so good. There were U-boats on the prowl, off Freetown in Sierra Leone and right down to lie across the shipping routes to the Cape, and north from the Cape to UK or across to the United States, the way the convoy was said to be going, though you never knew for sure until you were on the way.

The point was, after Simonstown the Old Man would be a bloody sight more occupied than he would be over the next few days before arrival: Porter's chance might be lost and by now he was beginning to worry himself sick. He didn't expect miracles, he just wanted to get things off his chest and feel that his worries had been shared: the voice of common sense might bring some balm. But in the upshot, partly because Dempsey remained on the bridge right throughout that day so wasn't available, and partly because Porter began to lose his courage for broaching fornication to the Captain, it was to the chief steward that he went. The chief steward was quite a fount of wisdom in his own right.

'Thought there was something up,' Chief Steward Lugg said, pushing aside his mountain of stores lists and ship's accounts. 'So it's a young lady. Now we know.' He pursed his lips. 'Got her in the club, would that be it?'

'Yes.'

'Bloody fool! Kiss 'em and leave 'em, lad, and nothing in between, that's the safest way. I don't hold with what goes on these days, everything's a sight too loose, no discipline.'

Porter shifted uncomfortably. 'It's not a case of discipline, Chief –'

'Oh yes it is, lad, *self* discipline. Keep your flies buttoned.' Grave-faced, Lugg stared disapprovingly over the tops of steel-rimmed spectacles. 'The war's no excuse,' he said, just as though Porter had said it was. 'We still have our responsibilities to face up to and that's what *you* will have to do, right?'

'You mean –'

'You know what I mean. Look, you said you'd thought of going to the skipper. If you're not plain daft, you know just what *he* would have said. He'd have said it was your duty to marry the girl, wouldn't he? Stands to reason: you can't let her down, not after what you done. What else were you thinking you might do, eh, lad?'

Porter, red-faced now, said, 'Well, I thought about – about an abortion.'

'An *abortion*! God give me strength.' Lugg wiped at his face with a handkerchief. He was thinking of that as yet unborn grandchild, the difficulties his daughter was facing in giving it birth, and he felt suddenly very angry that anyone could so casually use the word, abortion. 'What are you, a man or a worm? Get out of my cabin!'

'But –'

'Go on, get out.' Lugg got to his feet and waved his arms in the

air, in Porter's face. Porter got out, no argument: Lugg looked fit
to commit murder. Walking away from the chief steward's cabin,
Porter encountered Leading Seaman Sinker who was also looking worried, almost distraught. Porter scuttled past but Sinker
turned and called after him.

'Hey you, po bosun –'

Porter knew the Navy's term for officers' stewards. He
stopped. 'Yes?'

'You blokes act as kind of doctors, so they tell me.' Sinker
moved closer, confidentially. 'Never needed a doctor before, but
I reckon I do now. I was going to have a word with the chief
steward, but maybe you'll do. Less sort of official like. Got a copy
of that medical guide, have you?'

'Not me. Chief steward. What's the trouble, Mr Sinker?'

Stripey Sinker looked all around, making sure they were alone.
'You keep this to yourself, or else. Thing is . . . I had a woman
back in Sydney, down the Cross, know what I mean? Now I got
what you might call a reaction. Started some days ago it did, back
in the Bight.' There was real alarm in Sinker's face, and he had
started to shake. 'P'raps I'd best see the chief steward after all. I
s'pose he's got the medical chest, drugs an' all. Sulphur something I reckon cures it. It's like bloody broken glass every time I
pee. Can't take it much longer.' His courage screwed up, Leading
Seaman Sinker pushed on past before Porter could utter. Porter
went off shaking his head but with a glimmer of a smile in his
eyes. Poor old Lugg's principles were taking quite a battering
today.

iv

Below in the engine-room Evans, acting chief engineer, wiped his
hands on a bundle of cotton-waste and stared around somewhat
aprehensively from the starting platform. He felt at a dis-
advantage: no one of the black gang was really going to look upon
him as chief. For one thing he still wore second engineer's stripes,
gold with purple between, one stripe less than a chief's – he had
toyed briefly with the notion that he might use Warrington's
shoulder-straps when he was in his white uniform on deck but
had decided not to, that might bring bad luck – and, of course, he

knew his own lack of experience: he hadn't long had his chief engineer's certificate. The sea services were being diluted as a result of wartime pressures and the RFA was no exception. In peacetime it would have been years yet before he'd made even second engineer, and now here he was, chief aboard a big fleet oiler in waters that would soon become dangerous again and anything might go wrong in the engine spaces.

Would he be able to cope?

Of course. He braced his shoulders back, left the starting platform and walked around with an air of authority, the authority of the chief, the one who made all the decisions in his own kingdom of oil and grease, heat and noise, the man who made the ship go and without whom all would be lost. He knew that to be the fact and if he hadn't already he would have done by the time his father-in-law, a recent acquisition on his last leave, had expounded at much length, garrulous old sod . . . the father of Ruth, his wife, had been a chief engineer himself, in the Clan Line, and had a name to go with it, MacArthur, like that American general. What old MacArthur didn't know about engines and the vital importance of chief engineers hadn't yet been invented. Evans knew that he had to prove himself in his father-in-law's eyes, which meant Ruth's eyes also, for she fancied the sun shone out of her old man's backside and was accustomed to nod decisively at each of his dogmatic utterances. Evans, cringing inside, could hear the old geezer's reaction to the knowledge, when he got it, of his son-in-law's rocket-like projection to high rank. It would be a loud laugh like that of a horse . . . and, possibly from sheer habit since she was not in fact disloyal to her husband, Ruth would nod.

He was going to show them both. And the first thing he would have to deal with, in conjunction, of course, with Chief Officer Harlow, was a damaged cargo tank. That tank was currently being cleaned – properly this time . . . lucky in a way for poor old Warrington that he wouldn't have to face the enquiry into that improperly done job, which might yet rub off on himself, Evans, as the then second engineer of the *Coverdale*. When they eventually returned to the UK – or even in a few days' time at the Cape – the Admiralty would appoint some RN engineer officer, probably a captain(E), to investigate and ask searching questions and render his report. If any blame then attached to himself, old MacArthur would have a field day.

That must not happen. He could do worse than take a look at Warrington's engine-room logs and records, some of which would be in the chief's safe of which he now had the key. Just to refresh his memory. He returned to the starting platform and spoke to the new second engineer.

'I'm going up, Mr Vetch. Call me immediately if I'm wanted.'

'Yes, sir.' The 'sir' was pretty spontaneous and Evans felt pleased about that; it did something for his self-confidence. As he was climbing the ladders Leading Signalman Goodenough was making a report to the Commodore.

'Destroyer signalling, sir.' Goodenough made the acknowledgement and began reading the message off as it came through. 'Addressed Commodore, sir. "Radar indicates vessel bearing 325 degrees, distant thirteen miles, drawing aft." Message ends, sir.'

'Thank you, Goodenough. Cutler?'

'Sir?'

'Anything on the plot? Anything of ours?'

'Not a thing, sir. Just blank.'

Kemp frowned, watching the given bearing closely as though something might emerge. 'An unknown vessel, moving easterly. What does that suggest to you, Cutler?'

'Something scuttling away, sir?'

'Away from a virtually unarmed convoy? We can assume she'll have picked us up on her radar and identified us. She'll probably know the facts about the losses – we know *Kormoran* broke wireless silence once she'd engaged.' Kemp paused. 'For my money she's a supply ship for the *Kormoran*, making what would have been a rendezvous.'

Cutler said, 'Make a nice prize, sir.'

'Very nice! But somewhat unattainable so far as we're concerned. Even a supply ship –' Kemp broke off. 'Escort's signalling again.'

The message was flashed across the water: the unknown ship was now altering towards the convoy and the range was closing fast. Cutler believed Kemp could have been wrong; but the Commodore said, 'As I was about to remark, even a supply ship has guns of some sort and she could have got that report – that we're virtually without an escort now. Close up the guns' crews, Cutler. And pass the word as to what I expect.'

'Aye, aye, sir.' Cutler went down the starboard ladder fast, making for the flying bridge and shouting for Petty Officer Rattray. When Rattray got the word of possible action against a Nazi supply ship he spat on his hands, rubbed them together, and with a gleam of anticipation in his eye moved at the double to rouse out his gunnery rates.

Seven

Cutler asked, 'Do we scatter the convoy, sir?'

Kemp shook his head. 'No. Not this time. Somehow I still think it's a supply ship. Her captain may have ideas of heroics now the *Kormoran*'s gone. So far as we know, there's no other raider in the vicinity.'

Cutler looked dubious; but it was not up to him to question the Commodore's decision. However, he asked, 'Do we engage, sir? The *Coverdale*, I mean?'

Kemp said, 'If we're attacked, yes, of course. I dare say we can match a supply ship, gun for gun.'

'We're a tanker, sir.'

Kemp said evenly, 'I'm aware of the dangers, Cutler.' He turned to Dempsey. 'What do you say, Captain Dempsey? She's still your ship and your responsibility.'

'I'll go along with you, Commodore. We're in no more danger firing back than just sitting it out.'

'You can move out of range, remember.'

Dempsey gave a short laugh. 'Maybe I will if and when I think fit. But for now, well, I won't deprive the convoy of what our guns can do to help.'

Kemp clapped him on the shoulder, but didn't speak. He lifted his glasses again towards the expected bearing, watched the Australian destroyer moving to starboard under full power, cutting across the wind and the swell, throwing back a big bow-wave, her battle ensign streaming from the mainmast head. Below at the for'ard gun, Petty Officer Rattray also watched, many things running through his mind. That Aussie destroyer

70

had suffered during the attack by the *Kormoran*: two of her guns had been put out of action, there was a shortage of oil fuel, she had sustained a lot of casualties. It wasn't going to be any walkover and if the *Coverdale* was to engage they might all be going sky-high within the next few minutes and Doris would be a widow, all alone with her hypochondriac mother. Thinking of Ma Bates, Petty Officer Rattray shuddered. Maybe death would be better than going back to all that one day when the war ended; better a quick end than a long, slow one at the end of Ma Bates' tongue.

Home didn't always beckon. . . . Aboard a ship one was Petty Officer Rattray, gunner's mate, and very important in the lives of junior ratings. At home one was just 'that husband of yours' and a lifelong meal ticket. A crown above crossed fouled anchors on the left sleeve, crossed guns with crown and star on the right, all in gold when in Number Ones, didn't register in the home.

'Well, Leading Seaman Sinker, what's up with you, eh?'

'Nothing, PO.'

'Stop bloody twittering, then. All on top line?'

Stripey nodded speechlessly: he was on fire between the legs, having just taken a pre-action precaution, a leak. Broken glass wasn't in it; his feelings towards Feeling Deeling were sheerly murderous.

'Right,' Rattray said. 'Take charge aft and be ready to open the moment word comes from the bridge.'

Stripey nodded again. Trust Rattray to underline the obvious, he never left anything unsaid that didn't need to be said, it was all part and parcel of a gunner's mate's image, all gas and gaiters. Stripey Sinker carried his private agony aft along the flying bridge, another who with Rattray felt that a quick end might have its advantages. It wasn't just the broken glass either: not as such, that was. Back home, which was off the Ratcliffe Highway in London, Stripey had a wife. If ever she found out about his extra-marital activities, then he was for it. If he didn't find a cure for his current affliction, then she *would* find out, since it would go on getting worse and might even become incurable for all Stripey knew. She might divorce him and he didn't want that.

If he lived though what was coming.

Supply ships, if that was what this one was, didn't have much weaponry, just defensive stuff like any merchant ship in convoy,

71

but Stripey was as aware as anyone else aboard that all a tanker needed was just one projy in or near a tank.

Leading Signalman Goodenough prided himself on his ship recognition: he'd made a study of it, partly because it was his job to spot an identity if possible, partly because he was interested and had read every reference book he could lay his hands on. He knew all the pre-war liners – Cunarders, Union Castle and so on, and the foreigners – *Bremen*, *Ile de France*, *Normandie*, *Rex*, *Conte di Savoia*. The war had taught him more: the books of silhouettes of ship types had brought the smaller cargo vessels into his range. Thus, when the smudge on the horizon had grown into a ship, he was able to report at once to the Commodore.

'*Gerhardt Abusch*, sir. 3500 net register tons.'

'One of the *Kormoran*'s supply ships – just as I thought,' Kemp said, steadying his binoculars on the emerging ship. 'Armament's what – 3-pounders plus ack-ack?'

'Yes, sir,' Goodenough answered.

Kemp looked round: already Cutler was calling down to the guns' crews through a megaphone and as Kemp watched he saw both the ship's main weapons train round onto the bearing. The *Gerhardt Abusch* was coming on fast: *Coverdale* was her nearest target after the destroyer; and Kemp realized that the Nazi was making a bee-line for him and seemingly had the legs of the action-damaged escort, now opening fire with her remaining twin guns for'ard, pumping out shells that were so far failing to find their mark, though with water-spouts from near misses cascading like fountains over her decks, the onrush of the *Gerhardt Abusch* had all the appearance of a suicide bid. Kemp thought of his earlier remark about her captain having ideas of heroics. Currently, it was the sort of lunatic heroism that looked like paying off: flashes came from the Nazi as she turned slightly so as to bring her armament to bear, and more spouts arose astern of the *Coverdale*, which seemed still to be somewhat outside the German range.

Kemp passed the order to Cutler: 'Open fire!'

Fore and aft, Rattray and Stripey Sinker repeated the orders to the guns' crews. There was a shudder throughout the ship, a series of ear-splitting cracks as the rapid fire was kept up. Shell cases clattered down to the tank deck and the stench of cordite wafted across the bridge. The firing seemed almost frenzied: if the Nazi couldn't be held off, they were all due for a very nasty fry-up. Petty Officer Rattray gave a shout of joy as an explosion was seen on the Nazi's fo'c'sle, just for'ard of the bridge superstructure, orange flame followed by thick, billowing smoke.

'First blow to us,' Kemp said on the bridge. He was about to say something further when there was a high whine from immediately above his head and he went flat instinctively. There was the sound of splintering woodwork, the smash of glass, and a high, strangled scream from behind Kemp.

He pulled himself upright. Dempsey, who had been beside him, was running for the wheelhouse, which was a shambles. The Nazi shell appeared to have passed right through without exploding but had left havoc behind it.

And blood. The whole place was spattered: the chief officer, Harlow, lay on the deck, a gap where his chest had been. He was almost cut in two. The helmsman lay decapitated behind the wheel, which was spinning out of control; *Coverdale* was beginning to move in a circle. Dempsey himself grabbed the wheel, and brought the ship back on course.

'Steering all right?' Kemp asked breathlessly.

Dempsey nodded, looking out through the shattered side of the wheelhouse towards the *Gerhardt Abusch*. The German opened again and a moment later there was a big explosion aboard the *Bass*: something had landed on her fo'c'sle, and had taken out what was left of her main armament. It was a lucky shot from a pea-shooter that had perhaps scored its freak hit either just as a shell was being rammed home in the breech or more likely had landed on the ready-use ammunition in the racks. With probable subsidiary damage to her bridge and command personnel, the destroyer fell away, her head paying off to port with her engines still giving full power to her shafts. In the meantime the *Coverdale* was standing into danger. They had the speed to get clear of the German gunners and they were valuable to the war effort, more valuable than the problematic sinking of a supply ship. But there were those jam-packed troop transports for the Commodore of the convoy to consider. Captain Dempsey seemed to sense the way Kemp's mind was working, to sense his indecision, and he said promptingly, 'Just us and our guns between the liners and the Nazi. And as you remarked earlier, Commodore, the *Coverdale*'s my ship. I'm willing to take a chance.'

Kemp nodded his agreement: he understood Dempsey's attitude. In war you didn't run away. He went out into the bridge wing and watched the effect of the gunfire from both sides. *Coverdale* now alone against the German while the convoy, continuing on its steady course, moved westerly – well out of range by this time. Kemp believed he was now waiting for the end, and half his mind, at this late stage in which he could play no active role, went homeward across the waste of seas, home to Meopham and his wife, now facing a double tragedy – a son to be followed by a husband. Bleak thoughts, and so much to be laid at the door of Adolf Hitler, plotting mass murder from his eyrie at Berchtesgaden. Kemp's fists clenched hard behind his back: he felt so helpless, not for the first time as a convoy Commodore. He was nine-tenths a figurehead, though he could also be considered a rallying point when there was anything left to rally. In the last war he'd been active enough as a lieutenant RNR in destroyers and minelayers. Age went hand-in-hand with seniority and now he was too old and too senior for the more active role, an Ancient Mariner drifting across the last seas of life. . . .

Vengeful cracks, more acrid smoke, explosions aboard the *Gerhardt Abusch*, another awesome whine across the fore part of the *Coverdale* . . . a minute before, seconds before, the ship's bosun had been on the fo'c'sle, God alone knew what sense of duty had made him go up there to be an extra target. Now he was gone, taken out like Harlow by a shell that went on to hit the sea and send up another waterspout. Then an explosion by the after superstructure above the engineer's accommodation, a blast that cleared the poop of all the smaller impediments but so far as could be seen left the 3-inch intact.

After that the miracle, by courtesy of Petty Officer Rattray who had taken over personally as layer on the for'ard 3-inch – seeing as he knew best, as he put it later. His gun's crew put it down to sheer luck but whatever it was the result was satisfactory: two projectiles took the Nazi smack amidships, penetrated the unarmoured sides and caused havoc inside the hull. A magazine, was the general verdict. The *Gerhardt Abusch* erupted in smoke and flame and began to settle fast, with her back apparently broken, her stem and stern both pointing up to the skies until each part slid separately beneath the surface, leaving assorted wreckage and a handful of men struggling in the water. Away to the north-west, the Australian destroyer was still moving in circles, her helm stuck fast and neither her secondary nor emergency steering positions yet connected up.

A matter of minutes only since the action had begun, but to Kemp it had been an eternity.

He went into the wreckage of the wheelhouse. 'Captain, I'd be obliged if you'd send a boat away to pick up survivors. Cutler, make to *Bass* from Commodore, report situation aboard. And after that, my congratulations to Petty Officer Rattray –' He turned as he heard a step on the starboard ladder. 'Oh, there you are, Rattray.'

'Yessir.' Rattray never missed a chance of pushing himself forward. He saluted smartly. 'Come to report like, sir –'

Kemp smiled. 'I saw for myself. Very well done. You saved the ship. We're all grateful to you.'

'Yessir – thank you, sir.'

'All right, Rattray. My congratulations to all men of the guns' crews – they all did splendidly.'

Rattray saluted again and went down the ladder, making aft where the *Coverdale's* seamen under the third officer were sorting out the damage to the poop. The second officer had taken over the watch; Harlow's remains had been removed below to his cabin when the reply to the Commodore's signal came in from the Australian destroyer. The ship was seaworthy but virtually defenceless. There was some damage to the connecting links between the tiller flat and the secondary steering position aft of the searchlight platform but the warrant engineer expected to be able to report a successful repair shortly. HMAS *Bass* could continue to the Cape but with fingers crossed. If the warrant engineer should prove to have been over optimistic, the ship could be steered by use of the emergency steering in the tiller flat where, right above the rudder, the hands could move the rudder-head by means of heavy beams, like capstan bars.

Kemp, as the *Coverdale* lay with engines stopped, watched the progress of the ship's motor-boat as it moved in amongst the survivors from the *Gerhardt Abusch*. He counted only five out of probably forty seamen and engineers, being helped over the gunwale. For the rest, Kemp could feel no regrets. The Nazi philosophy had been responsible for the war. Let them get on with it and suffer with everybody else.

The motor-boat came back across the water and was hooked onto the falls aft. The survivors were hoisted on the falls and assisted from the boat to the after deck, some of them suffering wounds that still bled freely. They were met by the third officer and the chief steward, who would need to employ his medical skills as well as find the survivors accommodation. One of the Germans wore shoulder-straps with three gold bars: the chief officer, Kemp assumed.

Dempsey called down aft through a megaphone to the third officer. 'Mr Peel . . . send up the German officer.'

iii

Now the *Coverdale* had more deaths to assimilate: the bosun, Jack Pedley, had been a much liked man and a first-rate seaman. He was going to be missed. The feeling throughout the ship was far from good: yarns had circulated, however unfairly, however ludicrous, about Leading Seaman Sinker, these rumours having originated from that early careless remark by Petty Officer Rattray, overheard, repeated throughout the ship by the fo'c'sle hands and in the repetition exaggerated.

No one, as it seemed, paused to consider that a leading seaman might be an unlikely purveyor of useful information to the enemy, that a prozzy from the Cross might be an even more unlikely Berlin plant, making daily contact across the world by secret radio transmitter into the listening antennae of the German Naval Command. The seamen had a Johah, and that was enough. Somebody had to have the can fixed to them, and the somebody was Leading Seaman Sinker, the more so as word had filtered through from the Old Man's tiger, Porter, that Sinker had a dose of the clap. That proved something: it fitted the buzz about the prozzy, fitted the story they all wanted to believe. But all this might in the end have amounted to nothing more than dirty looks

76

and the cold shoulder had not something more positive taken place as the small group of survivors made their way for'ard under guard of four of the naval ratings and passed Leading Seaman Sinker on the flying bridge. It was spotted by Kemp among others as he looked over the after screen of the bridge, an apparent contact between Sinker and one of the Germans.

Eight

Kemp asked Dempsey to belay his last order: he would prefer the German officer to come to the bridge later. Then he leaned over the after screen.

'Leading Seaman Sinker.'

Stripey looked up. 'Yessir!'

'On the bridge, Sinker. Fast.'

'Yessir.' Still puzzled about what had taken place, Stripey put on speed and hefted his stomach up the ladders. That Jerry . . . odd, it was. He arrived on the bridge panting from his exertions, red in the face and dreading the next time he was forced to have a leak.

He saluted the Commodore. 'You wanted me, sir –'

'Yes.' Kemp led the way into the starboard wing of the bridge, motioning the signalman away. Dempsey, taking what seemed to be a hint, moved through the wheelhouse into the port wing as the *Coverdale*'s engines again went ahead and the ship moved fast to catch up the main body of the convoy. Kemp said, 'Now Sinker. An explanation. Do you know the man who spoke to you?'

Sinker shook his head. 'No, sir, I don't reckon I do. Not really, like.'

'Not really?'

Sinker licked his lips. The Commodore's tone was sharpish. 'He said –'

'Said, in English?'

'Sort of, sir. Pidgin English as you might say.'

Kemp nodded. 'Go on, Sinker.'

78

'Yessir. Well, sir, he said as 'ow we'd met. In Pompey . . . the fleet review, sir, the Coronation, 1937. Just before I went out on pension, like. Well, sir, me, I don't recall him, not personally that is.' Sinker lifted a hand and fingered his lurid birthmark. 'Mind, I did meet some o' the Jerry ratings, sir, from the *Admiral Graf Spee*. In the pubs, like – Queen Street, Commercial Road –'

'Yes, I see. So this man's a German naval rating, not a merchant seaman?'

'Seems like it, sir, yes, if he's got it right. About recognizing me, sir.'

Again Kemp nodded. 'That could be useful information, Sinker. Keep it to yourself for now – just in case I can make some use of it.'

'Yessir. Sealed lips, sir.'

Kemp smiled. 'That's the ticket.' He paused. 'That was all he said – all there was in it?'

'Oh, yessir! Me, I didn't say anything at all, bloody Nazi, if you'll excuse me, sir. I just give 'im a dirty look an' passed on aft.'

'Yes. All right, Sinker. I may send for you again – that's all for now.'

Stripey Sinker saluted again, a trifle unctuously. It wasn't by any means often that you had a private conversation with a Commodore, seldom indeed that you were able perhaps to be of some assistance to the brass, and Stripey rather liked his sudden leap from obscurity, it gave him something extra and in a sense could be considered one in the eye for that Rattray who acted as though he was the Holy Trinity at times.

Stripey lowered himself down the ladders and made for the messroom set aside for the guns' crews, thinking about the Jerry. He didn't recall the bloke at all though he quite likely had met him the time of the review – and Stripey was well enough aware that his birthmark made him more memorable than the majority of ratings in the Portsmouth Port Division. He did remember meeting quite a number of foreign seamen, Germans among them. There had been Frogs from the French battleship *Dunkerque*, Americans from the USS *New York*, Reds from the Russian battleship *Marat* though he didn't recall any of them being allowed ashore freely, Italians, Dutch, Norwegians, Japanese, Turks, Greeks, Argentinians, Cubans, Portuguese, Spanish . . . Queen Street and Edinburgh Road and Commercial

Road had been quite cosmopolitan and the hundreds of Pompey pubs had done a roaring trade.

Stripey remembered making some derogatory remarks about Adolf Hitler to a bunch of Nazis – it had been a time when the British Union of Fascists, the Blackshirts, had been a lot in the news and feelings were running high. But the Nazis had only smiled politely and although Stripey had intended causing trouble it hadn't come about.

Funny that one of them should turn up in the High South Latitudes and recognize him. Like his chat with the Commodore, it gave him a touch of mystique, actually to have hob-nobbed with the enemy in peacetime, but, of course, for a number of reasons it wouldn't do to talk about it. For one thing, Commodore Kemp was trusting him not to, and he'd find himself in the rattle for careless talk or something.

So he watched his tongue and went about with a knowing and furtive air. One that was not lost on certain members of the *Coverdale*'s crew who had, like Kemp, noticed a verbal exchange taking place. In the seamens' messroom other conversations took place shortly afterwards.

'Mate o' the Nazis – that Sinker.'

'Checks, don't it?'

'What we heard earlier. Rattray.'

'And the tiger.'

One of the speakers, a small, wizened man, a fireman who'd come along from the engine-room ratings' mess to stir up trouble about Leading Seaman Sinker, made a suggestion: there should be a deputation to the bridge, a report of their suspicions to the Old Man. More reasonable voices spoke against this proposal: neither Sinker nor the Nazi could do anything dangerous, and the prisoners would be kept under guard until they were landed at Simonstown, now not so far ahead. Better not to stick their necks out with unfounded accusations.

But no one was forgetting the men who had died as a result of the Nazi gunfire.

ii

The days passed towards Simonstown. Weary from long hours

on the bridge, Kemp was in his borrowed quarters below, sitting at his desk. There were reports to be written up before the ship reached the Cape about tank damage, the death of the chief engineer, the actions and the further deaths. Dempsey also would be compiling his reports from the ship's point of view, reports that would go ultimately to the Fourth Sea Lord at the Admiralty. Kemp's convoy report would go initially to the senior British naval officer at Simonstown and then to the Admiralty's Trade Division. Kemp, who disliked writing reports, indeed disliked all bumph, delayed his task. One of the things he would have to note would be the fleeting contact between one of his gunnery rates and a Nazi from the *Gerhardt Abusch*. It was interesting though not totally unexpected for a German naval rating, if such he was, to be aboard a merchant ship and not be wearing naval uniform which, supposing he was one of the gun's grew, he presumably would be. The Admiralty might like to know; but first Kemp would need to have further words with Leading Seaman Sinker. . . .

His mind drifted; his head fell forward and he brought himself up with a jerk. He ought to turn in for a spell or he would become useless, but sleep brought dreams, nightmares about sinkings in the Mediterranean. No news, and it had been such a long time now. Half Kemp's mind seemed to urge the convoy onward, to make Simonstown in the shortest possible time, the other half was filled with dread at the thought of what that arrival would bring. The end of all hope, the final confirmation?

He gave a heavy sigh: God damn the war! But he wasn't the only father in the world. Admirals had lost sons and had had to carry on with their high responsibilities, concentrating their minds for the sake of their commands. He was beginning very much to feel his age. He was about to call the bridge and say he was turning in for a couple of hours unless needed when Sub-Lieutenant Cutler knocked at his door and came in.

'Sorry to bother you, sir –'

'That's all right, Cutler. What is it?'

Cutler said, 'Well, probably none of our business, sir. Captain Dempsey's. But I thought I'd have a word with you.'

'Go on, Cutler.'

'Sinker's been moaning, sir.'

'Sinker? Oh, yes. Well?'

'Crew's been getting at him. They say he's a Nazi lover, sir.'
Cutler paused. 'He seems touchy about it. To that extent I reckon
it *is* our business.'

'You're suggesting I have a word with Captain Dempsey, I
suppose. You'll have to tell me more first. I can't go to Dempsey
and just say his men are teasing Leading Seaman Sinker.' Kemp
sounded edgy. His fingers tapped the top of the desk. 'Sinker's
not a babe in arms, is he?'

'No, sir. I'm sorry, sir –'

'Oh, all right, forget it!' Kemp smiled. 'I'm bloody tired, that's
all. It's not your fault, Sub. Only I don't like any suggestion of
interfering with the ship's master. It's not an easy situation.'
Once again Kemp brought himself up with a jerk: he was
excusing himself to a subordinate and that would never do. 'Let's
have it.'

Cutler elaborated. It hadn't been just name calling: Sinker had
said there was a nasty atmosphere, a feeling of being under
threat. The night before he had found a dead rat in his bunk; he
was certain none of his own messmates had been responsible.
He'd been given a number of vicious looks, too, and there was a
silence when he passed by small groups of crew members, and
loud comments when he'd moved on. He seemed even to be in
fear of physical attack.

'Tripe,' Kemp said. 'They would never risk it aboard –
Simonstown might be different, I agree, but I'm sure he's
exaggerating, Cutler.'

'I'm not so sure, sir. Quite a lot came out, sort of jumbled and I
don't know if I've got it right. Something about a woman in
Sydney.' Cutler gave a cough. 'Also he's got a dose, sir. Clap.
That's got around the ship too. He believes it came from Porter.
The information, not the clap.'

'I can't be responsible for the natural instincts of seamen,
Cutler, though I agree they're a bloody nuisance at times. Is he
being treated?'

'Chief steward's had a go, sir. But now we know, I guess Sinker
should be isolated.'

Kemp agreed; aboard a warship there was normally a CDA
mess – so named from the Contagious Diseases Act – where cases
of VD were kept apart, their mess utensils separately washed and
so on, the mess traps kept clear of the healthy men's stowages.

Aboard the *Coverdale* isolation wouldn't be so easy, since all the spare accommodation was occupied by the Commodore's staff and the gunnery rates. There was something else, and Kemp voiced it.

'The chief steward should have reported. It seems he hasn't or I would have been told – I hope!'

'I've had no report, sir. I guess the chief steward takes the medic's point of view maybe – professional discretion and not revealing secrets.'

Kemp snorted. 'I assume you're joking, Cutler. Any medical officer, the proper sort, knows he has to report to his CO.' Suddenly he yawned: he couldn't restrain it. He was almost out on his feet, or in his chair currently. 'Look, Cutler, have another word with Sinker and try to sort it out. If necessary I'll see him myself, but not just yet. It can rest for a while, like me.'

'Aye, aye, sir. I guess you need it.'

Cutler left the cabin. Kemp wondered wryly if the sub's last remark had held a sardonic touch, a reflection on the fact that Kemp wasn't reacting fully, wasn't thinking fast enough or something. Not on the ball. Well, if that was so, so be it. At any time there might be another emergency and the Commodore had to be fresh to meet it. The convoy's safety was of vastly more importance than a leading seaman's feelings of persecution or his shoreside peccadilloes. As he pulled his outer clothing off, Kemp reflected that if he had to practise abstinence there was no reason why Sinker shouldn't.

Three minutes later he was asleep.

iii

Chief Steward Lugg had been busy: wounded men, and never mind that they were Nazis, had to be seen to and he had done his best while Dempsey had eased his engines for the acting chief engineer to transfer oil fuel to HMAS *Bass*, herself wounded. When Evans' first ordeal in his new rank was over, Lugg's work went on, bandaging, applying ointment, sterilizing, administering aspirin, just filling in as best he could pending the removal of the Germans to hospital at the Cape.

One of his patients was Leading Seaman Sinker – had been for many days past. Sinker didn't seem to be responding to Lugg's limited knowledge, gleaned from *The Ship Captain's Medical Guide*: the principle ingredient of the cure was rest, not possible unless Sinker was put off duty and Sinker was adamant that he didn't want his condition known. Simple diet was indicated also, plus abstinence from all stimulants – that was easy enough. The *Coverdale* had some sulpha drugs in the medical kit but they didn't seem to be helping Sinker much. Perhaps, Lugg thought, the Australian gonococcus was a hardier germ than the home variety. If there was no improvement by the time the convoy reached the Cape, Lugg was going to report to Dempsey and never mind what his patient wanted: if the thing was left it could become chronic and in the meantime there were all the other men aboard to be considered; Lugg had warned Sinker to keep himself to himself as much as possible and wash up his own cups, plates and cutlery.

But those Jerries: they hadn't much English between them although one of them, a man with only a flesh wound from a piece of jagged steel, had said something about one of the British naval ratings, the one with the birthmark – Sinker.

'What about him, eh?'

The German hadn't seemed to understand and had just shaken his head and not pursued the matter. Later, Lugg mentioned it to Porter when the latter came down from taking cocoa to the bridge for the Captain and the others.

'Seems to know Sinker.'

'So I heard, from the deck mob. What did he say, Chief?'

Lugg shrugged. 'Very little. Just said his name.'

'Bit odd, isn't it?'

'Not really. We all get around, don't we, meet other nationalities. I remember in the old *Brambleleaf*, Med fleet pre-war, we took aboard a load of refugees from the Spanish Civil War, off Barcelona . . . ' Lugg screwed up his eyes and with his next utterance came right to the truth. 'Coronation review. I was there, again in the *Brambleleaf*. Met all sorts then, we did. Likely enough those two had a drink together.'

'Still funny,' Porter said, and went about his duties. Even back in 1937 you hadn't wanted to get tarred with the Nazi brush, not to the extent of making a mate of a Nazi naval rating. Porter had memories of the Blackshirts, the riots in London's East End and elsewhere, the vicious beatings-up from hard-fisted, club-bearing thugs, blood on the streets of peacetime Britain. Porter knew a young bloke who'd been almost killed by them and had never really recovered.

After Porter had gone, Lugg had another visitor: the Commodore's assistant. Cutler asked, 'Got a moment, Chief?'

'What can I do for you, Mr Cutler?'

'Leading Seaman Sinker. I guess you know what I mean.' Cutler stood just inside the cabin door, leaning up against the doorpost. 'I've heard things . . . things that should have been reported.'

'Yes. Don't worry, Mr Cutler, he's been warned.'

'Not good enough, Chief. He'll have to be isolated. You should know that.' Cutler paused. 'Any suggestions as to where he can be berthed?'

Lugg didn't like being told off by the Navy. His tone was stiff when he said, 'Engineers' accommodation – cabin going spare now. The junior engineers can shift up one. We can disinfect after.'

'After Simonstown?'

'Not Simonstown. They won't put him ashore, Mr Cutler, not for clap. They'll put the proper drugs aboard us and we'll carry on. At least, that's what I reckon.'

Cutler nodded. 'Okay, then. I'll suggest to Captain Dempsey we have him in that spare cabin aft. And in the meantime I'll be having a word with Sinker. I guess I don't have to involve you – my information came from Sinker himself.'

Cutler left the chief steward's cabin and went in search of Leading Seaman Sinker, finding him off-watch and staring broodingly aft from the poop, at the *Coverdale*'s streaming wake. He told Sinker of his new accommodation and Sinker seemed grateful.

'Safer I reckon, sir. From the ship's crew.'

'Safer for your messmates, that's the point. Let's have the other story, Sinker. In full this time.'

'The other story, sir?'

'Come off it, Sinker. That Nazi.'

'Oh – yessir. No more in it than what I told you, sir, honest. I just don't know how anyone can make anything of that, I really don't.'

'Juxtaposition,' Cutler said.

Sinker looked puzzled. Cutler went on, 'Your woman in Sydney, and overhead remarks. Then this. People put two and two together and most times get it wrong.'

'Yessir,' Sinker agreed doubtfully. Cutler, like any other RNVR subby, hadn't been at sea a dog watch yet and just didn't understand. One thing he didn't understand was the essential difference between some merchant seamen and naval ratings. The men who sailed before the mast in merchant ships, in which term Sinker included the RFA, were more independently minded than the dragooned bluejackets aboard the warships, and independence of mind could often lead to independence of action as well. Funny things could happen. Many of the older seamen – and in the merchant ships a lot of them were a sight older than naval ratings who mostly got chucked on the beach by forty if not sooner – many of those older men were inward-looking and filled with seafaring superstitions of many sorts, the Jonah business being but one. And that was bad enough.

Stripey Sinker knew that to be rated a Jonah was more than just a misfortune.

Cutler said, 'See the chief steward, then get your gear together and be ready to shift as soon as I've had a word with the Captain. And I'd advise you to keep away from that Jerry, all right?'

Sinker nodded; the prisoners wouldn't be allowed much liberty in any case, just exercise periods probably for the fit ones and the rest of the time in somewhere like the forepeak or the bosun's store maybe, all stench of paint and deck-cleaning gear, best place for the sods especially in anything of a sea.

Cutler went back to the bridge: Kemp was still below in his cabin. Cutler wouldn't disturb him; he did need that sleep. Cutler began to think ahead to Simonstown and a bit of shore leave, getting to grips with some nice cold beer or scotch-on-the-rocks, maybe find a girl. And then on for the States, real civilization again and with luck a few days back home in Texas with his folks. But he knew he mustn't tempt fate. The worst, the most dangerous part of the voyage, was yet to come. They'd barely started yet and never mind the *Kormoran*. Once into the South Atlantic and steaming north, they would come into what could be called Hitler territory insofar as the U-boats were concerned. And Hitler wasn't going to let a big troop convoy reach USA if he

86

could do anything to stop it in its tracks.

For no apparent reason Cutler, as he paced the bridge wing with the third officer, suddenly thought about that sealed canvas bag locked away in the chart room.

Nine

Kemp hadn't visited the Cape for very many years: not since his apprentice days with a company running small cargo liners. As he brought the convoy with its limping destroyer escort up towards Cape Agulhas, with something over a hundred miles yet to go for False Bay and the naval port of Simonstown, he felt a number of things: interest in seeing again a place that had been, from time to time, a part of his youth; nostalgia for days past linked with memories of the men who had been his shipmates then and of runs ashore when he had taken part to the full in the usual shore-side activities of seafaring men of the age he had then been, activities which in many cases were not left behind with the passing of youth. But over all the gnawing anxiety that had been with him ever since that night in Sydney's Hotel Australia and which would soon be settled one way or the other. Youth again: perhaps, all said and done, it was better to go in the full flush of the early twenties rather than to live on and in the end look back to what could never come again, an old man of the sea reliving his memories to the boredom of those around him. . . .

Kemp stayed on the bridge for most of the way after the *Coverdale* had made her landfall, picking up the marks –Danger Point, Walker Bay, Cape Hangklip at the eastern arm of the land enclosing False Bay, the Cape of Good Hope itself being to the west. The landfall had been made in the early hours, before the dawn was up: it was in mid morning of a splendid day that Kemp came up towards False Bay with Simonstown on its western shore and looked north-westerly towards the great eminence of Table Mountain surmounted by its thick, misty tablecloth of cloud.

Dempsey was at his side as the convoy made inwards. He said, 'The troops, Commodore. Will they be given shore leave?'

'Not up to me,' Kemp said. 'When the convoy rests, so largely does the Commodore! OC Troops'll have to make that decision, though he'll be guided by what the shore authorities have to say. You know Australians, Captain.'

Dempsey nodded. 'High spirited!'

'There are two sorts: the ones who don't drink and get God Almighty puritanical about it, and the ones who do –'

'And don't do it by halves.'

'Exactly. And one guess as to which sort those transports are likely to be mostly filled with.'

Dempsey laughed. 'What you're saying is that they may not be too welcome ashore. But I wouldn't care to be their officers if they're to be confined aboard.'

Kemp didn't make any response; he was watching out ahead, still with all those thoughts running through his mind. A couple of minutes later a signal was made from the shore, indicating the Commodore's berth along with all the others. Dempsey moved into the wheelhouse, ready to con the *Coverdale* through to the berth, which would be alongside the wall in the dockyard. As the oiler made her way inwards there was more signalling from the naval port and Leading Signalman Goodenough reported.

'FOIC to Commodore, sir. "You are required to wait upon me soonest possible after berthing." Message ends, sir.'

Kemp, grinning, caught Cutler's eye. 'Somewhat peremptory, I fancy!'

'Stuffed shirt,' Cutler said in agreement. He looked sideways at the Commodore. That grin had been a shade tight, no humour in it. Kemp was on edge and no wonder, dreading the next hour or so. The *Coverdale* moved on under Dempsey's orders, her engines now at half speed until Dempsey brought them down to slow once they had the tugs buttoned on for the final approach to the dockside.

ii

Ambulances were alongside for the wounded soon after the ship had berthed, asked for by signal as the *Coverdale* had entered

False Bay. All the Nazis were removed under a naval guard supplied by the Flag Officer in Charge ashore, belted and gaitered seamen, some of whom travelled in the ambulances as escorts to the wounded prisoners. With them went Leading Seaman Sinker, not in his official capacity as such but as an invalid.

He had asked formal permission from Petty Officer Rattray. Rattray had looked him up and down. 'Walking scran bag once again. Where's your lanyard, eh?'

Sinker felt in front of his seaman's jumper, where the loop of the scrubbed lanyard should have showed around the knot of the black scarf worn in memory of and in mourning for Lord Nelson. 'Forgot it, PO.'

'Go and get it, then, if you want to go ashore . . . and what do you want to go ashore for, may I enquire, Leading Seaman Sinker?'

'Things to do,' Sinker muttered, not meeting the PO's eye.

Rattray snorted. 'Get on with you! Think it hasn't spread, do you? The word – not the clap, God forbid. Go ashore and get bloody well *cured*, all right?'

Rattray had turned away and gone off muttering about dirty rotten matlows who weren't particular where they dipped their wicks. Stripey Sinker had caught that remark and muttered other sentiments about petty officers who thought they were immune to what bothered junior ratings whereas he, Sinker, knew Rattray wasn't always as continent as he made himself out to be. An anonymous letter home to Rattray's wife could cause the bugger bother and Sinker was half inclined . . . but knew he wouldn't. They were all in it together and he wasn't the sort to bring harm to anyone. He went ashore and climbed aboard one of the ambulances, heaving his gut up the rear step, and was driven off to naval sick quarters to see the quack. Or more likely just an SBA. Clap and the pox were not uncommon afflictions in the fleet and quacks had more important things to do.

Soon after the ambulances had gone, the mail from home came aboard, some of it official for Dempsey and the Commodore, most of it personal to bring happiness and anxiety in more or less equal measure.

Chief Steward Lugg had had a grand-daughter: that was cause for celebration, the more so as his daughter had come through

90

well and there were no more worries on that score. Lugg brought out his whisky bottle and sent for his second steward to join him. A toast was drunk and Lugg revealed the chosen names of his new descendant, not particularly euphonious: Clementine Lugg Earwicker.

'Ah,' the second steward said non-committally. 'Funny name, Earwicker.' That, about a son-in-law, was safe enough.

'Yes. Clementine after Mrs Churchill, Lugg after me of course.'

'Decent of them, Chief.'

Lugg made a sour sound. 'Daughter's idea. Earwicker wouldn't have, you can bet your bottom dollar.'

'In the services, I s'pose?'

'Not on your life! Fishmonger. Got a gammy leg, or so he says.' Lugg turned to other matters. 'Now, those stores lists. NSO's bum boy'll be aboard next thing, asking for 'em. When he appears, bring him straight to me and I'll bash his ear till he passes every last item we've indented for.'

The second steward tried to be funny. 'Not his earwicker, Chief?'

Lugg glared. 'Don't joke. I don't like it, all right?'

In the Captain's pantry, sitting as tense as a spring by a cupboard of crockery bearing the Admiralty crest, Porter read a letter from Rothesay. He'd hoped, he'd prayed on his knees that the bun hadn't really been there at all, that it had been a false diagnosis; but it was there all right and growing. The mother-to-be was in a right state. She had yet to tell her parents – she was on the plump side anyway and her stomach wasn't so big yet that they'd noticed anything amiss – and what was she going to do?

The letter was an appeal from the heart: Porter, she knew, would fix anything. She simply awaited his word. He hadn't a clue what that word was to be. He still wouldn't let her down but, if marriage was to be the only answer, he wouldn't be home for quite a while yet, if ever, and weddings took time to arrange even if you went to a register office; and the result of the union was going to be a pretty obvious illegit – or rather, a pretty obvious dummy run before the off, since holy matrimony would pre-sumably legalize it in the eyes of the law. And he would have the wrath of the grandparents to face. The old man was formidable and very large, played the bagpipes, ate haggis and attended the kirk. He also drank whisky but only in secret, fondly imagining that no one could smell it on his breath. When he had done this he was touchy and dangerous. More immediately so than Hitler, who hadn't yet come to England; grandfather-to-be was poised to cross the border at any moment he chose, and Porter's home, was in Carlisle.

Nevertheless it was Beryl herself who was Porters' chief worry. So far away, the war standing between them just when she needed him most.

iii

Two days before the Simonstown arrival Kemp had had those promised further words with Leading Seaman Sinker about the German who had appeared to recognize him; but Stripey Sinker had nothing to add to what Cutler had already got out of him. It all seemed to amount to very little and Kemp found no reason to catechize the German naval rating involved. Interrogation wasn't in his line and the naval authorities at the Cape could be relied upon to do all that was necessary once Kemp's report had been assimilated.

In obedience to the signal received on arrival, Kemp left the ship in a car to wait upon the Flag Officer in Charge, a rear-admiral of the British Navy, at Area Combined Headquarters in Cape Town. The South African Naval Service had not yet taken over.

It was a longish drive with time to think about many things: Kemp was scarcely conscious of the passing scenery, of the route through the Cape Town suburbs, of the immensity of Table Mountain looming over the city and the bay. Leaving the car and entering the HQ building to be directed to the office of FOIC he was aware of the thump of his heart, of some constriction in his breathing. He was one of those who had had a letter from home, from Mary. It had been written before news of the sinking of the *Burnside*. Mary wrote simply that she hadn't heard from Harry for some while and hoped he was all right. Christopher, the other son, had been home on leave from another destroyer acting as convoy escort out of Scapa. Granny – old Mrs Marsden, Kemp's nonagenarian grandmother – was as well as could be expected but was getting more and more fractious. She kept asking when

Kemp was coming home and seemed never to take in the answer; and she had been having trouble with her false teeth – the dentist was an old man come back from retirement to stand in for the practice, the partners having joined one or other of the services, and granny's teeth didn't have much priority. The result was that she was kept going on pap – soups and porridge, Bovril and Benger's Food. There had been the usual air raids, largely the jettisoning of bomb loads before the Luftwaffe crossed the coast for France. But all was well.

Teeth and bombs, old ladies under threat from Goering . . . Kemp cast all but one thing from his mind as he was admitted to the presence of the Flag Officer.

'Ah, Kemp. Sorry to send for you so soon.'

'That's all right, sir –'

'You had a disturbed trip, I know that. The German wireless signals, the *Kormoran*.' The Rear-Admiral seemed ill-at-ease and Kemp, guessing why, felt as cold as death. 'Your report should be valuable.'

'I have it with me, sir.' Kemp reached into the inside pocket of his uniform and brought out a buff manila envelope with the Admiralty crest on the flap. He laid this on FOIC's desk.

'Thank you. Sit down, Kemp.'

Kemp sat, feeling the shake in his fingers as he crossed his arms. The Rear-Admiral went on, 'You'll want to know . . . I've had a signal from the Admiralty. Perhaps you'd like to read it yourself.' He handed over a signal form. Kemp read, his vision jumping about unsteadily. 'Inform Commodore Kemp . . . Sub-Lieutenant H.G. Kemp RNVR missing presumed drowned.'

That was all; stark, simple, cold. Kemp swallowed hard and felt his eyes mist over. FOIC said, 'I'm very sorry, very sorry indeed. Remember, though, it's not final. Missing . . . there's always hope. *Burnside* went down off Pantelleria.'

Always hope? Was there? Missing at sea meant only one thing to Kemp: death by drowning. What hope could there be out in the Mediterranean during heavy attack, probably by combined air and surface forces plus U-boats, and never mind an apparent proximity of land? Pantelleria, a great dry rock currently held by the Italians.

All the same, it was perhaps something to cling to – or to prolong the agony right across the South Atlantic to Chesapeake Bay.

FOIC was on his feet and crossing the room to a mahogany cabinet. He was at Kemp's side with a glass of neat whisky. He said, 'Get that down.'

Kemp did so. He closed his eyes for a moment, felt the room sway round him, then he steadied.

He said, 'My report, sir. There's a good deal to discuss.'

iv

Soon after berthing, shore leave was given to the Australian troops after all. They surged down the gangways. Like the *Coverdale*, the transports had taken up berths alongside, other vessels being shifted out to the anchorage to make room for them, since to disembark thousands of men by tender and re-embark them again would take far too long. Simonstown and Cape Town filled with khaki uniforms beneath bush hats, and the bars did a ferocious trade in beer, whisky and gin. The shore patrols were kept busy as a result. Leading Seaman Sinker remained aboard the *Coverdale* after returning from the shore sick bay, finding it safer than risking his life if any of the crew decided to beat him up ashore. Sinker was not a fast-moving man and was no fighter. So he remained, after delivering drugs and instructions to the chief steward, in his CDA cabin in the engineers' accommodation. There was no mail for him and he felt forgotton, and grew maudlin about home, his wife and his physical condition.

Petty Officer Rattray had mail, the usual: two letters from his wife full of news about Ma Bates, who'd had a nasty turn in the first letter but had recovered by the second. Just his bloody luck, Rattray thought, and when leave was granted went ashore to drown his sorrows.

Among the rest of the mail were letters for Chief Engineer Warrington and Bosun Pedley. They wouldn't be opened until they had gone back to their writers, sad boomerangs of the war at sea. Sub-Lieutenant Cutler had quite a batch of mail, from his parents, from an aunt in Wisconsin and an uncle in New York, and from a number of girl friends in both the USA and Britain.

Cutler had been distressed at Kemp's news when the Commodore returned aboard. He had felt at a loss, not finding the right words, and had been cut short by Kemp.

'Thank you, Sub. I appreciate . . . ' Kemp's voice broke a little and he didn't go on. 'From tomorrow there'll be a lot to do. Not today. Get ashore and make the most of it while you can.'

'I'm not particular about going ashore, sir, if I can –'

'I shan't want you, Sub.' Kemp had turned away as he spoke and Cutler fancied he understood: the company of a sub-lieutenant RCNVR of about the son's age wasn't quite what the Commodore wanted at that moment. So he went ashore in a clean Number Thirteen white uniform of shorts and shirt and circulated around the bars until he fell in with a gaggle of English girls, all except one third officers WRNS out from the UK, sitting on a bench in a park looking out across Table Bay. It wasn't long before he had cut a Yankee dash and separated one of the girls, the one who wasn't WRNS but was English and worked for the South African administration, suggesting that she should act as personal escort for a little sight-seeing. Just in from a perilous sea voyage from down under, he couldn't go wrong.

Ten

There had been another interview in Cape Town, one that Kemp said nothing about to Cutler or to anyone else. After he had gone through his convoy report with FOIC, Kemp had been told that a high-ranking civilian had asked to see him, and he had been taken by a petty officer writer to another office one floor down. Here a short, thick man with a hectoring Australian voice rose briefly from behind a desk before sinking back onto a well padded backside.

'Commodore Kemp?'

'Yes.'

'Matthew Grout, Australian High Commission. Sit down.'

Kemp sat. The man looked like a bully, one who no doubt terrorized his subordinates. Grout said, 'I don't beat about the bush, Commodore. Too bloody busy. In your possession you have a sealed canvas bag.'

Kemp stared. 'May I ask how you know that, Mr Grout?'

'No, you may not. Point is, I do – too right, I do! You were handed it by Hennessy, back in Canberra. I reckon you won't know what's in it. Eh?'

Kemp hesitated: he felt matters moving a little way beyond him, that he was being caught between the military and civilian authorities. Hennessy had made no secret of his views as to the troop lift out of Australia, and the wisdom of leaving the continent stripped of fighting men when the Japanese armies were poised for an attack. As Kemp saw it, the only thing to do was to be truthful in his answer to Grout. He said, 'Only very broadly.'

'Hennessy told you?'

'Yes.'

'Then maybe you'll see the implications.'

'I don't know that I do.'

'Listen and I'll tell you.' Grout leaned across his desk, heavily, a scowl darkening his fleshy face. 'What's in that bag is dynamite, or could be, right?'

'Perhaps.' Kemp remembered that 'dynamite' had been his own mental simile when he'd come away from the offices of the Military Board in Canberra.

'No perhaps about it. The military down under, they want to put a spanner in the works, they want those troops back under their own command –'

'Not surprising, Mr Grout.'

'Eh? Now look.' Grout's face darkened further. 'I'm not asking your bloody opinion, Commodore, I'm just telling you, that's all. There's good reasons, political reasons, why those troops have left Australia for the USA. And –'

'And you represent the political aspect?'

'I represent the High Commission, I represent our Government, the Commonwealth Government in Canberra. Get it? I don't want that bag to reach the Pentagon. So I'm telling you to hand it over to me. I override the military – you'll understand that.'

'Perhaps. But I'm personally responsible for that bag and for its delivery as entrusted to me by Brigadier Hennessy.'

'It's right and proper you should say that. I appreciate your position.' The Australian was keeping his temper with difficulty. 'But I'm telling you I want it delivered, by you personally, right here – and as fast as possible. All right?'

'Not all right at all,' Kemp said crisply. 'I'm under no duty to take orders from you and it would be totally wrong of me to accede to your request –'

'Request be buggered, it's an order and in fact you are obliged to –'

Kemp got to his feet, his face set hard. 'I repeat, I take no orders from you, Mr Grout. If the order comes to me from FOIC, then of course I should be obliged to take a different view. But I rather fancy no such order will come. Unless and until it does, the bag remains with me.'

He turned for the door. Matthew Grout sat like a motionless toad with dangerous eyes. He said in a low voice, 'By God, Kemp, you're going to regret this.'

Kemp made no answer beyond a shrug as he left the room. He believed he had Grout's measure, that he had been right when he'd said no order would be forthcoming from any naval source. Grout had his axe to grind and he was grinding it clandestinely: Kemp was caught up in internecine warfare between the Australian military command and the civilian administrators. It might well prove an uncomfortable situation but in his mind his duty was clear, and it was to Brigadier Hennessy alone. Leaving HQ, he told the staff car to wait and he walked for a while, trying to clear his thoughts, trying to acclimatize to his personal bad news. By now Mary would have been told . . . he must write to her, a first priority when he got back aboard. He pushed through the crowds in the streets, almost unseeingly, found he needed a drink and went into a bar where he threw back a whisky. As he finished it a surge of bush-hatted troops came into the bar, the advance guard of the liberty men from the transports, loud voiced, thirsty. A hefty arm went around his shoulders and a hand tapped his commodore's broad gold band on the shoulder-straps of his white uniform.

'Navy, eh? Commodore.' The speaker, a man well over six feet, was an infantry lance-corporal. 'From the convoy, are you, eh?'

Kemp said, 'I am.'

'The bloke that got us here. Well, good on yer, cobber!' A huge hand smote Kemp's back. 'Reckon you did all right by us even though the poor bastards in the escort took a bloody beating. You'll have a drink, mate.' The soldier shouted across to the bartender and another whisky came. Kemp drank it but refused another: this could go on all day. He had work to do, he said, and he had to remain fit to do it. There was laughter and more shouting, but they understood. They were a free-and-easy bunch, no awe of rank, and the encounter cheered Kemp a lot: it was nice to be appreciated. But he got a good deal of unsolicited comment from the Australians, comment that made him more thoughtful as he walked back to HQ to pick up the staff car for Simonstown and his ship. As Hennessy had hinted in Canberra, the troops were reacting to their situation, to the uncomfortable knowledge that they were needed back home to fight the Japs more than they were needed in the United States, a cushy billet until more orders sent them into the firing line, maybe, in Europe, while Australia bled. That brought him back to Grout, who also had a soft job in Cape Town, and who clearly didn't want information to leave Australia and perhaps be the means of the troops being sent back. The politicians again, and their private axes. Butter up Whitehall and even an Australian could get a knighthood. . . .

ii

A knock came at Kemp's cabin door: Dempsey. Dempsey said, 'It doesn't do to brood alone. Have a change of scene – come along to my quarters and have a drink. Do you good. And you won't be needed tonight.'

It was dark now, though the moonlight showed up the great mass of Table Mountain in the distance and the lights of Simonstown glittered like a fairground as Kemp looked out of his port. He said, 'Right you are, Captain, and thank you.'

He went along to the master's day cabin, a spacious affair with a row of square ports facing for'ard across the tank deck and the flying bridges. It reminded him of his own peacetime quarters aboard the Mediterranean-Australia Line's *Ardara*. As they entered, Porter came in behind, his cloth over his arm.

'Whisky?' Dempsey asked.

Kemp nodded. The steward went to his pantry and came back with a bottle of Dewar's and a siphon, plus a jug of plain water. He poured two stiff drinks and went away again.

Dempsey lifted his glass. 'To hope,' he said. 'There's always that, believe me.'

'You sound as if you really do believe that.'

'Oh, I do. My elder brother . . . like me, he was in the last lot. Only he was army. His battalion was overrun by the early German advances across the Marne. We got the usual telegram, of course.' Dempsey's face had a faraway look, remembering trauma. 'We all thought that was that.' He laughed suddenly. 'He turned up two years later . . . kept himself going with the help of the French, never got caught by the Huns, and got away through Belgium. Pinched a fishing boat and got picked up by a destroyer of the Dover Patrol.'

Kemp was about to comment when a racket was heard from the quayside, raucous singing and shouting, a party of drunks returning aboard. Some of the noise came aboard the *Coverdale*, most of it went on past towards the big transports berthed astern. Kemp and Dempsey exchanged glances, grinning: the words of the song were loud and clear and they were not those of *Waltzing Matilda*. They brought back memories: neither Kemp nor Dempsey had been puritanical in their younger days. Then, from the after decks of the *Coverdale*, a loud voice was heard, an angry and slurred voice.

'Bugger the Commodore. Bugger you too. Le' me be.'

Dempsey lifted an eyebrow. 'Recognize the soft and gentle tones, Commodore?'

'Yes. Petty Officer Rattray, being persuaded to go to his quarters quietly.'

'And you didn't hear a word.'

'Not a thing. Rattray's a good PO if a trifle set in his ways, his pre-war ways. At a guess he's in the hands of Leading Seaman Sinker. I wish Sinker luck!'

'Me, too. It's not an easy life.' Dempsey pressed a bell-push and Porter appeared. 'More whisky, Porter. Bring the bottle and leave it. Then go and get turned in.'

'Aye, aye, sir. Thank you, sir.'

Dempsey looked at his steward critically: Porter seemed preoccupied and anxious, not an unusual thing just after mail from home had come aboard. 'Anything up?'

'N-no, sir –'

'All well at home?'

'In a manner of speaking, sir.' He didn't appear to want to say more, perhaps because of Kemp's presence.

'I'm glad to hear that. All right, Porter.'

The Captain's steward went off, came back with the bottle and left again. Dempsey poured two tots. He said, 'It's not an easy life for any of us, is it? We deserve a few drinks as much as anyone else. Helps things along.'

'An anaesthetic.'

'And why the hell not?'

Kemp took his glass in his hand. Why not indeed? The convoy was secure for now and they would be back at sea soon enough. He was about to go back to the subject of Dempsey's brother and his happy ending when there was a sharp knock at the cabin door and the third officer came in.

'Captain, sir –'

'Yes, what is it, Peel?'

'Sorry to intrude, sir –'

'All right, I'm not a young woman in her boudoir.'

'No, sir. It's Leading Seaman Sinker, sir.'

Kemp asked, 'What about him? Having trouble with my PO?'

'Yes, sir. Petty Officer Rattray fell down a ladder and he may have broken a leg. It seems he's currently too far gone to make any sense.'

Kemp said, 'God damn and blast! Now he's going to have some unavoidable explaining to do. Captain Dempsey, can you have word sent ashore for a doctor?'

iii

Stripey Sinker had had a difficult job if not an unaccustomed one: in his years at sea he had gone many times to the assistance of drunken messmates. Petty Officers were different: the drunker they were, if Rattray was anything to go by, the more officious and rank conscious they became. Rattray was very abusive and at the same time insistent that he was far from drunk. Having invited fate to bugger both the Commodore and Sinker, he had gone on to shout that he was effing sober, hadn't had enough effing cash to get effing drunk and how could a bloke get effing pissed on sodding sixpence, which Stripey Sinker took to be a monumental exaggeration of Rattray's financial state. Rattray was a mean sod with short arms and long pockets and saved his pay like Shylock. The shemozzle had brought more ratings to the scene, those few of the guns' crews who were not ashore, but it didn't help much. Rattray flailed about with his arms and they scattered, which was just as well. It would never do for a PO to strike a junior rating, this being a court martial offence just as much as the other way round.

'Bloody eff off the lot o' you. . . .'

'Stupid sod,' Sinker said.

'Wha' wash that, Leading Sheaman Shinker?'

'Nothing, PO.' Sinker took a deep breath and put his arms

around Rattray's body, pinning him against his stomach. He lifted like a human derrick, got Rattray's feet into the air, and lurched along the flying bridge.

'Effing let go! Thash a norder, Leading Sheaman –'

'Put a bleeding sock in it!' Sinker hissed in his ear. 'Blimey O'Riley, you're as pissed as a bleeding newt! Chancing your rate, you are. Smell like a combined brewery and distillery, you do!'

One of the guns' crews said, ''Is flies are open, Stripey. . . .'

'Do 'em up, then.' There was a delay while this was achieved against Rattray's struggles.

'Peed in the dock,' Rattray said. 'Forgot I 'ad. Leave me alone, dirty buggersh.' Suddenly, as though given extra strength and some return of co-ordination under a mistaken sense of nasty goings on, Rattray leaned forward, using all his weight and muscle, and heaved Sinker up until he lay like a crab on the PO's bent back. In danger of being toppled over the flying bridge to the hard metal of the tank tops below, Sinker let go his hold and dropped backwards. Rattray took his chance and lurched for'ard along the flying bridge, making for the midships superstructure. Going after him, Stripey Sinker slipped on a patch of oil and went headlong.

There was a laugh from Rattray. 'Serve you effing right's what I shay. Goin' to report you to the C-Commodore.' He put on speed and vanished into the superstructure before Stripey could catch up. And that was when it happened, as Sinker reported soon afterwards, first to Third Officer Peel and then to Commodore Kemp and Captain Dempsey when the two senior officers went to view the damage.

'Lorst 'is balance like, sir.' Rattray was now out cold.

'I see. What was his condition, Sinker?'

'Condition, sir?' Sinker looked virtuously blank.

'You know very well what I mean, Sinker.'

'Oh yes, sir. Yes. Well, sir, I reckon he'd ate something that disagreed like, sir.'

'He was unwell?'

'You might say so, sir, yes.'

'I think I might.' Kemp, bending over Rattray's motionless form, sniffed the air.

Sinker saw the sniff. He said, 'Smell o' alcohol, sir. 'E explained that, sir. One o' them Australians, sir, upset a pint o' beer over 'im.'

102

'And a bottle of whisky too?'

'Yessir.'

Kemp hid a smile; he appreciated loyalty and he had no wish to see Rattray run in and be disrated. There could be ways around Rattray's condition though whatever happened he wouldn't escape a tongue lashing from the Commodore in private. Kemp said, 'All right, Sinker. Leave him where he is until a doctor arrives. But see he's made comfortable and kept warm.'

'Aye, aye, sir, just leave 'im to me, sir.'

Kemp walked away with Dempsey. Rattray would be very far from the only casualty tonight, or any other night while the convoy remained in Simonstown. The Military Police would be having their hands full, likewise the naval town patrols, marching the streets with belts and sidearms. Drink and women, the twin curses of the sea and the soldiery. That was, in excess. Kemp was glad to reflect that Rattray had probably been too drunk to indulge in women: Sinker's case was quite enough to be going on with, quite enough to carry across the war-torn seas to America. It had already been confirmed that he wouldn't be kept ashore. Kemp excused himself to Dempsey and went to his own cabin; there would be much to do tomorrow, though he himself wouldn't be concerned in the first work item, which would be the shifting of the *Coverdale* to the oil berth for discharge and then after tank cleaning to the repair berth for her damaged summer tank and hull to be made good for the next part of the passage.

Kemp turned in after he'd had the doctor's report: a surgeon lieutenant had come from the base with commendable speed and his verdict wasn't too bad. Nothing serious, no concussion – the PO was already coming round, noisily. He had expressed the view that all effing quacks were effing useless. The leg was not broken but was badly strained and Rattray should attend the shore sick bay next morning to have it strapped up. An ambulance would be sent for him. Thereafter he would be on light duty for perhaps a fortnight, which left Stripey Sinker as acting PO. The surgeon lieutenant said that Rattray had only just escaped alcoholic poisoning.

Next morning that was what Rattray felt like: he woke with a violent headache, a terrible pain in his right leg which felt as though it had been wrenched from its socket and miraculously – since it was still there – replaced. Rattray's mouth felt full of garbage, like the bottom of a bread barge. And he had the usual, overriding anxiety of anyone who'd been dead drunk the night before: what, exactly, had he done? From about 2100 hours on, his memory was blank.

He was racking that useless memory when Sinker looked in.

'All right, PO?'

'What d'you mean, all right?'

'After last night's what I mean.'

'Oh, yes.' Rattray winced as pain shot through head and leg simultaneously. 'Had a drink or two. . . .'

Stripey Sinker knew the drill: no drunk ever admitted that he couldn't remember what he'd got up to, he just fished around for information to fill in the blanks unasked. Stripey, with a certain amount of relish, obliged.

'Fell down a ladder, PO.'

'Get away with you! Which ladder, eh?'

Stripey told him and added, 'Peed in the dock – you said.'

'I never!'

'Just repeating what you said.'

Rattray closed his eyes and groaned. 'Met a bloody Aussie pongo, I did . . . got me, well, a bit tiddley, like, I don't deny.' He paused and looked suspiciously at Sinker. 'Anyone else get to know, did they, eh?'

'Some o' the guns' crews. Captain Dempsey. Commodore.'

Rattray said bitterly, 'God, you bloody fat ullage!'

'No option. Hurt yourself. We thought you'd broken your leg. Quack was sent for . . . ambulance'll be alongside 0900 sharp.' Sinker looked at him closely. 'What's up, PO? You look –

'Get a bleeding po for God's sake, I'm going to puke.'

Stripey was just in time, and in the ensuing couple of minutes sent up a prayer of thanks that fate had made him a seaman and not a poultice walloper.

At 0900 Petty Officer Rattray was carried down the accommodation ladder to the waiting ambulance and departed for the shore sick bay; and half an hour later, in the care of the dockyard tugs, the *Coverdale* was moved off the berth and taken under tow the short distance to the oil jetty where acting Chief Engineer Evans saw to the pipe connections for a full discharge of the tanks. As the pumps got to work and emptied the ship, she rose slowly to her marks, showing a weed-covered line below her boot-topping: the ship, Dempsey remarked to Kemp on the bridge, had been too long without a bottom-scrape.

'Exigencies of war. We have to keep the seas even when the weed cuts our speed. I'll see what can be done about it while we're here.'

'Dockyard labour?'

Dempsey nodded. 'It may have to be, even though my crew could do some sort of a job working from bosuns' chairs. It all depends what the union situation is out here. You know what it'd be like at home.'

'Yes, unfortunately I do.' Certain jobs were the province of the dockyard workers, who tended to go on strike if their cherished functions were usurped by seamen. In the middle of the world war for survival it didn't make any kind of sense, but there it was. Kemp had some stronger words for it than just senseless, and one of them was treason.

Kemp went below to his cabin to write another letter to his wife. By an automatic reflex he checked the safe: in port, the sealed bag had been transferred back from the chart room. Kemp wondered again about Matthew Grout of the Australian High Commission. So far, no orders of any kind in relation to the bag's contents had come from Naval HQ. In the event, they never did.

iv

Two days later the *Coverdale*'s tanks were both emptied and steam cleaned – and afterwards flushed through with seawater, plenty of it, before shifting once again, this time to the repair yard. In the meantime a number of dockyard officials had come aboard and had poked and pried into everything they could find; the damage to the hull had been inspected, as had the fractured summer tank once the cleaning process was complete. Dempsey and Evans had been in the thick of it, answering questions from civilians who, had they been in Portsmouth, Devonport or Chatham, would have worn sober suits and bowler hats in indication of their status as management. A captain(E) RN had, as anticipated, come aboard with them and Evans had spent some uncomfortable hours with him, being catechized as to his report and all the circumstances leading up to the death of the chief engineer and Dempsey's dangerous descent into the gas-filled tank.

Evans, young and inexperienced, was out of his depth; when the naval officer had at last gone ashore, he felt that his job might well be in danger even though he had not been acting chief at the relevant time. There were always unfairnesses at sea; someone always had to carry the can and, of course, as second engineer at the time he did have some responsibility himself. It was clear enough that there had been some slackness in not clearing the tank of every last bit of sludge. There was going to be a board of enquiry; it was due to sit the next day and the sorting out would not be a fast process, but the convoy's sailing would not be put back because of it. The final conclusions might not come for months, with Evans sent back from the UK or somewhere to resume his evidence. And whatever happened it was certainly going to be months before they announced their findings, so a long time of worry loomed ahead – unpleasantly to an acting chief with his career at stake.

Worries had come also to Sub-Lieutenant Cutler. Commodore Kemp was an understanding boss, far from stuffy, with plenty of sympathy for the desires of a young officer to make the most of his time in port. Kemp had had plenty to do in the way of attending conferences, discussing his route diagonally across the South Atlantic with the Naval Control Service officers, being apprised of such as was known of the movements and current positions of German raiders and U-boat packs and so on; but he had felt able to dispense largely with his assistant's help. As a result Cutler had seen a good deal of the English civilian girl by the time the tank and hull repair had been made good; and, somewhat precipitately, he had fallen in love.

Her name was Natalie Hope-Wynyard. Not that alone: she was Lady Natalie Hope-Wynyard and her father, an earl, was an admiral. But it wasn't the difference in the respective ranks that worried Sub-Lieutenant Cutler. It was his own parents. Both his father and his mother disliked the British; in the past they had expressed their views with force. Britain was going to drag the United States into the war – that had been before Pearl Harbor – just as had happened back in 1917 when Uncle Sam had had to pull the British chestnuts out of the Kaiser's fire, a fact that

Cutler's father, who had lost an arm and a leg in the last of the fighting, had never forgotton. Cutler's father had grudged having his son join the RCNVR in order to get into Britain's war.

Worse: the Cutler parents couldn't stand the British aristocracy. They were effete, gormless, an anchronism, typical of the huge division between an old, worn-out system and the vigour and thrust of a young country of opportunity and vision. Titles in themselves were an abomination. Cutler's father called them all Lord Tomnoddies and said that only God was entitled to be called Lord. The British were blasphemers.

Trouble loomed. Cutler had talked of it, more or less vaguely at this stage, to Natalie. He'd started by asking what her British admiral father thought about the Americans. Did he like them?

'Oh yes, awf'ly.'

Cutler could hear that coming out in front of his father. He said, 'I'm glad to hear that, I guess.'

'Daddy says we couldn't do without you. All those destroyers you sold us –'

'I thought we gave them?'

'Oh no, not actually *gave*, according to Daddy. But he says it was awf'ly sporting. He thinks President Roosevelt is wonderful.'

Cutler's father didn't; but this wasn't the time to go into that. Natalie went on with her father's sayings; they were all complimentary to the Americans but he did seem to have said one hell of a lot over the years, about other things as well as Americans: he disliked socialists, beards, what Natalie called chichis, most young men under thirty, and his wife; disliking his wife was a bore, Natalie said, but she did in fact see his point because Mummy was utter poison and when his flagship was in port in peacetime had tried to run the whole show, going over the head of the Flag Captain and causing ructions. Since Daddy had other interests lined up, a divorce was pending but might have to wait until the war was over.

Worse and worse: the Cutler parents – of whom Cutler was fond – tended to go bonkers at the mention of the word divorce. But maybe they would come round . . . just maybe they would, no certainties, though Dad had always had a soft spot for a pretty girl, and Natalie was certainly that and very sexy.

The day before the troop convoy was scheduled to leave

Simonstown, Cutler went ashore with Kemp and Dempsey to attend the final sailing conference and take the last-minute orders and situation assessments. When the conference was over Cutler asked if he might remain ashore: fond farewells were looming, though this he did not say. Kemp nodded his permission, and went off with Dempsey in a staff car. Cutler, meeting Natalie in a hotel bar as already arranged on the assumption he would get leave, fancied he had seen the last of the two senior officers until next morning.

But he had scarcely settled down with the girl in a corner of the bar when Kemp and Dempsey walked in. The bar was not full and they could not help but catch eyes.

Cutler got to his feet. 'Evening, sir.'

'Hullo there, Cutler. Sit down – don't let me interrupt.'

'You're very welcome, sir. We'd like you to join us.'

Kemp glanced at Dempsey: neither wanted to play gooseberry but neither wished to appear churlish. They walked across and Kemp said, 'Just the one drink, Cutler. And it's on me.'

'Why, thank you, sir.' Cutler made the introductions, adding that the girl's father was the Earl of Truro.

'Truro,' Kemp repeated. 'The admiral?'

'Yes. That's Daddy. Do you know him, Commodore Kemp?'

'Only by name, I'm afraid, Lady Natalie.' They chatted; Natalie dropped a number of naval names, mostly lost on Kemp, though Dempsey was familiar with some of them. There was a good deal of talk about the girl's father, in fact, quite an earbashing until Natalie delivered her *pièce de résistance* as Kemp thought of it later.

She said, 'Daddy thinks you RNR people are absolutely splendid.'

Kemp, caught a little off-balance, said, 'Ah. Really?'

'Yes. He's often said so. He thinks the convoys are *tremendously* important. Well, of course . . . they are, aren't they?'

'Yes, they are,' Kemp said, at a total loss for words. The girl was very enthusiastic and obviously considered himself and Dempsey as a couple of fuddy-duddies in need of cheering up. It made him feel very old. He noticed that Cutler was looking embarrassed. He drank up quickly, caught Dempsey's eye again, and got to his feet. 'We'll have to be getting along,' he said. They took their leave and outside the hotel Kemp grinned at Dempsey and said, 'A penny for 'em, Dempsey. A pretty child, don't you think?'

'Very. Well, we were all young once, but for Cutler's sake . . . I mustn't be unkind, though.' Dempsey frowned. 'What was this Bodders she kept on talking about?'

'Didn't you get the reference, Dempsey? Bodmin – the family place is near Bodmin, in Cornwall. Bodders . . . we're just getting old, you and I.'

Eleven

At 0750 next morning the departure reports reached Captain Dempsey, on the bridge with the Commodore: all crew members aboard, the naval party present and correct – they were all fallen in for leaving harbour, under Leading Seaman Sinker acting for the PO, along the starboard after flying bridge – and the ropes and wires singled-up to the springs ready for casting off.

The main engines had already been rung to stand by; on the starting platform Evans wiped his hands on a ball of cotton-waste and watched the telegraphs and a number of dials and gauges. The engine-room was as spotless as ever, the metalwork gleaming, the bearings all with their due coating of oil. There was a hot oily smell and a sense of power. The telegraphs rang and Evans repeated the order.

'Slow astern.'

There was an increase in the sound level as the shafts began turning slowly; a small shudder ran through the ship as the screws bit into the water. On the bridge Dempsey, watching carefully as his ship slewed her bows round against the backspring's checking of her sternway, passed the order aft: 'Let go all!'

'Let go, sir.' There was a splash as the heavy hemp backspring, its eye cast off from the bollards on the quay by the unberthing party, dropped into the water and was winched aboard dripping foul harbour water. 'All gone aft, sir!'

Dempsey, from the bridge wing, raised a hand in acknowledgement, moved into the wheelhouse and passed the next orders: 'Engines to slow ahead. Wheel amidships.'

'Engines to slow ahead, sir. Wheel's amidships, sir.'

The traditional repetitions of the sea. Each order repeated back so that there was no mistake, no mis-hearing. The *Coverdale*, under five degrees port wheel a little later, moved out and away from the berth. After her the big troop transports came off the dockyard wall, to be followed by the grain ships and the others of the convoy. The warship escort had already moved out and were steaming slow down False Bay: the damaged Australian destroyer was no longer with them – she would need an extended refit. But for the dangerous part of the run the escort had been strengthened beyond that originally provided for the run from Sydney. They now had two County Class cruisers, *Staffordshire* and *Northampton*, one Colony Class – HMS *Nassau*, wearing the flag of the Rear-Admiral commanding the escort – and four destroyers: *Newbury*, *Leyburn*, *Meriden* and *Melton*.

Still far from a strong escort, as Kemp had stressed at the convoy conference; but all that could be provided by a navy stretched almost beyond its limits, a provision only made possible at all by keeping the ships at sea month after month when by all normal peacetime standards they should have had time in port for all manner of small defects to be attended to. The same with the ships' companies: the men had been and would continue to be driven hard to their own limits of endurance.

So the convoy moved out to come around the butt of the Cape of Good Hope.

'Well, Cutler?'

'Sir?'

'You look pensive.'

'Sorry, sir –'

'Oh, don't worry, I'm not criticizing. Sympathizing, rather. She's a good-looking girl.'

'Guess so, sir. Awf'ly good sort.'

Kemp stared. Was Cutler being tongue-in-cheek, sardonic . . . or was it love, expressed in adopting his idol's modes of speech? Cutler looked too honest, too fresh-faced and frank, to be sardonic. It had to be love.

Kemp said, 'Don't drop your Americanisms, Cutler. Sometimes I've criticized . . . but it's all been a lot better than – well, British expressions that don't suit you. D'you get me? Just a friendly word.'

111

Cutler grinned. 'Guess I get you all right, sir, Commodore. Something else too: my dad – he'd say the same.'

'Sensible man.'

Kemp lifted his glasses towards the exit from False Bay.Some fifteen minutes later the *Coverdale* swung to starboard to make the turn, followed in succession by the troop-laden transports, moving out behind the Flag and the rest of the escort. Out for the turn north eventually into the South Atlantic, to head up for the latitude of the British port of Freetown in Sierra Leone from which, it was expected, more destroyers would join for the final leg, the leg where U-boat attack would be most likely.

After that, a straight dash for the Virginia Capes, Cape Henry and Cape Charles, and a safe berth in the James river. That, at any rate, was the hope of everyone in the convoy. And there was an extra worry for Kemp and the masters of the transports: at the conference those masters had reported bad feeling along the troopdecks. There were agitators spreading despondency about Australia's defences. None of the liner masters had hinted at anything like mutiny; that was unthinkable – the men were loyal enough, no question. But there had been rumours circulating in all the ships that the Australian high command was split on the issue and that had worsened the soldiers' fears and doubts. It wasn't a happy situation.

ii

Far to the north, in the heart of Germany, the Führer was on a tour of inspection of his troops, having left Berlin by heavily guarded train for the military garrison at Minden in Prussia, on the left bank of the River Weser. Herr Hitler reflected that Minden was a name that had happened to figure much in British history, in wars long past: among others the British Hampshire Regiment had gained distinction when in 1759 they had routed the French cavalry, and as a result had added the Minden Rose to their cap badge, something that the Führer regarded as an impertinence. Now, of course, the British were very conspicuous by their absence; and Minden, that day of inspection, resounded to the tramp of marching German feet, to the thunder of the gun-carriages and the splendidly stirring sounds of the military bands as they came past the saluting platform to receive their Führer's lifted-arm acknowledgement. From Minden the Führer was driven in a Mercedes to inspect the garrison at Rinteln, also upon the Weser. Before carrying out the inspection, Hitler insisted upon walking, with a fat and heavy-breathing Field Marshal, to the top of some hills from which he could look down on the barracks, built only fairly recently in the form of a large Nazi swastika, potent symbol of the victorious Third Reich, the symbol that before much longer would bring down the wretched Churchill, humbling his conceit in the dust and chaos of total military and naval disaster.

For the Third Reich was on the march now to the victory that Herr Hitler had known all along must come. The British, despite their best efforts, were making no progress in the North African campaign against the master tactician Rommel; the Americans had entered the war it was true; but their fleet lay shattered by the gallant Japanese on the bottom of Pearl Harbor, or sticking up from it in jagged pieces of steel. There had been rumours of a second front one day but the Führer considered that merely boastful: the British Army was a ragged and broken force that could never again attempt to stand up to the might of Germany. And in the meantime the detested Russians, with the Führer's generals hard upon their heels, were in retreat towards Stalingrad and Moscow even if not so fast as had been expected.

And the British Navy?

Hitler gave a laugh and danced a few steps, a sort of jig, stared at by the fat Field Marshal. The British Navy was a joke: had not the great battleship *Royal Oak* been sunk early in the war inside its own base of Scapa Flow, by the gallant Kapitan-Leutnant Prien's U-boat? Had not the aircraft-carrier *Courageous* – which its own ship's company called the Curry Juice, thus demonstrating their frivolous attitude towards war – also been sunk very early after hostilities had commenced? And of course later the *Hood*, and so many other ships as well; and the U-boats of the Reich were winning the Battle of the Atlantic, going in amongst the British convoys and sending the merchant ships and escorts alike to the bottom.

It was splendid.

It was certainly true that the sinking of the *Hood* had been followed by the end of the *Bismarck*, but that was a different story and one written only via the sheer obstinacy of the terrible Churchill, who had diverted every ship in the British fleet to the chase, the act of a madman who was prepared to leave the seas naked so that he could serve his own overweening arrogance and self-satisfaction. In any other circumstances, the *Bismarck* would not have been sunk. Everyone knew that.

The Führer was thus pondering the war at sea when a corporal of signals approached – a despatch rider from Minden, who had left his machine at the bottom of the hill.

'Mein Führer –'

'Yes, what is it?' Hitler's voice was an irritable snap; he disliked being interrupted in a pleasurable reverie.

'Mein Führer, a message to be delivered personally.'

'Give it to me.'

An envelope was handed over and the Führer ripped it open. The message was from the Admiralty in Berlin, from Grand Admiral Raeder himself. Hitler read, then conferred with the Field Marshal.

'An immediate reply is clearly needed,' he said. 'See – Raeder has intelligence from the British base at Cape Town. A large troop convoy has left and has turned north around the Cape of Good Hope. And something else. You may read it.'

The Field Marshal did so: German intelligence had reported a most vital despatch known to be aboard the Commodore's ship. Grand Admiral Raeder wished to attack the convoy and seize the ship carrying the despatch, the contents of which were not known but again the likely importance was stressed, as was the destination, as believed, of the troop convoy: the United States of America.

Before the Field Marshal could utter, the Führer spoke. 'Raeder is wasting time by asking my permission. This is of course granted – see that he is told at once. The withdrawal of forces from the North Atlantic is approved. He should have known my wishes! The convoy is to be destroyed.'

The Führer had become angry, but the Field Marshal sympathized with Admiral Raeder, who was not clairvoyant. Only a suicidal fool would act on his own initiative when it was well known that the Führer insisted on making all large decisions himself.

The Führer's answer was passed to the despatch rider, who left

114

immediately. Hitler became sunny again, looking down at his barrack buildings.

'Another blow to the heart of Churchill,' he said. 'And the wretched Roosevelt!'

iii

'Leading Seaman Sinker?'

Stripey Sinker looked up towards the bridge from aft. 'Yessir?'

'On the bridge,' Cutler called down. 'Smart!'

'Yessir.' Smart, eh! Young shaver. It was all very well for him – no gut to carry around. Feeling his responsibilities as acting PO, Stripey bore his stomach along the flying bridge and up the ladders at the end, thinking of the constant adjurations of Petty Officer Rattray from his sick bed, or more precisely the couch provided for the support of his leg by the chief steward.

Rattray had been fretful from the start, not trusting anyone else to do his important job. 'Keep 'em up to the mark, Leading Seaman Sinker, or you'll get what for once I'm back to duty, where I should be now, by rights.'

'You can't walk proper, PO –'

'Bloody hobble, can't I?'

'Not if the weather gets up.'

'If, if,' Rattray said scathingly. 'Flat as a virgin's stomach, it is, and likely to remain that way. Now then: plenty of gun drill, right? Quarters Clean Guns likewise. Them guns got a proper overhaul in Simonstown after the bad weather . . . or I hope they did.'

'I reported –'

'Yes, I know you did. What's reported, Leading Seaman Sinker, and what's done, is sometimes two different things, right? What I was going on to say,' Rattray continued, wiping his sleeve across his nose, 'is, see that they stay that way. The guns. Plenty of greasing an' that, keep the weather out. And chase the hands like I said.' He paused. 'Any buzzes going around? Me, I'm out of touch like.'

Stripey said, 'No buzzes, PO. Not that I've heard.'

'That's odd. There's always a buzz. When there isn't . . . well, I don't like it.'

115

'I don't reckon 'Itler knows there isn't a buzz.'

Rattray looked blank. 'Eh? What's that supposed to mean?'

'Nothing, PO.'

Rattray had started to simmer and Stripey had invented a job to be done and had buggered off out of range of Rattray's hectoring voice. Now, making for the bridge, he reflected on the fact of his standing in for the PO. True, there was no one else to take over, he being the next senior, so it wasn't all that much of an accolade. But if he did well, came out of it without any mishaps, well, he might be in line for PO himself. If Kemp put in a good report he might be rated up once they got back to UK and the Pompey depot put his name on the roster. Or maybe Kemp could rate him up all by himself – Stripey wasn't sure about that. If he made PO, his wife would live a bit better. A leading seaman's pay wasn't too hot and he could do with the extra, a bob or two more for himself and the rest on his allotment note to go home to the old lady. Life wasn't funny for the civvies in wartime, all the rising prices and that, to say nothing of shortages and power cuts and the air raid warning sirens going half the night if you lived anywhere with a target value. At sea, until you came under attack, you didn't do too badly. Plenty of food, warmth off watch in the messdecks, fags ten for sixpence, a daily tot of rum for free. Uniform more or less provided by the initial free issue supplemented thereafter by the Kit Upkeep Allowance, although that didn't amount to much and what there was of it was spent by most ratings on fags and, when ashore, beer. Sinker reckoned that Rattray saved his and spent it on what it was supposed to be spent on – he was that sort of bloke, apart from the odd booze-up.

'Wanted me, did you, sir?'

'Yes.' Followed by Sinker, Cutler moved across to the port wing of the bridge. 'That trouble you had before Simonstown. I'm talking about the crew – understand?'

'Yessir –'

'Quietened down, has it?'

'Yessir, I reckon so.'

'Good.' Cutler looked out across a blue sea, flat calm although there was a fairly heavy swell that was making the *Coverdale* roll heavily. Cloud drifted high across the sky as blue as the sea; it was a welcome contrast to the Great Australian Bight and the roaring forties. Cutler grinned. 'Maybe it's the weather.'

'Yessir. Or p'raps it's because. . . . '

'Well?'

'Because we're all peaceful, like, sir.'

'Let's hope we stay that way, Sinker. There's a long way to go yet. All right, that's all.'

Sinker saluted and went back down the ladder, thinking about officers, a weird bunch. You thought they weren't bothering about you but all the time they remembered and kept an eye lifting; it was quite flattering really. And could be just as well: although there had been no further manifestations of hostility from the crew, Stripey Sinker didn't feel safe yet. There was indeed a long way to go – he knew from one of the quarter-masters, who'd had a look at the chart, that the convoy was currently a little north of the latitude of Cape Lopez in French Equatorial Africa and coming up between the African continent and Ascension Island. Six days out from Simonstown, something like fifteen more days to Chesapeake Bay.

Plenty could happen yet. The crew were quiescent only; they might not remain so if Adolf Hitler showed his hand again.

117

Twelve

This was easy, Cutler thought, making home for the States across a somnolent sea, a burning sun overhead, the blue water broken only by the wakes of the ships in convoy and their escort. The tropical heat was uncomfortable certainly, but there was a wind made by the ship's passage that brought a little relief from that. Kemp had yarned to him during one of the quiet spells on the bridge about his early days in sail, how the windjammers had lain for days, sometimes weeks, in the Doldrums, waiting for a wind to carry them on down to the passage of Cape Horn with its eternal storms and lashing rain. The Doldrums had been hell enough then, Kemp said, a time of lost tempers, of shipboard feuds coming to breaking point as the sun blistered, the sails slatted against the masts, and the general airlessness made the ship into a torture chamber below decks until a sudden, brief squall struck when it was a case of all hands to tend the sails and try to use the tearing wind to carry them on a little farther while it lasted.

But in those days they hadn't had the enemy to cope with.

Cutler paced the bridge wing, his thoughts now veering between two opposite points: home, and Cape Town. Would it be a case, as with Kipling's East, of never the twain shall meet? Probably: wartime romances were fragile things, usually very temporary. Not always, though. Cutler was seeing a vision of the girl when he was interrupted by Leading Signalman Goodenough.

'Flag calling, sir.'

Cutler looked ahead towards the *Nassau* and the signal lamp

118

winking from her flag deck. Goodenough had already sent the acknowledgement and was reading. It was a short signal: Goodenough reported, 'Commodore from Flag, sir. "Am about to close your starboard side." '

Cutler was puzzled. 'What the heck?'

'Something to tell us, sir, very likely too long for a signal. He'll use his loud hailer.'

Cutler shrugged and spoke down the voice-pipe to Kemp's cabin. Kemp was on the bridge with Dempsey within half a minute and was levelling his binoculars. *Nassau* was coming round under full starboard wheel, heeling sharply until she straightened and came down on the convoy, her signal lamps busy again, passing messages to the other warships of the escort. Within the next few minutes, astern now of the Commodore's ship, she had turned again and was coming up rapidly on the *Coverdale*'s starboard side, easing her engines as she began to come abeam and then taking her way off with a short burst of stern power.

Kemp flicked on the loud hailer in anticipation of a verbal exchange. As he did so an amplified voice came across the gap. 'Commodore, please.'

'Listening,' Kemp called back.

'Trouble ahead.' The Rear-Admiral's voice came over loud and clear. 'A long cypher from Admiralty. It seems the German Naval Command has got word of the troop lift. Or may have – it's being assumed so, because an unusual load of operational signals has been intercepted though not broken down. Our cypher boys haven't cracked the new codes yet – pity!' There was a distorted buzz from the loud hailer. 'Are you hearing me?'

'Loud and clear, sir.'

'Right. Now, here's the point: Naval intelligence believes those signals to have been addressed to the U-boat packs operating across the North Atlantic convoy routes. For the last three days there's been no U-boat activity up there, no attacks at all on the convoys other than by air when they've been in the zone from the airfields in occupied France. It's thought that they've been diverted towards us. Understood?'

'Yes, sir.'

'If our boys are right, I think we can expect attack, a heavy attack, after we haul away from the African coast. The area of most danger will be from Freetown onwards. A long haul, Commodore. I'm expecting an extra destroyer escort to rendezvous off Freetown.' There was a pause. 'I'll leave it to you to inform the convoy accordingly. All right? Now there's something else. I'm about to send a heaving line across with a message, so have your hands standing by for'ard.'

The loud hailer clicked off. Dempsey, at Kemp's side, called down to the fore deck. Hands moved to the fo'c'sle-head and along the tank deck. Stripey Sinker was working on the for'ard close range weapons. He had a nasty feeling in his gut, a kind of premonition. When the heaving-line snaked across the fo'c'sle behind the monkey's-fist that gave it carrying weight, it was Stripey who caught it; he heaved in and brought a light canvas bag aboard. Cutler had come down from the bridge and was standing by to take it. As the heaving line was cast back to the cruiser, Cutler went up to pass the bag to the Commodore.

'Not another,' Kemp said. He opened it. Inside was a sheet from a signal pad. His face set hard as he read the message. Dempsey was looking at him but Kemp avoided his eye. 'Cutler, a word in my cabin.'

When they reached his cabin Kemp came straight to the point, tight-lipped, angry. He waved the signal form. 'The Admiralty reports that German naval intelligence is aware of the existence of the sealed bag. The one entrusted to me. Not many people – on *our* side – know about that bag, Cutler.'

'No, sir.' Cutler's voice was quiet, but there was a sudden shake in his fingers. 'Do I take it you're accusing me of something, sir?'

'You were, are, one of those who know.'

'And so you're suggesting –'

'That girl, Cutler. Lady whatnot. Did you ever speak of the bag to her?'

Cutler had flushed deeply. 'I did not. Never. To her or anyone else. You have my word on that. I wouldn't be that kind of a fool.'

Their eyes met and held. Cutler's gaze was level. There was clear honesty there. The gaze held for half a minute, then Kemp gave a short, rather embarrassed laugh and said, 'I accept that, Cutler. Fully. And I'm sorry.'

'That's all right, sir. You were bound to ask. It's obvious someone's talked out of turn. So what happens now?'

120

'The Nazis are going to try to get hold of the bag. *Coverdale* will be the principle target when the attack comes. I've half a mind to dispose of the damn thing now . . . but if they don't find the convoy – *if* – then I'll have mucked up someone's –' Kemp broke off from a near indiscretion. Aboard the *Coverdale* only he was aware of the nature of the bag's contents. 'Anyway, there'll be time when the attack comes.' He paced the cabin, backwards and forwards, hands clasped behind his back, his weather-beaten face troubled. 'Look, Cutler. For now, we keep mum. I'll take Captain Dempsey into my confidence, of course, and after that, we'll see. All hands will have heard the Rear-Admiral on the loud hailer, so they'll know that part of it. I don't suppose you'll need to chivvy the guns' crews in the circumstances. How's Rattray, by the way?'

'Still on the sick list, sir. I guess Sinker can cope.'

'If we're attacked, then the sick list goes by the board.'

'Yes, sir.' Cutler paused. 'Talking of Sinker, the Rear-Admiral spoke of the Nazis having got the word about the convoy. That could be enough to kind of sink Sinker.'

ii

Stripey's thoughts were similar: the dirty looks had started up again and he was a worried man, casting looks over his shoulder, fearing a knife in the back when below decks, fearing to be on the tank deck or the flying bridges during the dark hours when all manner of things could happen at sea. He'd known, or anyway he'd heard, of unpopular bastards of petty officers who'd ended up gagged and tied with rope and battened down into a wash-deck locker which had then been conveniently 'lost' overboard in bad weather and not a man of the ship's company but had kept his lips sealed thereafter. It was easy to lose men at sea, the sudden curling wave that swept aboard to engulf the ship and take its toll, breaking hand-grips on lifelines or stanchions. Stripey thought again about Jonahs, and the often superstitious natures of seamen, not that superstition came into it this time, but still – it was all of a piece, and any suggestion of being a spy was worse than being an ordinary Jonah. It was just as ridiculous as ever, of course: anyone should know that Stripey was in no position to gain information, let alone pass it on, and also if they'd kept their eyes open they'd have seen that he hadn't gone ashore in Simonstown.

Except to the quack.

The sweat of fear broke out all over Stripey's vast body, adding to the sweat of the tropical heat. After seeing the quack in the shore sick bay he could have gone anywhere, made any sort of clandestine contact. And of course he *did* know, like everyone else, that the convoy carried a big troop lift and was bound for the US. *Like everyone else.* Surely that let him off the hook? The whole of Simonstown would have seen the transports entering and leaving again. So why pick on him?

Stripey knew the answer to that: because they'd been after him ever since leaving Sydney, all because of bloody Rattray's daft remark. They would be like terriers, never let go once the teeth were in.

The glances followed him along the deck. Not glances: bloody long, lingering looks, the fat bugger who'd put all their lives at risk. He wanted to shout out at them, ask what about his own life? He was just as much at risk, wasn't he? He didn't want to come under attack any more than they did, but he knew from past experience that some people were thick as planks, not taking anything in except what they wanted to take in. Jonah. A marked man. Stripey quaked on aft to his cabin, his CDA mess, his limbs shaking. Someone had got there before him, losing no time after that loud hailer had shattered his peace. Once again, like before the Cape arrival, there was a dead rat in his bunk: he could smell it, though he didn't see it until he'd ripped the sheet back.

iii

Now it was dark: the convoy steamed on, the shaded blue stern lights assisting the station keeping. The days had passed, the ships were now well north. From Freetown two more destroyers had joined the escort, taking up their positions on the port and starboard wings, their asdics searching continually through their arcs. The sea was calm though there was still a swell: near perfect weather for the U-boats. More signals had come in from the Admiralty: more indications via intelligence reports that the Nazi

Rattray gave a jeering laugh. He hadn't liked what Lugg had said – the way he'd said it, rather – about things being better and so on. It had sounded bolshie somehow. He said, 'You don't fight a war by running away. Convoys . . . they 'ave to go across and we 'ave to fight. Bloody 'Itler, 'e'd only lie in wait. Fighting through, that's what we're here for.'

Lugg sighed, a heavy sound. He shoved the snapshots back in a drawer, then took them out again and crammed them into his wallet, which he kept in a pocket of his white uniform shorts. If he had to swim for it, he wanted to take his mementoes with him.

'Watch that leg,' he said. 'Still looks swollen. I s'pose you think you know best.'

iv

The worries out at sea were reflections of worries back home, a two-way business. In spite of the difficulties of civilian life in wartime, of the air raids and the gloom on the BBC News broadcasts, of ever-rising prices and the shortages of virtually everything; in spite of the adjurations of one set of food experts to eat plenty of nourishing potatoes, of which at one stage there was a glut, and then the advice (when a shortage came) of another bunch of experts not to eat them since they contained fattening starch; in spite of Lord Haw-Haw and his 'Jairmany calling', the traitorous tones announcing, with the aid of his town maps and his Kelly's Directories, that Mrs So-and-so down the street was going to get Hitler's full attention that night, and his continual claims that such-and-such a ship had been sunk; in spite of strikes that interrupted war production and put the fighting men at greater risk – in spite of all this and much else beside, the over-riding worry of the women left at home was for husbands, sons, fathers and brothers facing shot and shell on land and sea. Some of the civilians hadn't seen their men for two years or more; and letters were sometimes infrequent.

Rattray didn't write often and when he did, not much: he was no literary man and his imagination was stunted and in any case what could you write in wartime? You couldn't say where you were for one thing, or what you'd seen and done ashore – if you did the officers who censored your letters before they left the ship

packs were dropping south from the North Atlantic. It was to be a massive blow, the prize the destruction of an entire Australian division. To help counter it, a cruiser force of the US Navy, with destroyer escort, was preparing to leave Norfolk, Virginia to steam towards the convoy, still so many days away to the south-east.

'They can't get to us in time,' Kemp said when the word came in by lamp from the *Nassau*. 'Too much to hope for!'

'Just to pick up the pieces,' Dempsey agreed.

Kemp looked sideways at him. 'You fellows have the worst job of the war – tankers, my God!'

'This time, you're with us.'

Kemp needed no reminder. He thought of the cargo tanks beneath the clamped-down hatches, the immensity of the explosion that could come, the shooting flames, the spurting, burning oil that would spread its blaze all around the ship to fry any survivor of the main blow-up, or, on the fringes perhaps, to sear the lungs and guts of any man who got that far. Kemp felt in his bones that the convoy was virtually doomed: at the very least there were going to be heavy losses. He had passed the initial warning to all the ships in his charge. It was up to each master to make his own arrangements, to decide for himself how much he made known to his crew and, in the case of the transports, to the soldiers, in consultation with the OC Troops in each ship. Already Kemp knew the situation was dodgy, that the Australians were far from happy with the overall military decision that was sending them across the world.

Would there be trouble? No, surely not. They were all disciplined men and in any case had nothing to gain by adopting any stroppy attitudes. All the same, the knowledge that they were steaming slap into Hitler's U-boat packs – and there was no possibility of taking any avoiding action since no one had a clue as to the actual positions of the packs – that knowledge wasn't going to ease anything. Kemp remembered his conversations in Cape Town with the liner masters and with the military officers. There had been a lot of disgruntlement around and bad feeling had spread amongst the soldiers. One of the colonels had said, tongue in cheek, that he wouldn't blame the troops if they mutinied.

That sealed bag again.

Some of the colonels aboard the transports might be in Hennessy's confidence for all he, Kemp, knew. But where did that lead anybody? No OC Troops could take it upon himself to divert a ship from known attack, and save his men to fight another day, in another land – in Australia, against the Japs. And supposing he could – what would Matthew Grout of the High Commission in Cape Town think of that one? Lay the blame on the Convoy Commodore, probably, for not delivering the bag to him for destruction and obliteration of Hennessy's schemes.

Thoughts bordering on the fantastic: Kemp gave a laugh, shaking his mind free of useless speculation. He heard a step on the starboard ladder and he turned. Rattray was coming up, stiffly. Kemp heard the PO report to Sub-Lieutenant Cutler.

'Back to duty, sir.'

'Chief steward say so?'

'No, sir. I did. Can't loaf about now. The leg'll work good enough, sir.'

'Sinker can cope.'

'Can he, sir?' The voice said clearly that he could not. 'In a dream, sir, and scared of 'is own shadow –'

'He reported there'd been another rat.'

'That's correct, sir. And I'd like to get me 'ands on the rat as put it there.'

'Any ideas as to who it was?'

Rattray shook his head. 'No, sir. Soon as I get something, I'll be dealing with it. Or him.'

'Take it easy,' Cutler said. 'Report to me first, all right?'

Rattray's answer was wooden. 'If you say so, sir.'

'I do, Petty Officer Rattray. This isn't our ship. Captain Dempsey'll deal with any trouble from his own crew. If it is one of the ship's crew.'

'Wouldn't be any o' the gunnery rates, sir. They all know Leading Seaman Sinker. Slow but sure, if you get me, sir. Not a lot on top but – well, honest.'

Cutler nodded. 'All right, PO.'

Rattray saluted and turned away for the ladder, thinking about Sinker and his woes. Thinking also about the attack to come, wondering who was going to get through. An oiler was a nice target, but so, of course, were the crammed transports. They had a reasonable escort though Rattray would have liked to see a

bigger anti-submarine screen to cover such an important c̶ But even if they'd had that, there was always the bugger t̶ through to loose off his tin fish and create havoc. Petty Rattray went below for a word with Chief Steward Lugg, him he'd put himself back to duty. Lugg was in his cabin, l̶ at some snapshots of home. Pompey: there was a snap c̶ Rattray took to be Mrs Lugg, standing with her back to a P̶ tram, near South Parade Pier.

'Pompey trams,' Rattray said nostalgically. 'Remember ̶ you?' His mind went back into the past. Fratton Park whe̶ was a big match on, the enormous crowds, the way th̶ clanging electric trams used to come up one after a̶ clearing the crowds as if by magic, each one crammed fu̶ standing passengers clinging to the straps dangling ove̶ the bench seats packed like sardines – like troop transpo̶ piping days of peace, no Hitler to loose off bombs and torp̶ Red Corporation trams, green ones run by the Horndea̶ Railway Company, all gone by the middle thirties. Rattra̶ courting had taken his intended out for an afternoon on ̶ tram, all the way from South Parade Pier, out through No̶ past what had been the Town Hall before Pompey had be̶ city, through Cosham and over Portsdown Hill and̶ Horndean, a small country village noted only for Gale's Br̶ Gale's Ales, Rattray could taste them now. They'd̶ through to Rowlands Castle – a three-mile country walk̶ place but four pubs – The Railway, The Fountain, The Cas̶ Staunton Arms. A drink in each then, giggling together,̶ Pompey by the Southern Railway, for Rowlands Castle̶ railway station as well as four pubs. That jaunt – fares,̶ fish-and-chips afterwards in Arundel Street before del̶ Doris back to Ma Bates – had cost Rattray most of a ten-bo̶ He'd never been so spendthrift since.

'Good days, eh.'

'They'll come again. It needn't all be in the past.'

Rattray scratched his cheek. 'I dunno so much. Things i̶ to be different when this lot's over.'

'In some ways, yes, probably. Better, maybe, for the̶ you and me . . . if ever we get through. Tell you somethi̶ don't the Commodore, or the Rear-Admiral, divert us b̶ Freetown? Eh? Just till the panic's over?'

would cut it out. And in Rattray's case you didn't want to invite too much in return about Ma Bates and her disabilities.

Porter's girl-friend in Rothesay hid his letters from her parents after she'd read them for the umpteenth time. They might pick up hints if they found them lying about, though she had as yet had no response from Fred Porter to her most recent letters about the definite pregnancy. She longed desperately for that response as in the afternoon she left the Victoria Hotel, where she worked, and sat in the summer sun by the shore of Rothesay Bay and looked across at HMS *Cyclops*, depot ship of the Seventh Submarine Flotilla, and sometimes at aircraft carriers lying at anchor until a wind tore down Loch Striven and sent them scurrying out to sea in the Firth of Clyde rather than drag their anchors onto a lee shore.

She liked looking at ships: it made her seem somehow closer to Fred Porter as she nourished their secret and hoped to God it wouldn't show too soon. She would probably get the sack from the Victoria Hotel, to say nothing of what Dad would say. As she sat she thought bitterly of Dad and his bagpipes and his church-going, Presbyterian old bugger. She knew all about the whisky; she'd used it against him when he tried to forbid her working at the Victoria Hotel, which naturally had a bar – two bars, one used by Naval officers, the other by ratings. According to Dad's bigotry, all hotels were sinks of iniquity where such things as unmarried coupling – his phrase – took place.

She worried ceaselessly about Fred Porter and his dangerous life aboard the *Coverdale*. If anything happened, if he didn't come back, she would do away with herself, another sin. Two sins, for the unborn baby would die too, but she knew she would never be able to carry on. But surely all would be well; Fred had had permission to take her aboard the *Coverdale* when the ship had last been in home waters, at anchor off Greenock – indeed she believed that conception had taken place in the Captain's pantry while Captain Dempsey was ashore at a convoy conference – and later, when the Captain had returned aboard, he'd seen her on deck and had spoken very nicely to her and she thought he was a decent old stick and looked reliable, so he'd probably keep his ship safe.

There were those who knew by now that their men would not be coming back: Mrs Warrington and Mrs Pedley among them.

The chief engineer's widow sat in her wheelchair, outwardly calm but the look in her eyes showing the turmoil within. Her sister-in-law grieved for a lost brother but kept occupied in looking after his widow. It would be drudgery for as long as it lasted but she wouldn't let her down now. She looked out for letters from overseas each time the postman came along the street. There would be some from Walter to make sad reading, and one from Captain Dempsey, something perhaps to treasure through the empty years, something saying Walter had died for his country. There had been no mention of an illness in the Admiralty's telegram so the ship had probably been attacked by the Nazis. Walter Warrington's sister always thought of them as Nazis, not Germans. The Germans were a decent people; in the late twenties, early thirties she'd spent some years in Germany, secretary to a British businessman in Berlin, and she'd seen at first hand the rise of Adolf Hitler and his goose-stepping SS guards, and had seen what Nazi-ism had done to Germany, and had now done to her brother.

In Meopham in Kent old Granny Marsden banged on her bedroom floor with her stick and Mary Kemp went up to see what it was all about this time. She climbed the twisty cottage stairs slowly: there was a stiffness in her knees and often there was pain. She wasn't getting any younger.

'Well, Granny. What is it?'

'My pillows.' The voice was still strong but lately a petulance had developed. It wasn't surprising really: Granny Marsden was far from the sort who would have wished to live on into decrepitude and dependence. Mary fluffed up the pillows and settled the thin white hair comfortably. The old lady asked fretfully, 'Still no news of the boy?'

Mary took a grip. 'I told you. The telegram.' She said it all over again, feeling tears start. 'Missing presumed drowned.'

'I know that, Mary dear. It's the presumed part, don't you see? They ought to *know*. I still think you should telephone to Sir Edward.'

'Sir Edward telephoned me – I told you that too.'

'But not with news, Mary –'

'Not with news, no. Sympathy.'

'I think he should be specific. He's always been so good.'

Mary sighed and suppressed a strong desire to snap,

remembering that John was fond of his grandmother. 'Sir Edward's the chairman of the Line. He's not the Admiralty.'

'There's no need to sound so irritable, Mary dear. I may not be here much longer.'

'I'm sorry, Granny.' After all, the poor old thing was devoted to her great-grandson. The news had left fresh lines on her face if such was possible. Mary Kemp fluffed again at the pillows, checked that the water-bottle was full and the pills prescribed by Dr Hawkins were not available for inadvertent over-dosage, opened the window a fraction, was sharply told to shut it again, did so and went down the stairs to listen to the BBC News. Today it was not all gloom: the troops were in good heart in Egypt, eager to mount a fresh offensive some day soon, they were having a great time on the whole, there was plenty of sport available and a new Army Commander had been appointed, a lieutenant-general named Montgomery whom Mary Kemp had seen recently in a newsreel at the cinema when she'd managed to fix a granny-sitter. A cocky little man wearing a beret covered with badges, with a somewhat hectoring voice that had spoken of knocking Rommel for six. Mary wished him luck. The news-reader, Gordon MacLeod, said now that Montgomery was already known to his troops as Monty and that this was a good sign. Mary didn't hear any more because the stick banged again, urgently.

v

Captain Dempsey was on the bridge when the signal was flashed from the Flag; Cutler was down aft with Rattray, putting the gunnery rates through their paces. Dempsey called down the voice-pipe to Kemp.

'Asdic contact, bearing green four-five, distant eight miles, closing.'

Thirteen

With the ship at action stations Kemp leaned from the after screen of the bridge. 'Cutler!'

'Sir?'

'Warn the guns' crews, U-boat contact, action imminent. Then get up here.'

'Aye, aye, sir.' Cutler turned to Rattray. 'Well – you heard, PO.'

'Looks like this is it, sir.'

Cutler grinned. 'You can say that again. All I can do is wish you luck – wish us all luck. I know the lads'll do their best –'

'They will, sir, they will.'

Or you'll know the reason why, Cutler thought to himself. Rattray's face was like a vice, hard and unyielding. He hated Nazis and he knew just what they all faced if a single torpedo took the ship, knew too that no gun would be likely to stop a torpedo once on track. The only real defence would be hawk-eyed lookouts and immediate responses from Captain Dempsey, who would be doing the dodging.

Rattray looked round when Cutler asked, 'Where's Sinker, PO?'

Rattray said, 'Sinker, he'll have gone for'ard, sir. Must have, if he's not here.'

Cutler nodded and doubled away along the port side flying bridge. Dempsey and Kemp were covering the bearing with their binoculars; the leading signalman was watching out for further signals from the flag or captain (D) in the destroyer leader, now moving to attack. The Officer of the Watch, Third Officer Peel,

130

was standing by in the wheelhouse ready to pass Dempsey's helm orders to the able seaman at the wheel, and telegraph orders to the starting platform below in the engine-room. The lookouts on the bridge and at the foremast head were scanning the sea for the tell-tale streaks that would indicate the oncoming torpedoes: the flat calm conditions would help in this but as if to negate such assistance the day was fading, fast as it always did in the tropics; there was a many-coloured splendour across the sky as the red of the sun declined below the horizon, and a deep purple light over the sea . . . very romantic, Cutler thought, if times had been different and the *Coverdale* a liner with girls in ball gowns and a band playing.

But not now.

There was a stillness: no one spoke. So far there were no more signals. Kemp was like a statue in the starboard bridge wing, as though he felt that any movement might attract a torpedo, a statue that had no current bearing upon events other than to wait and then, very promptly, to react. Dempsey, standing beside the Commodore, was equally still. Like Kemp, he had no current function other than vigilance. The *Coverdale* was as ready for action as was humanly possible: which in Dempsey's mind meant she was ready to be blown sky-high with all hands. There was nothing anyone aboard a laden tanker could do other than pray and hope to take that vital avoiding action in the very nick of time.

Cutler looked for'ard towards the gun's crew on the fo'c'sle: he noticed he couldn't see Leading Seaman Sinker, who might have gone to the after gun after he, Cutler, had left it. If he hadn't –

'Cutler.'

'Yes, sir.' Cutler moved across towards the Commodore.

'That bag, Cutler. I see no point in ditching it. If we come through, we come through. If we get hit . . .' Kemp shrugged. There was no need to put it into words. 'All the same – stand by to get it out from the chart room. Here.' He passed over his keys. 'Unlock the drawer, Cutler. We just may have to act in a hurry after all.'

'You're thinking of that hand message, sir?'

'Yes.' Kemp didn't elaborate. Cutler went thoughtfully into the chart room and unlocked the drawer. Kemp had a boarding party in mind, armed Nazis with orders to get hold of the bag, men

131

covered by the torpedo-tubes and guns of one of the U-boats. But surely not in the middle of a full-scale attack on a convoy? A surfaced U-boat would never stand a chance; the warships of the escort would be on her like a pack of hounds. Cutler gave a shrug and went back to the bridge wing, where he returned the key of the drawer to Kemp. He looked around at the convoy, still in its formation, the big troop transports, *Asian Star*, *Asturias*, *Carlisle Castle*, *Southern Cross*, and the armament carriers, and the three big grain ships that had not yet broken off for the United Kingdom. The Nazis had chosen their time nicely, they had plenty of targets.

'Scatter, sir?' Cutler asked.

Kemp shook his head. 'Not a good idea against U-boats. Surface attack is different. We keep together and leave it to the A/S screen. I –' He broke off, looking up from his binoculars. 'They're attacking now. The destroyers.'

Cutler saw the great spouts of water rise from the flat surface, just visible in the last of the daylight as the depth charges, released from the racks and projected by the throwers, exploded on reaching their settings. At the same time a lamp began flashing from the flagship. Kemp called to the leading signalman.

'Reading, sir. Further contacts port, sir.'

'Buggers,' Kemp said grimly.

ii

Rattray spat on his hands, then wiped them on the seat of his white shorts. If one of the U-boats could be forced to the surface within range of his guns he was going to have a field day and he wouldn't be waiting for any order from the bridge before he opened. He wondered, as he waited, about Leading Seaman Sinker. Bloody blockhead, he should have reported for action and not just gone for'ard all on his own initiative. But now wasn't the time to go for'ard himself and give Sinker a bollocking: that could wait. Rattray's fingers itched to press the tit and kill a Jerry. He'd always hated Nazis but more so since Cape Town. After that first run ashore early on, when he'd got so pissed that he'd gone arse over bollocks down that ladder, he'd faced the prospect of being shipbound all the time in port, which was largely why, in spite of the indignity, he'd consented to being carried down the accommodation ladder one afternoon and placed in a wheelchair for propulsion to a sort of garden party organized by a group of Cape Town lady do-gooders to bring some joy into the lives of sailors in from the sea, a strictly no booze affair, but still. Chief Steward Lugg had been insistent that it would be better to go than to mope around on his bunk in stifling heat, and the quack, come aboard to look at the leg's progress, backed Lugg's opinion; the quack happened to be on the do-gooding committee. So Rattray, on the appointed day, had been shoved, chairborne, into the back of some sort of ambulance where his conveyance was snugged down with lashings to stop it charging about the vehicle, and driven into Cape Town to be deposited in the big garden, with marquee, of some local notable.

As he had half expected and looked forward to, Rattray attracted immediate attention: the wounded warrior, home from the sea and combat. Women, young and old, clustered to ask questions. One of them, an old bag he thought her, clutched his hand and leaned across him dripping diamonds.

'Were you shipwrecked, you poor, poor man?'

No, he wasn't shipwrecked.

'But hit by shells?'

'Attacked,' Rattray answered truthfully. 'Casualties, like.'

'And your wound?'

'Me leg.' Rattray screwed his face up as though in pain. No need at all to mention ladders and getting tanked up in the bars of Simonstown. The old bag almost swooned with emotion and was forced to let go of Rattray's hand by a press of other women anxious to be able to say they'd shaken the hand of a British hero, badly wounded in action against the enemy. Cups of tea were brought, and buns. Rattray munched and preened; it was nice, being a hero. He didn't feel any sense of guilt – after all, he could become a real hero at any moment once the convoy sailed again, or anyway could catch a packet and there was no harm done in having the adulation in advance. He half wished Ma Bates was present, just to see him getting all the attention. At one moment, while talking about his wound to a bright young girl dressed as he imagined a southern belle from the USA might dress, all flounces beneath a sunshade and a big picture hat, he heard a suppressed hoot of laughter from behind, from one of the wheelchair attendants – two able seamen from the *Coverdale*'s naval party, detailed as PO's nurses for the spree if you could call it that.

Rattray twisted round. 'Shut it,' he said. 'Or else. Right?'

'Right, PO.'

His tone had been harsh; the southern belle twittered a little. A bully? That wouldn't be nice . . . but of course the poor man was in pain so it was understandable. Rattray read all this in her face, and again manifested pain with a grimace. Not that it mattered; someone else turned up and there was a strong stench of rum that scattered the ladies.

'Ratty! Well, I'll be blowed if it's not Ratty, the old bugger!'

'Christ above,' Rattray said wonderingly. 'Shiner White! What you doing here, then?'

'Come down from Freetown for a boiler clean. In the old –'

'Pissed as usual,' Rattray said. 'You don't fit with a bleeding garden party.' He lowered his voice. 'Got any with you?' he asked. They hadn't met for years; but in the past, Petty Officer White had always bottled his tot, illegally saving it up for a good free piss-up ashore where you didn't get run in for being three sheets in the wind. Shiner White, not changed over the years, produced a lemonade bottle, half full of issue rum, the real hard stuff that you didn't get ashore.

Rattray took a swig. 'God, that's better.' He wiped the back of a hand across his lips.

'Got another an' all,' White said. 'What's up with you, eh?'

'Hurt me leg,' Rattray said dismissingly. 'But don't let it obtrude.' He twisted round again. 'All right, you two, you can bugger off and enjoy yourselves if you can find any talent. Report back when the show's over.' He settled back for a yarn with his old mate – shared commissions China-side, in the Med, West Indies, Atlantic Fleet in the days before it had been redesignated the Home Fleet, Pompey barracks. Whale Island, too – Shiner White was a fellow gunner's mate. There was plenty to talk about; and there was plenty to drink. The ladies of the garden party tut-tutted a little but kept the condescending smiles intact on their faces and left them to it. You always had to stretch a point with sailors, a roughish lot but good-hearted. They simply made way when White decided to push his old mate around a bit and get to meet some of his own shipmates. And that was when it happened. Rattray's wheelchair struck a tall, distinguished-looking man in a white sharkskin suit, who went down flat.

'Pardon me,' Shiner White said.

The man swore. Rattray gave a start. The man, picking himself up, said, 'Clumsy idiot.'

White pushed the chair away, fast. Rattray said, 'He spoke German, Shiner!'

'Eh? Clumsy idiot, that's English enough.'

'Not that. *Before* he said that. A Jerry swear word. I met a Jerry cruiser squadron once, China-side, got to know some of 'em. Look, Shiner, that bloke could be a bleeding spy –'

'Just because 'e swore –'

'Caught on the hop, see? Automatic reflex, you swear in your own bleeding language. There's Nazi spies everywhere, you know that. Besides, when he said clumsy idiot, it come out guttural. Bloody swine!' The rum was surging by now; Petty Officer Rattray saw himself as a real, genuine hero, the bloke that had bowled out one of Hitler's spy rings operating in a vital naval base. His duty, he said indistinctly to Shiner White, was clear: they had to report the man to the brass, and there was bound to be some brass present, the high-ups always liked slumming and putting on a friendly face to the lads on occasions like this. And sure enough, half-way through the afternoon there was a stir as the Admiral arrived, white Number Tens, double row of gold oak leaves on his cap-peak, gilded shoulder straps with crossed swords and stars and all. Many medal ribbons, and a flag lieutenant in attendance. The do-gooders loved it. And Petty Officer Rattray, spycatcher, took his chance of glory.

Now, back at sea and waiting for the first of the torpedoes to go in amongst the ships of the convoy, Rattray shuddered in recollection. Pushed, egged on even, by his old mate PO White, he had bearded the Admiral, saluting stiffly from his wheelchair and being very much the gunner's mate in adversity. There had been a great hoo-ha and the gutteral-voiced man who had sworn in German was brought along. To Rattray's astonishment the Admiral saluted him: it turned out that he was indeed a German, at any rate by extraction, but had for many years been a South African by nationality, a good citizen of the Empire and a bigwig in the South African government. To Rattray's further morti-fication, the quack who'd seen to his leg had been present and had explained to the Admiral. That was all right so far as it went: it got Rattray off the hook so far as discipline and charges were concerned. It was fair enough that a man in from a convoy should have a drink or two and the Admiral happened to like being seen to be democratic and tolerant of ratings' foibles. But the quack – the bloody quack had come across loud and clear, that the wounded hero had slipped arse over bollocks down a very peaceful ladder. . . .

In Rattray's mind it was all the German's fault. It added fuel to the flames. He patted the breech of the after 3-inch, muttering to himself as he did so. He was going to give the sods what for.

Then, across the dark water with its gleam of phosphorescence, he saw the twin tracks heading for the convoy and he yelled a warning to the bridge.

iii

Dempsey too had seen the trails. No avoiding action was necessary: the torpedoes were passing across his stern, harmless to the *Coverdale*. He passed an order to ex-yeoman Gannock, his own signalman: a warning signal to the port column of the convoy.

Kemp said, 'Shallow settings. We'd not have seen them otherwise.' Within a minute the first of the explosions came, an almighty bang and an upsurge of red and orange flame in the middle of which the outline of one of the grain ships was clearly seen, with debris falling like rain over a wide area of the sea. Heat beat across the water: the grain ship had been steaming on the port quarter of the *Coverdale* and not very distant.

Dempsey said, 'Two hits, fore and aft. She hasn't a hope.'

True words: in the hellish glow of flame and red-hot metal, the ship could be seen to be settling on an even keel, filling at both ends. She was ablaze from stem to stern and steam was rising as the sea encroached. Dempsey glanced aside at the Commodore. Kemp's face was set, no emotion visible as the *Coverdale* moved on, no word about survivors. Not that there would be many – but a life was a life, someone's husband or father, son or brother. Someone left to die in agony, perhaps, or just to drown while the convoy passed on, each ship an automaton with no voice for the dying. This was the fear faced by anyone who sailed in convoy and it was an accepted fact that the convoy as a whole was of more importance than those who fell by the wayside. But Dempsey had come to know Kemp well since the departure from Sydney and he was aware of the mental conflict that would be in the Commodore's mind. His own too, though with a difference. The unspoken order to leave the survivors to die was not his to decide. He wouldn't be carrying it to the grave as he suspected Kemp might be. In Dempsey's view the job of Commodore was a bastard.

Below in the engine-room acting Chief Engineer Evans was listening to the reverberations of the torpedo hits and of the explosions of depth charges as the destroyers of the escort pressed home the double attack on the two U-boat packs. Evans' metallic, oily kingdom shuddered and rang as the shock waves reached the hull and he began to worry about sprung plates. From time to time the electric lights dimmed but always came back to full power. The shafts turned on, disdainful of outside interference. Evans left the starting platform to his acting second engineer, and made his way around, watching, feeling joints and bearings, wondering if he would be able to cope if anything went wrong. That was always the test, when things went wrong and you had to think fast and think correctly to put them right – that was one of his father-in-law's pearls of wisdom and Evans knew it happened to be dead right.

He looked up through the maze of steel ladders leading to the air-lock: the only way out and a long way up, and many men to be got up there before the chief engineer made it himself, the shepherd of his oil-streaked, sweaty flock in pants and singlets.

Not that any of them would, if the ship was hit – not unless there was a miracle. One big bang and that would be all they knew about it.

Evans went back to the starting platform and stood beside the acting second. A huge eruption came from close by, made the ship lurch so that both men were flung from the platform to fetch up in a heap on the greasy deck plates. As they scrambled to their feet the lights dimmed once again and this time went right out. As Evans shouted for the electrician the voice-pipe from the bridge whined at him. He put the tube to his ear.

'Chief here.'

'Bridge.' It was Dempsey's voice. 'Close shave, that's all. Another grain ship . . . swung close astern of us just as she took a fish. All well below?'

'Lights gone, sir, otherwise OK.'

'We still have power on the steering, Chief, so it must be just local, the lighting circuit. Report when all's well.'

'Yes, sir.' Evans had just replaced the tube when the lights came up again and he breathed a heartfelt sigh of relief, found he was bathed in sweat just as though he'd stepped out of a bath. Even his shoes seemed to squelch . . . he looked down and saw blood. He must have damaged something when he was propelled off the starting platform but he hadn't felt anything. Now that he'd seen the blood, however, he felt the pain. A torn leg, bleeding freely, but nothing to be done about it at the moment. You had to carry on in action and that was that.

'Getting a shade too close, Chief.' Vetch, acting second engineer, noticed the blood. 'Better get that seen to. I'll take over if –'

'No, I'm all right. It'll keep.' Evans looked around the engine-room: no sprung plates, no leaks. Like the Light Brigade, they moved on. Evans said, 'You're a praying chap. Now's the time, if ever there was one.'

Vetch nodded, but didn't appear to be praying. Evans said, 'Or d'you think God knows, without being asked?'

'I reckon He knows we're busy, Chief.' Vetch belonged to the Elim Tabernacle where members of the congregation got to their feet and spouted when they felt the irresistible urge. At the moment, he didn't know why, he didn't feel it. Maybe that was because there was so much he wanted to pray for, and he might not have much time, and his mind was in a jumble, a kind of torrent in which his family and the ship and himself were whirling around. It was best left to God to sort out. He always knew best, that was one thing that was sure and unequivocal.

The *Coverdale* steamed on, so far unscathed. On the bridge there was partial relief – only very partial so far as Kemp was concerned. They were not coming under direct attack and obviously there was intent behind that fact: they were wanted for other things. Any moment now it might become necessary for that sealed bag to be ditched. Kemp was about to tell Cutler to stand by in instant readiness when someone came up the starboard ladder to the bridge, swayed at the top and then collapsed in a heap, blubbering like a child.

Leading Seaman Sinker.

Fourteen

There had been more dead rats; it had become in fact a daily occurrence, a daily nightmare, a daily torture of the innocent. Stripey Sinker, knowing just how horribly unfair it was, had shaken like a leaf each time he entered his cabin. Rage and fear were uncomfortable bedfellows in themselves, to say nothing of the succession of rats and their stench. Someone was deliberately keeping corpses until they stank. Stripey had become a bag of nerves. He had kept watch when he could, but he couldn't all the time, and whoever was doing it knew when the cabin would be empty. Stripey had no idea at all as to who the culprit might be. It could be any one of the crew.

But tonight had been different.

Stripey had turned in during the late afternoon, off watch and dead tired from many sleepless nights. Before turning in he'd gone along to see the chief steward for his continuing dose of sulpha whatsit and he'd come out with his troubles, man to man. Lugg had said he'd best have a good, stiff slug of Scotch, or better still some of the Van der Humm he'd been able to bring aboard in Simonstown. Stripey had agreed; and the Cape brandy, a really big double, had done the trick. He'd gone out like a light after a while and he was still asleep and breathing like a steam engine when the alarm had come; and he'd remained unaware in his bunk. But when the racket started outside, the thump of explosions and so on, he'd come awake with a bang. And when he did so he knew there was someone in his cabin, someone moving stealthily towards his bunk. That someone would believe that he, Sinker, was at his action station: another rat for delivery?

Stripey's mind moved with unusual speed: there was no rat smell and if the intruder believed the cabin to be empty why didn't he flick on the light, and why the stealth?

It was more than a rat, this time. In the heat and kerfuffle of action, murder could be done. Someone had gone round the twist. Stripey heard heavy breathing and then moved his unwieldy body as fast as his mind. He came off the bunk like an elephant and threw himself towards the breathing sound. He made contact and came down hard on top of the intruder. They both crashed to the deck of the cabin and Stripey's beefy hands found the throat and squeezed, and went on squeezing.

When the body went limp Stripey knew he'd gone too far. Shaking, giving a high sounding moan of anguish, he found the light switch. One of the engine-room gang, a bloke named Passmore he believed. The eyes staring, the tongue lolling, garish red marks around the throat, all the limbs still. No heartbeat. He had become a murderer. He couldn't hide from what he'd done, everyone would know. And you didn't kill people just because of stinking rats. There was a rat beside the man's body, probably a fresh one since there was no smell, and there was no sign of a weapon such as a knife or a belaying-pin. Stripey wouldn't be likely to get away with self-defence. But there had been a lot of torment and maybe Commodore Kemp would understand.

ii

Kemp was watching out for a surfacing U-boat: Cutler took Stripey Sinker over. Sinker was like a jelly, eyes large, limbs all over the place, a jelly-octopus talking in a high voice about victimization and the ends of tethers, dirty looks and rats and veiled threats and what he'd believed to be an attempt at murder. There was currently no point in trying to sort out the facts and in any case, with the ship in danger, this was no time for an investigation.

Cutler said, 'Hold it, Sinker. Shut your gob. I'm taking no note officially of what you've said – you're in a panic right now. It'll be gone into later. I –'

'I didn't mean to do it, sir, honest I didn't!'

'Maybe not –'

'It's all right for you to talk. They got their bloody knife in me, drove me bloody mad they did.'

'Yes, all right, Sinker.' Cutler was thinking fast while Stripey Sinker went on. He had to be placed in restraint for his own good but you couldn't shut a man in, say, the fore peak with the ship liable to go sky high at any moment. There was only one thing for it and Cutler made the decision without reference to the Commodore or Captain Dempsey, who each had other worries. He interrupted what had become an incoherent ramble, using the voice of authority. 'Get down to your gun, Leading Seaman Sinker. We're in action. You'll help fight the ship – all right? Just one moment.' He went to the after rail of the bridge and shouted down for Petty Officer Rattray to come up at the double. Officers, Rattray thought to himself, bloody officers just don't think . . . double, with his leg? He went for'ard and climbed the ladders as fast as he could. When he arrived Cutler told him the facts as briefly as possible.

'Keep an eye on him, PO. Detail a hand to be with him all the while. When we come through, we'll see what's to be done. In the meantime, don't let him do anything stupid.'

'Like going overboard, sir?'

'Yes –'

'Best thing for 'im if 'e did, sir.' Rattray sucked at a hollow tooth. 'Best for 'is family too. Better than swinging, is lost overboard in action.'

Cutler's voice was hard. 'See that it doesn't happen that way, Petty Officer Rattray. There could be a case for manslaughter. The poor bugger's been hazed too far. As you should have known – as you should have prevented.'

'If you say so, sir.' Rattray turned away and shouted at Sinker to get below to his gun as ordered. He kept close behind as Sinker stumbled blindly down the ladder. Cutler went across to join Kemp, and made his report. Kemp nodded but didn't comment at first.

Cutler said, 'I guess he was driven to it, sir. That's if I've got the facts right. And we did know about the rat in the first place. Maybe we're all to blame. Not just Rattray.'

'All the facts'll come out, Cutler, at the proper time. At this moment, I can say nothing more.' Kemp turned to Dempsey. 'Your man Passmore, Captain. What's he like?' He added, 'What *was* he like, I should say.'

141

'On the bolshie side – not amenable to discipline, as reported by Warrington. Also a natural chip on his shoulder about the Nazis – they bombed his house in Stepney.'

Kemp nodded again: it seemed to fit. And every man had his limits, the point beyond which he would retaliate. Leading Seaman Sinker was a harmless, good-natured man by all accounts – Kemp had always made it his business to familiarize himself as quickly as possible with the men under his command and although the guns' crews were, in the case of the *Coverdale*, strictly part of the ship's wartime complement and not part of his own staff as Commodore, he knew that much about Sinker, a three-badgeman of previously excellent character. Rattray, according to Cutler, was disparaging about his capabilities but that was a different story and Rattray was inclined to be disparaging about everyone other than himself, another thing that Kemp knew.

He lifted his glasses again, stared intently through the encroachment of the night. So far the transports were moving along unscathed; and the destroyers' attacks on the U-boats had achieved some success, Kemp believed. At any rate there were no more hits. Perhaps the Nazi packs had withdrawn, gone deep to lie doggo for a while – but as sure as fate they would resume the attack before long. Kemp lowered his glasses and rubbed wearily at tired eyes. You could go on looking out for too long, until you began seeing things that weren't there.

And murder, in the middle of an attack. If murder had to be done at all, what a time to choose!

Binoculars up again, and something obtruding, right astern of the *Coverdale* . . . Kemp used the old seaman's trick of looking away and then back again, looking slightly to one side, obliquely.

'Cutler. . . .'

'Sir?'

'Dead astern. See anything, or is it my eyes?'

Cutler was onto the bearing pronto. 'Feather of water, I believe, sir. Can't be sure.'

'Periscope. Or our wake, playing funny buggers with our vision? Keep on it, Cutler.'

From behind Kemp, Dempsey spoke. 'Something black emerging, getting bigger.' He paused, looking hard through his binoculars, oak-leaved cap-peak low over the eyepieces. 'It's a surfacing U-boat – slap in our wake.'

'Where the A/S screen's Asdics can't pick her up,' Kemp said. 'And for my money she's not going to fire off any fish at us. Cutler?'

'You reckon the time's come, sir? That bag?'

Kemp nodded.

'I'll go get it,' Cutler said, took the key from Kemp, and moved fast into the chart room. Coming back with the sealed bag, he stood beside the Commodore. 'Say when, sir.'

Again Kemp nodded, watching the emerging submarine, its outline blurred by the disturbance of the ship's wake. He was about to pass the order to Leading Signalman Goodenough to warn the senior officer of the escort of the U-boat's presence when the main attack was resumed with startling suddenness and devastation. There was a colossal explosion away on the *Coverdale*'s port beam, a huge blaze of light, red and orange and purple with shafts of searing white, a conflagration from which shoots of fire appeared, as though some gigantic firework display had been set off.

'One of the armament carriers, sir, *Bull Run*.'

'Poor buggers.' It would have to be the *Bull Run*, one of those that had left Sydney in ballast . . . she'd loaded ammunition in Simonstown, just one out of the three with a cargo, and had been under orders to detach for the Windward Islands, which in a few more days she would have done. Kemp watched in awe, helplessly. This was not the first time he'd had to witness such a sight; but it was one that he never grew hardened to. All those men . . . now disintegrated, the flesh burned from their bones virtually in the wink of an eyelid. A mercy, of course, that it should be fast. There could be no survivors. Scorching heat came across the moving convoy, the terrible fires continued, the pieces of debris came down like rain. Something large and red-hot took the after tank deck, right on the tank tops between the flying bridges. Dempsey took charge, going down himself to get the fire parties on the job before the heat could get through to his lethal cargo. Petty Officer Rattray stood by his gun, watching the half-surfaced U-boat and lining up his sights ready to open the moment he had the Nazis where he wanted them. Any second now. He was about to give the firing order and bugger the bridge and the Commodore when he saw a light flashing from the conning tower.

Funny, was that! U-boats, they didn't waste time in making signals. There just might be something on that he didn't know about, and it wasn't for a gunner's mate to bitch up anything. So he didn't give the order to open fire.

The Nazi signal was read on the bridge and Goodenough reported to Kemp.

'Heave to or be sunk, sir.'

Kemp met Cutler's eye. 'Right, Cutler.'

Cutler moved to the port rail. 'Just hold on a moment, sir? Till the situation clears?'

Kemp's mind went to the importance of the bag's contents, the importance to many highly-placed officers in Canberra, to the lives of thousands of Australian troops, to the security of Australia itself at any rate in the eyes of those who disagreed with the movement of so many men out of the Commonwealth. There was time in hand perhaps, time while he played games with the U-boat's commander, time in which the senior officer might pick up the U-boat's presence and detach a destroyer to blow her out of the water. And there were the *Coverdale*'s own guns.

'All right, Cutler. Hang on.'

Cutler remained ready at the bridge rail, the canvas bag balanced on the teak woodwork. Kemp took up a megaphone; there was a lot of noise around, more explosions, continual depth charging from the destroyers and gunfire from the cruisers: probably something else had come to the surface, a damaged U-boat to be finished off by the big guns – no quarter would be given tonight, Kemp knew. Through the megaphone he spoke to the guns' crews.

'I believe there'll be an attempt to board us. All men –'

He was interrupted by the leading signalman. 'Flashing again, sir.' Goodenough read off the message as it came through. ' "You have sixty seconds to stop your engines." '

For Kemp, time seemed to stand still: so many considerations, and the moment of final decision had come. He turned to Dempsey. 'All right, Captain. We'll do as he says.' He added, 'For now.'

Dempsey moved into the wheelhouse and himself pulled over the handles of the telegraphs. Bells rang on the bridge, and were repeated in the engine-room. The big shafts idled to stop. There was near silence. Gradually the way came off the ship and she lay

144

rolling in the ocean swell, on an otherwise flat sea with a bright moon coming up to lay a silver sheen across the water. From the bridge, from the upper deck, the watchers saw the U-boat, still with little more than her conning tower above the surface, move across to starboard.

Kemp called down again. 'All close-range weapons' crews stand by!'

Rattray's voice came back. 'Permission to open fire, sir?'

'No. It'd be a very lucky shot that got her first time. And the moment we open, we're done for. We'll play this differently.' Kemp paused. 'Stand by for further orders, Rattray. When she approaches too closely for a torpedo attack, I intend to rake her with the close-range weapons. And then you may get your chance with the 3-inch as well.'

iii

To a large extent Kemp had been relying on the emerging moon: in that light the U-boat's conning tower must surely be seen by the escort. He had refrained from making a signal asking for assistance; to do that would be to invite the torpedo that would send them all blazing into the heavens as surely as the armament carrier. But the moon failed him. With the devastating suddenness to which the sea area was prone, a squall came up. Clouds where there had been none only minutes before, and a screaming wind that brought the sea up into heavy waves, from the tops of which the spume blew like a carpet to hide the U-boat. Teeming rain, so fierce that as the slashing water-slivers took the decks they bounced back up again to a height of some three feet, drenched the men from below as well as from above. Visibility was brought down to a matter of yards.

Salvation in itself? Perhaps. Certainly it would aid the convoy. The main attack would be drawn off again until the visibility cleared. There would be no point in the Nazis loosing off their torpedoes, blindly into the night. And with luck their close companion would go deep – but, again, only for the time being. Basically the threat remained. But there was something that could be done, a delaying tactic.

'Captain Dempsey . . . I suggest we move on out. Fast!'

145

Dempsey rang the engines to full ahead. Noise came back to surround Evans as the shafts turned and bit. The *Coverdale* moved on, keeping the course of the invisible convoy. Along the upper deck the tanker's crew and the naval ratings shivered in the now icy cold. The rain had soaked into everything: white shorts and shirt stuck to Petty Officer Rattray as though he personally were being laundered. Stripey Sinker shook with more than the cold and wet: a murderer, all set to hang when the ship reached dry land, or anyway, UK. They wouldn't land him in the States, he imagined; he was a British problem. He felt the unfairness: he'd been driven to it, all those rats, stinking buggers. And all, in the last analysis, the fault of bloody Rattray's big mouth and the daft remarks that had issued too loudly from it. Now this attack on the *Coverdale* itself, singled out from all the others in the convoy, the ship in which he, the Nazi spy so called, was sailing. He'd be lucky not to be murdered himself. Well, it wouldn't be any worse than waiting bloody months while all the formalities of charge and prosecution took their lengthy course and in due process of the law he was made ready for the hangman and felt the rope go around his neck.

On the bridge Kemp spoke again. 'The Rear-Admiral will have broken wireless silence, Dempsey. Once attacked. . . .' Kemp looked around the close horizons that hemmed them in. 'How long will this last, d'you suppose? I'm not too familiar with this part of the world.'

Dempsey said, 'It could be over within half an hour. But there'll be more behind this one. Once they come, they tend not to come singly.'

Kemp grinned. 'But in droves . . . Shakespeare, I think.'

'Not exactly droves.' Dempsey sounded a little on edge and Kemp knew why: a prudent master didn't push his ship at full speed into nil visibility, not when there were other ships in the area. The radar was all very well; it was never one hundred per cent to be relied upon. If the *Coverdale* should slam into another ship it would be reckoned against Dempsey: he was not obliged to obey the Commodore's order when it came to ship safety. He still commanded the ship: no one could take over that responsibility. With the lookouts, with all the bridge personnel, Dempsey was straining his eyes through the deluge, watching out for the loom of a ship's hull as the big oiler moved on through the night.

So many ships, so many echoes for the radar to report, those bearings constantly shifting as the vessels, running blind, altered their relative positions in the convoy pattern. They would be dead lucky to get away without a collision somewhere in the formation.

Sub-Lieutenant Cutler was still standing by the guardrail, still holding the vital sealed bag: just as well, he thought, that he'd suggested to the Commodore that he should hang on a while longer. The squall had mucked up the Nazi's plans quite nicely. Cutler believed they were going to get away with it; thoughts of home came back to him, and thoughts of Cape Town as well. One day he might go back to the Cape. Not that Lady Natalie would be waiting around for him: there were too many other men handy in Cape Town, and more convoys, out and home, arriving to bring fresh blood. . . .

'Cutler?'

'Yes, sir?'

'That bag.' Kemp had already had a discussion on tactics with Dempsey: his intention, when the U-boat reappeared, was to let the Nazis come alongside. They would be lulled; once close, as Kemp had said to Rattray, they wouldn't be in a position to fire off torpedoes. There was, of course, her gun; but Kemp didn't believe it would be used when close, any more than torpedoes. The subsequent explosion would involve the U-boat as well. Dempsey had been in full agreement with Kemp's plans. Kemp now said, going back to the bag, 'We have to choose our moment right, Cutler. I want to hang onto that bag if at all possible. But if it has to go, then go it will. After that, the ship's the main consideration.'

'Sure it is, sir –'

'What I mean is, we may let the Nazis board rather than risk the ship. It's the bag they're after – not us as such. When they know it's gone – once they've searched the ship – they won't hang about.' Kemp was still clearing his own mind. 'They'll go back and shove off. Go deep if the A/S screen's around. That's when our gunners'll have to be fast – before they either dive or put a fish in us.'

Cutler didn't say anything. Kemp, water streaming from him as from a duck's back, resumed his watch ahead, binoculars peering through the filthy weather. The cloud seemed to be right down on the water now, bringing a thick murk even though the wind was still at screaming pitch: there must be one hell of a lot of cloud around, Kemp thought, more and more of it being hurled about them by the wind. He felt as though he was breathing water like a drowning man. Dempsey was standing by the fore rail, close to the wheelhouse door, ready to pass instant orders to the helmsman and the engine-room. Below, Petty Officer Rattray moved with difficulty along the flying bridge, still to a large extent a dot-and-carry progress, keeping tabs on the alertness of his guns' crews – and on Leading Seaman Sinker, murderer-at-large.

He found Sinker by the for'ard 3-inch, holding onto the gunshield and staring out into the teeming rain, not seeming to be aware that he was as full of water as a sponge. Close by was Able Seaman Parsons, detailed as guard, watchdog, nanny or whatever you chose to call him.

'All right, Parsons?'

'All right, PO.'

'Don't take your eyes off him, Parsons.'

Parsons shifted uncomfortably; he didn't relish his job. 'Poor sod,' he said.

'Not the way to speak of a leading hand, Parsons.'

Parsons stared: the pusser bugger! Well, of course, poor old Stripey *was* still a leading seaman . . . but still. His remark had been one of sympathy, but bloody Rattray would never understand that. All gunners' mates were the same, not human. Quarried, not born of woman. Ice water in their veins, gunpowder instead of brains, and did everything, but everything, by numbers. Even when on leave. Wife and kids to have breakfast, one-one-two. Fall-in for washing-up, muster for housework. Family to dinner, tea, supper, then pipe down. Then the other thing: they did that by numbers too. Parsons gave a sudden chuckle. Rattray on the job . . . it would be a routine process like shoving a projy up the breech of a gun.

'What's funny, eh?'

'Nothing, PO.'

'Laugh at bloody nothing, do you?'

'Just thoughts.'

'Shouldn't have thoughts, not at sea, Parsons.'

'Sorry I'm sure,' Parsons said. Why didn't the stupid prat eff

148

off? Suddenly the stupid prat seemed to widen his eyes, not that Parsons could exactly see that in the prevailing conditions, but Rattray had stiffened his body as he watched out ahead, past the shivering figure of Stripey Sinker.

'*Jesus Christ!*'

Parsons saw it and moved fast, grabbing at Sinker and hustling him aft as the *Coverdale* swung heavily to port. Dead ahead of their track a huge shape had loomed through the murk, a vast counter, the stern, Parsons believed, of one of the troop transports. The *Coverdale*'s plates shuddered and rang as the engines went to emergency full astern and the heavy swing increased.

iv

'Close,' Dempsey said. His face was expressionless: they had just about grazed past, a scrape of hulls before the full port wheel and the engines had done their work, and done it just in time.

Kemp said, 'Nicely done, Dempsey.'

'Thanks be to God.' Kemp glanced at Dempsey: he'd sounded as though he really meant that, a kind of genuine thanksgiving for salvation. God was often enough there with seafarers: Kemp had had some narrow escapes at times and had a strong fellow feeling for Dempsey and his evident belief. The majesty of sunrise and sunset in all the quarters of the world, the brilliant colours, the often amazing cloud effects; the sheer strength of angry waters, of howling winds, the peace of calms, the very look of the waters off Cape Horn, or the North Atlantic where the waves could rise well above the bridge of the biggest ship afloat, sending her down into the depths of a valley only to pass beneath the hull and lift thousands of tons of steel to the heights, so that her company could look straight down a hillside . . . these things were not of man, they were of the elements, and God was the elements. Kemp was not a churchgoer, though in the days of peace he had taken many a Divine Service in the first-class lounges of the liners of the Mediterranean-Australia Line and the act had always meant something to him. It had been conducted with full reverence and never mind that the surroundings were unchurchlike in the extreme: the lounge, place of drinking and dancing and of the arrangements made preparatory to sea seductions. On Sunday mornings, God took over and cleaned things up, for however short a time . . . after the service the stewards who largely formed the choir were given their beer money from the collection. Officially the collection went towards Marine Charities, but it was always accepted that beer money was a marine charity of a sort. Kemp had a feeling that God would understand that, and give the mild deception a wink and a nod from on high.

Standing beside Dempsey now, Kemp said quietly, 'I think God's with us, all right. The visibility's improving.'

'Yes.' Dempsey had his glasses up: the ships of the convoy were coming into view, great shapes not where they should be. But they would soon re-form into convoy columns. The destroyers of the escort were away ahead and on the flanks, but there was no more depth charging. Dempsey eased his engines to drop the *Coverdale* back into the Commodore's position: they had overtaken a number of ships and Dempsey remarked on this.

'Sheer luck we didn't hit anyone.'

'Divine intervention again?'

Dempsey gave a short laugh. 'Could very well be. And perhaps God's taken care of the U-boats as well.'

'Just a respite.' Kemp gave a huge yawn, one that he was unable to smother: he was dead tired, but knew he couldn't go below until the convoy was in the clear, and no more could Dempsey, who looked equally tired. 'They've gone deep, but they'll be back –'

He broke off suddenly: there had been a curious sound from below, from deep down in the ship. A second later the decks gave a very heavy lurch to port and the bow seemed to rise, to lift high and then drop back. Dempsey and Kemp both found themselves staggering, and Kemp fell heavily to the deck of the bridge: no damage except to his dignity.

Dempsey helped him to his feet. 'Hit something, Commodore. How much'll you put on it that it's a U-boat?'

'Can't be anything else.' Kemp was breathless. 'We'll not have done it much good, that's for sure.' He was wondering if the submerged object might be the shadowing U-boat, and deciding that it most likely was. If so, that particular worry was now past: anything hit like that would be so badly stove in that it would go down like a stone, flooded within seconds. But the relief didn't last long. As Dempsey passed the word for the carpenter to sound round below there was a shout from ex-yeoman Gannock. The half-surfaced shape was back and was lying off to starboard.

Fifteen

'Signalling,' Dempsey said. 'It looks as though he means to lie off.'

Kemp said between his teeth, 'I might have known it.' The U-boat's signal, as reported a few moments later, indicated that the tubes were lined up on the *Coverdale* to act as cover for a boarding party, who would be expendable if the British Commodore should wish to commit suicide after they had come aboard. Soon after that the watchers from the bridge saw something moving between themselves and the Nazis: two inflatable rubber dinghies being pulled across the dark water and already close. Rattray saw them too, and called up to the bridge.

'Seen them,' Cutler called back.

'Open fire, sir?'

Kemp heard. 'No!' He spoke to Cutler. 'All right, this is it. Ditch the bag, Cutler.'

'Already have, sir.' Cutler had been sweating, now felt a strong sense of relief that his clumsiness didn't matter: when the ship had hit the underwater obstruction he, like Kemp, had lost his balance. The bag had shot from his hand, over the canted starboard guardrail, and plummeted down towards the sea. Now, Cutler started to explain.

'Clumsy oaf,' Kemp said. That was all. There was only one line of action left now, the second of his two alternatives. The U-boat was not after all taking the risk of closing within gun range, and since the bag had gone and its vital secrets with it, Kemp would simply let the Nazis board. There was no other way, short of allowing the *Coverdale* to take a gutfull of torpedoes, and that would help no one. 'Brains before brute strength,' Kemp said. He gave a harsh laugh. 'I haven't an idea in the world what happens next, but something'll turn up!'

Dempsey said, 'Whatever turns up isn't going to be much use to us now.'

Kemp didn't respond to that. He knew, as Dempsey knew, that the moment the frustrated boarding party left the ship, the U-boat would send in the torpedoes. Meanwhile the main attack on the convoy was being resumed: the destroyers of the escort were moving fast on the flanks and the sea's surface was being broken again by the upheaval as the depth charges exploded beneath. As the rubber dinghy closed the gap, there was a white flash from one of the troop transports, the *Asian Star*, taken on her port side for'ard, then a second later another amidships. Kemp watched the spreading fire, the red glow from her plates. In the fires he could see the lifeboats, swung out ready from their davits and lowered to the embarkation deck, with the Australian soldiers milling about, caught up in an unfamiliar situation in an unfamiliar world, far from the homeland they would not have left if Brigadier Hennessy had had his way. Really, that bag's contents had been too late all the way through, certainly too late to be effective for the troops aboard the *Asian Star*.

And something else stood out a mile: with a troop transport in difficulties the attention of the senior officer and the escorts would be heavily concentrated, and not upon events around the Commodore's ship, though they might wonder at the Commodore's silence in an emergency.

ii

Along with two seamen of the *Coverdale*'s crew Petty Officer Rattray stood by the lowered Jacob's ladder sent down from the after tank deck for the embarkation of the armed Nazis.

'Dirty bastards,' he growled as a German officer came over the side.

The officer, a man in his early twenties, skinny and bird-like, smiled. 'There is a war on, my friend,' he said.

'Speak English, do you?'

'Yes. Heil, Hitler! Take me to your Commodore. Quickly!'

153

Rattray pointed. 'Bridge. Up there, see?'

More men came over the side: fifteen all told, armed with sub-machine guns. As the last man embarked, the dinghies stood off to starboard to become lost in the darkness. The Nazi officer spoke again to Rattray: all hands were to stand away from the guns. If there was any trouble, a signal would be flashed to the U-boat and the torpedoes would be fired.

'After you've hopped it over the side, I s'pose,' Rattray said sourly. The Nazi didn't bother to answer, and Rattray was aware he'd talked nonsense: the spreading, blazing oil when the *Coverdale* went up wouldn't leave anyone alive in the vicinity. Back in Germany, this lot would be rated bloody heroes who'd sacrificed their lives for the Fatherland. Rattray felt a sense of grievance: only the British were supposed to be heroes. He wondered fleetingly what it would be like to be a Jerry, facing the same dangers, praying for deliverance to the same God, all the flipping padres busy on both sides, spouting praise and glory. All that aside, he reckoned these Jerries were bluffing. In due course they would piss off out of it and only then would the *Coverdale* be sunk. Rattray felt a familiar itch in his trigger finger as the Nazi officer left the tank deck and climbed up to the bridge.

He watched the Nazi salute Dempsey and the Commodore, all very formal and polite. The Nazi had a narrow, unpleasant face – looked like Gestapo but wasn't. What a bunch, salute and fire. Still, all officers were the same, velvet glove and iron fist. Rattray moved away from the Jacob's ladder, making across to the flying bridge where the naval party had been told off to muster to the Nazis' instructions. He was followed by a German seaman, who went on aft to the deck above the engineers' accommodation where he took charge of one of the close-range weapons and lined it up on Rattray and his gunnery rates. Rattray was wondering just what all this boarding was in aid of: before the Nazis had come aboard, he'd had a word with Porter, the Captain's steward, asking what was going on. But never mind big ears, Porter didn't know a thing. Or wasn't saying. Porter had looked dead worried, which wasn't surprising, they were all worried, all in the same boat. Literally. Rattray, however, didn't know what Porter's personal worry was: when the baby was born, it was going to be not only a bastard but a fatherless one, and what would happen to Beryl?

On the bridge, Kemp, also formal, had returned the Nazi officer's salute and uttered formalities. 'What's the meaning of this? What do you want with me?'

'You have a bag, with intelligence.'

'No.'

'Do not try to delay, Commodore. The facts are known.'

Kemp laughed. 'They may be. I accept that. But you're too late. Do you take me for a fool? The bag has gone overboard. I'm afraid your journey wasn't really necessary.'

The German stared back at him: the moon was once again shedding its light, and the angular, bony face, thin-lipped, arrogant, could be seen quite clearly. Another thing the moon had shown Kemp was that the U-boat had submerged again, down to periscope depth: where she had been on the surface was a thin feather of spray from the periscope as she kept level with the *Coverdale*'s bridge. The German said, 'I do not believe you, Commodore Kemp.'

Kemp gave a start. 'You know my name?'

'Yes. And mine is Cramm. *Leutnant* Cramm. This will not have been known to you.'

'Is it significant?' Kemp stared the Nazi in the eyes. 'How do you know my name?'

Cramm shrugged. He held a revolver loosely in his hand, and behind him, covering all the bridge personnel, were two of his armed seamen. He said, 'Our German intelligence is good, that is how.'

'Agents planted everywhere –'

'Precisely, yes. Everywhere, Commodore Kemp. And our allies, the Italians . . . they also make reports on certain matters, and certain things have been relayed to my submarine. You understand?'

Kemp said, 'That bag. I say again, you're too late.'

'Not the bag – that too, yes, of course – but other things.' The Nazi brought up his revolver and levelled it at Kemp's chest. 'There is need to hurry, you will understand that. To search the ship will take time, but this will be done if necessary. You will not have disposed of what is in that bag, Commodore Kemp, of this I am certain. Now I have something else to tell you.'

'Go on, then.'

For a moment or two Cramm remained silent, staring back at Kemp. Then he said, 'Your son's life.'

'My son –?' Kemp felt the sudden lurch, the thump of his heart. What was this man talking of? How did he know, what did he know? The urge to ask many questions was almost overpowering, but Kemp resisted it. He had to remain calm, in control of himself and his emotions. It was a time for waiting. All he asked was, 'What is my son to do with you?'

Cramm spoke steadily. 'A destroyer in the Mediterranean, sunk in combat. Many men lost. Two of them swam away after the destroyer went down. They reached the island of Pantelleria. One of them was your son.'

Kemp swallowed hard. 'My son – is alive?'

'He is alive, yes. He was taken prisoner by the Italian garrison. Lists are rendered to Berlin of prisoners taken by our allies, Commodore Kemp. When your name became known as Commodore of this convoy, orders were issued from Berlin. Sub-Lieutenant Kemp is being transferred to Germany.'

Kemp's voice was hoarse now. 'In heaven's name . . . what for?'

Cramm smiled. 'Certain things are required of you, Commodore Kemp. Not just the bag.'

iii

'I'll be buggered!' Petty Officer Rattray pushed his cap back from his forehead and scratched at his head, glancing up at the close-range weapons aft as he did so. The Nazi gunner was on the ball, watching closely, and the look on his face said he would scarcely wait for an excuse to open fire. 'Just you keep it right where it is, Leading Seaman Sinker, all right?' Stripey had hidden the bag inside the top of his workings overalls and in the general fatness the bulge was not particularly noticeable. 'How did you get your hands on it, eh?'

Sinker said, 'Just 'appened to be passing, like, when the ship give that lurch. Something come down from the bridge . . . got caught up in the falls o' the seaboat. I grabbed it – that's all. Then the panic started, with the bloody Jerries coming across from –'

'All right, all right, I got the picture.' Rattray looked for'ard, up towards the bridge. The officers were still yacking and no orders had been passed from either side, British or Nazi. The *Coverdale* was continuing on course. On the flanks the British counter-attack was also continuing, but Rattray had no idea as to how the destroyers were doing. As he looked ahead he saw a shaded blue lamp flashing from what he believed was the *Nassau*: a signal from the senior officer to the Commodore? If that remained unanswered, help might soon be on the way. He turned back to Stripey Sinker. 'You're valuable property now, Leading Seaman Sinker. Or what you got is.'

'The Nazis'll bloody –'

'Skin you alive – yes. Not that we know what's in the bag, but we can make guesses. Secrets, right? What those buggers come aboard for. All as clear as flippin' day, it is, now. So what do we do, Leading Seaman Sinker?'

'I – I dunno.' Stripey chewed at his lip. 'Chuck it over the side. That's maybe what the bridge intended.'

'Yes. No doubt they did, unless someone was flippin' careless when that lurch came. Either way, it's not a decision I can take. Apart from which, Leading Seaman Sinker, unless you or me wish to commit immediate suicide, it wouldn't be exactly bloody wise, now would it?' Rattray jerked a thumb towards the hawk-eyed Nazi behind the gun. 'Hang onto it for now. Then we'll see. Maybe we can hide it away safe, pending orders from the bridge.'

'Hide it where?' Sinker asked dismally.

'Search me,' Rattray answered, looking around. He caught the eye of the Nazi gunner and swore beneath his breath. It was a question not only of where but also how. He looked again towards the bridge. A signal was being made, the message from the senior officer being acknowledged, presumably. Wool being drawn over his eyes, by order of the Nazi lieutenant? Rattray surveyed Stripey Sinker, looking more than jaundiced. 'You bloody would,' he said witheringly, 'wouldn't you, fat bag o' lard!'

iv

As Rattray had surmised, the Nazis on the bridge had dictated the response to the signal from the flag, which had been merely to convey information: six U-boats were believed to have been destroyed by depth-charge attack or by gunfire after surfacing following damage. Not surprisingly, this news was badly received by the German officer. But he said, 'You will signal your congratulations, Commodore. That only, very briefly, the one word, "Congratulations". If there is trouble, your ship will be sunk. You will be the first to die, you and all the others on the bridge.' He prodded with his revolver. Kemp passed the order to Leading Signalman Goodenough.

He said, 'Exactly as ordered, Goodenough. Nothing more.'

Goodenough obeyed the Commodore. Kemp could be presumed to know best, though Goodenough had an idea that if he signalled not 'Congratulations' but 'Bollocks' then something would be known to be amiss aboard the Commodore's ship. Command wasn't all that simple and straightforward and Kemp had the ship and her company to think about – and, it seemed, his son. Goodenough had heard all that and if Kemp was going to lean over backwards so far as possible for his son's sake, then it was wholly understandable. Goodenough was certain Kemp wouldn't lean over far enough to go arse over tit. Even a son wouldn't finally stand between him and his duty.

So the signal was made; there was no further exchange. The Rear-Admiral in the *Nassau* was well known to be one who gave commodores their heads and didn't interfere unnecessarily. And the convoy was still in its formation, minus the *Asian Star*, abandoned and left behind to sink, many of her troops picked up by other ships in convoy, many cramming the lifeboats to await succour when the attack had been beaten off. Until then, until he had to redispose the convoy columns when the attack was over, there was in fact nothing for the Commodore to do other than to plod on. Which, under German orders now, he was doing.

Once the congratulatory signal had been made, the world, for Kemp, seemed to have been stood on its head. The Nazi expounded: the U-boat pack was under orders to destroy the convoy; that was normal enough, of course. The particular U-boat shadowing the *Coverdale* was under orders to take possession of the sealed bag from Australia. Also a facet of war, though Kemp believed that Berlin had been misinformed and was reading much more into the bag's contents than was the actual fact.

But that was not all.

The *Coverdale* was to detach from the convoy and steam for the

port of Brest in Occupied France. A prize of war, a big fleet oiler with a part cargo of valuable fuel oil in her tanks. And, that apart, the mere fact of taking out a ship from a convoy and delivering her to the Fatherland would be a pinnacle of achievement, a glowing beacon in the German Navy's annals, a feather in the Führer's monstrous cap, a blow to the morale of the British.

And Kemp was to assist. Kemp would know how to do it without arousing suspicions. He could drop astern, making reassuring signals to the warships to keep them from intruding, and could deal with any allied convoys or escorts that they might meet as they came further north. Kemp could get them safely through as they neared the Western Approaches to Britain.

Knowing what the answer was going to be, Kemp asked, 'And my son, Lieutenant Cramm?'

'Your son will be well treated if you assist us. We do not wish to harm your men – and for you and the senior officers in particular we have a use, since the ship must be steamed. You as Commodore, I repeat, know the proper routines and require-ments to deal with interference. You are indispensable. Your son is not. I think you will understand, Commodore Kemp.'

Sixteen

'No surrender,' Dempsey said. His face was set hard; steel was showing. 'I'm sorry, Commodore. I know the – fix you're in. If it was my son –' He threw up his arms. 'Who's to say, until it happens? But you must see my point as well. I'm in command –'

'I've never disputed that.' Kemp felt his nails dig into his palms as he did his best to keep his tone level and reasonable. The Nazi officer was behaving very properly, so far at any rate. Although he had disposed his men about the ship so that all vital areas were covered by the sub-machine guns, although the officer of the watch and the helmsmen were under constant surveillance, although two Nazis had taken control of the engine-room, the Commodore and the Captain had not been unduly interfered with. Kemp had asked for some time alone with Captain Dempsey; and this was allowed. Hot cocoa was brought to the chart room by Porter, whose fresh worry about being a prisoner of war for an indefinite period was making him all thumbs. There was an armed guard on the door to the wheelhouse and that was all. But Kemp was now under immense pressure: he had understood very well what Cramm had meant: he, the Commodore, could assist; but he could also act the other way and give the alarm to the senior officer while appearing to fake a reason to detach the *Coverdale*. And he could do the same all the way to Brest if they encountered a British ship. Kemp's son was the guarantee that he would not do this.

To Cramm, he had invoked the Geneva Convention, the proper treatment of prisoners of war. That had cut no ice. And Kemp knew that the Nazis would have many ways of covering

160

up when they were brought to book after the war was over.

Porter spilled some cocoa. 'What's up with you?' Dempsey asked testily.

'Sorry, sir.' Porter was shaking like a leaf in a gale, and his face was pinched.

'We're all in it, Porter.'

'Yes, sir, I know. But for some it's worse. Them bastards – they don't know what they're doing, sir.'

Dempsey gave a short laugh. 'On the contrary, Porter. They know very well indeed. Now then – what's worse, in your case? Better come out with it.'

Porter did; his tray and glasses rattled and he set it down on the chart table. The story poured out; Dempsey listened without expression. He didn't say a word but when Porter had had his say there was a difference. The steward said, 'It's better for talking about it to you, sir. Thank you for listening, sir. I'd got all sort of bottled up, like.'

'All right, Porter.'

When the man had left Dempsey said, 'What a time to choose! My fault, of course. And it's done some good. Now: where were we?'

'You said you're in command. You said no surrender. I go along with you, of course I do.' Kemp was sweating freely, and not from the chart room's closeness alone. 'All I'm asking for is time. Frankly, it's inevitable now. Suppose I make some sort of warning signal. What does that U-boat do, the moment the escort's seen to react? She's still got us all under periscope watch.'

Dempsey rasped at his chin: the question needed no answer. He sighed, heavily. 'You're right on that,' he said. 'So what's your proposal, Commodore?'

'We appear to accede, that's all. We're seen to realize we have no option. Then we bide our time.'

'We don't go all the way to Brest?'

'We do not. That's a promise, Dempsey. We'll not surrender the *Coverdale*. Far from it – we'll get her back.' Kemp took a pull at his cocoa, emptying the mug. 'One thing – we've got rid of that damn bag. Now it's time to tell Cramm we're co-operating.' He went to the door and with Dempsey pushed past the German sentry.

Dempsey's face was still hard as the mendacious signals went out to the flag: he detested allowing the Nazis their gloat, and he saw little prospect of Kemp's being able to bring off any recapture of the ship. True, the Nazis were outnumbered, but they had the U-boat – which, still at periscope depth, had shifted back into *Coverdale*'s wake for security from the asdics aboard the destroyers – they had a full U-boat's crew to call upon; and there would always be the big threat of the torpedoes.

In the meantime it was going to be a hard job to let his own crew and the naval gunners know the true score: indeed it might be better to keep them in ignorance for the time being, in case mouths were shot off. Rattray for one: Rattray was never slow in coming forward and might not be able to restrain himself from having a jeer in advance. That was something that must yet be discussed with Kemp. Dempsey watched as the leading signalman flashed the Commodore's signal: 'Flag from Commodore, am turning back to pick up any survivors from *Asian Star*.' The Rear-Admiral might have his objections, although the escorts appeared by now to have the attack held despite their own losses – two of the destroyers had gone, so had the two ballasted armament carriers, and another of the transports had been hit although she was still seaworthy and limping along. Kemp would disregard the senior officer's objections: as Commodore he could decide his movements for himself, and to have a regard for survivors might be foolhardy but would be seen as perfectly natural. So the *Coverdale* would drop astern and would not rejoin the convoy; she would alter course to Cramm's orders and head for the port of Brest, to take service under the German ensign, her crew transferred to the Fatherland as prisoners.

Within two minutes of the signal being made, the Rear-Admiral's reply came back: 'Commodore from Flag, you will proceed at your own risk. Cannot spare an escort.'

As expected, Dempsey thought: Kemp had worked that one out for himself. An escort would be unwelcome to the Germans.

'Excellent!' Lieutenant Cramm said.

Under orders, Dempsey brought the ship round to a reciprocal of her course. He called the engine-room. Evans answered from the starting platform, sounding what he was – under duress.

'Reversing course, Chief. All well below – within limits?'

'Within limits, sir, yes.'

'Keep your chin up, Chief.' Dempsey slammed down the voice-pipe cover. He was aware of having uttered a platitude, but what else could you do? And it just might give a hint that all this wasn't being taken entirely lying down . . . Dempsey recalled his own earlier doubts about letting anything be known. He'd believed in a clamp-down, but you had to allow hope.

Dempsey went out to the starboard wing and joined Kemp as the *Coverdale* steadied on her new course. They stood together, not speaking, each according the other silence in which to sort out his thoughts and emotions. After a few minutes Cramm came up behind them. He said, 'After dawn, Captain, your radio room will send out a signal, a Mayday call which will of course not be answered by your convoy. You are under attack. The transmission will be suddenly broken off.'

Dempsey said nothing. That signal would finally dispose of the *Coverdale* in British minds. In the, by then, far distant flagship, there would be visions of a last-gasp radio message before the big bang that closed the matter.

iii

From the decks the hands watched as the convoy vanished astern: the buzz had spread, the rumour that the Commodore was co-operating with the Nazis and pulling the ship out. Dempsey too: they were in cahoots. The opinions polarized: Kemp and Dempsey were shit scared and saving their own skins; alternatively, they'd had no option.

Whichever view was right, there was a loneliness now. Just a solitary ship, with that U-boat escort. Once the convoy was safely out of the way, the U-boat would presumably come to the surface and remain immediately handy with her gun and her torpedo-tubes. Chief Steward Lugg had come up for a look-see: he was thinking of his new grand-daughter . . . he wouldn't be seeing her for bloody years, if ever. If the Nazis won the war, and it was on the cards they might even though deep down in your heart you knew they never could win against the whole British Empire's might plus the men and munitions from the United States . . . if they *did* win, then you could kiss the past goodbye –

his wife, his daughter, his home, the baby, the lot. Freedom, too. No freedom under the Nazi jackboot, not for those British who came through in the POW camps or anywhere else. Hitler, triumphant, driving along Whitehall and the Mall to Buckingham Palace, heiling himself like all-get-out, that daft-looking arm raised and the moustached face one bloody big gloat as he hustled the King and Queen out. *They* wouldn't surrender. They wouldn't co-operate.

Not like some.

Lugg looked towards the bridge, saw in the moonlight the glint of gold oak-leaves from the two uniform cap-peaks. Christ, he thought, there could have been some attempt made, some sort of fight-back while they had the escorts handy. On the other hand, Lugg was well aware of the potentialities of oilers, not the best places to pick a fight. Even a chance bullet striking sparks off a tank top could be disaster. Funny things, unexpected things, could happen. Two of the *Coverdale*'s tanks had recently carried high octane stuff, aviation spirit, to Sydney. Those tanks were empty now, and had of course been cleaned, but Lugg remembered that summer tank not being properly cleaned. Any lingering fumes . . . maybe Dempsey and Kemp had had that in mind.

At the after end of the port-side flying bridge Petty Officer Rattray spoke to Stripey Sinker. He'd seen some of the Nazis mustering for'ard and he made a guess. 'Search party,' he said. 'That bag.'

Sinker gave a sound of terror. 'Best chuck it over, PO.'

'Don't be more of a prat than you can help, Leading Seaman Sinker.' Rattray rose and fell on the balls of his feet, hands clasped behind a stiff back, shoulders squared: once a gunner's mate, always a gunner's mate and sod Hitler. 'The buggers are still behind the gun, up there. Any move like that, and we've all had it. Which is why they've mustered us here, right?'

'What, then?'

'First of all, Leading Seaman Sinker, don't bloody *panic*. Bag's hidden for now, but not secure – easy to find in a search. What we got to do is to make it harder to find. So far as it's bloody possible, that is. Turn your back to the stern and face for'ard.' Rattray prodded two of the other ratings. 'You an' you, get round Leading Seaman Sinker. Cover him like, see? Now then.' He

164

reached into a pocket of his white shorts and produced his knife, which was attached to a lanyard around his waist. He removed the lanyard, slid it free of the knife's ring, and passed it to Sinker. Sinker stared at it, puzzled. Rattray said, 'Lucky you're wearing overalls.'

'Why?'

'Use your loaf, Leading Seaman Sinker. If it weren't for overalls, you couldn't have bloody hid it in the first place. Now the overalls are going to provide even better cover – if we go on being lucky. Now – bring the bag out, secure the lanyard to it, then shove it in your flies, right? Join your cock in seclusion.' Rattray gave a coarse laugh. 'Thereafter, try not to waddle like pregnant duck.'

'They'll see –'

'No, they won't, not if you don't draw attention.'

'But a bleeding personal search, PO –'

'Clamp your legs together. It's a better chance than up by your tit, right? If they get that far, well, it's just too bloody bad. Things do happen in war, you know. We can't all win, but we can do our best, right? Now – move!'

Stripey uttered a strangled bleat but was quite dextrous: the bag was tied and deposited uncomfortably between his legs in quick time. Not a moment too soon: the German seamen were coming aft, along the flying bridge. They pushed past towards the door into the after superstructure, no doubt to carry out a search of the engineers' quarters. Rattray assumed a similar search for'ard in the seamen's accommodation, another in the officers' cabins amidships. Then the store-rooms and such. They'd be unlikely to open up the tanks, of course, except maybe the empty ones. In any case they'd have their hands full and Sinker might be able to relieve himself of the bag by shoving it into an already searched section later. Meanwhile, Rattray cast about for some way of letting the bridge know that the bag was in good hands. Hands? Rattray chuckled to himself: between good legs.

The *Coverdale* moved at full speed on her temporary southerly course, the moon-streaked water swishing past her hull plates, the thump of the engines loud in the otherwise silent night, a light wind, made largely by her own speed, sighing through the standing rigging. It was, Rattray thought, a peaceful enough

165

scene for what amounted to a time-bomb to steam through. He thought in terms of a time-bomb because he was convinced that Commodore Kemp wasn't going to take the situation lying down, and no more was Captain Dempsey. Rattray considered himself a good judge of men, and anyway you didn't reach command by turning the other cheek too often.

On the bridge, Dempsey and Kemp paced, scarcely able to keep their eyes open, falling asleep for fractions of a second whilst on the move, coming to with a start to find themselves cannoning into each other or into the bridge screen. The Nazi seaman on guard followed their movements. Neither of them would admit the weakness of exhaustion: their place was on the bridge and there they would stay.

'Talk about something,' Kemp said suddenly. 'Anything, just to keep us awake.'

So Dempsey did. He talked about the past, repeating things that Kemp knew already. He'd had a varied life, starting off like Kemp in the sailing ships, the old square-riggers largely out of Liverpool for Cape Horn and Chile and across to Australian ports. He talked of Liverpool as he'd known it nearly forty years before, in the first decade of the century. A real sailors' town, more than sixteen hundred acres of docks, thirty-six miles of quays, any number of bars. Seamen from all the world rubbing shoulders in such public houses as the Bear's Paw, shipmasters and agents conducting their business largely in the saloons and dining-rooms over whisky at three-and-sixpence a bottle, everywhere thick with pipe or cigar smoke. The old-time music halls, too – a wonderful atmosphere, Dempsey said, and Kemp, who recalled it himself, agreed in a slurred voice. Dempsey had been an apprentice then; the Great War had seen him with a temporary RNR commission as a sub-lieutenant, serving the King in Q-ships and later minelayers. After the war he'd joined the RFA; and his first appointment as master was aboard an old gunboat, HMS *Racer*, salvaging gold bullion from the White Star liner *Laurentic*, sunk by a mine off Lough Swilly in Donegal. It had been a record at that time, he said, five million pounds worth recovered by the naval diving teams.

'I had a steward called Joss,' he rambled on, nearly asleep again. 'Had the curious habit of saying yoss instead of yes. Took my nephew aboard once, my brother's boy, the one . . . told you

166

about him, ex-POW. Four years old . . . Lad went around the ship saying "Joss says yoss" in a loud voice, quite embarrassing. . . .'

His voice trailed away. Kemp had crashed into him again; he took his arm and steered him. Kemp hadn't heard a word and the object of the exercise hadn't been achieved at all.

iv

The petty officer of the German boarding party reported to Cramm as the moonlight gave way to the first dawn of captivity; and Cramm confronted the Commodore.

'The search has produced nothing, Commodore Kemp.'

'You'd better search the floor of the South Atlantic.'

'Do not make jokes, please. I am convinced the bag is still aboard the ship.'

'You're entitled to believe that if you wish.' Kemp staggered, lurching back against the bridge rail. The dawn was fresh and spectacular, a sky shot with red and green and orange, over a sea beginning to shimmer to the sun's rays, stretching to far horizons, a flat calm . . . Kemp's mind reeled, he had the curious feeling that this was no longer the world, that he had had a glimpse of a better place where there were no Cramms, no Hitlers, no wars, no more responsibility for a convoy commodore. He wrenched himself back; back to the bridge of the *Coverdale* and Cramm's revolver. Cramm was speaking again, ironically solicitous.

'You are very tired, Commodore Kemp. You should sleep. You are no longer young. But you will not sleep. You will remain here until you tell me where the bag is.'

'I've told you. There isn't anything else to tell. The bag's gone.'

Cramm scowled, biting his lip. 'Let us suppose, just for a moment, that that is the truth. You will know what was in the bag.'

'No.'

'That also is a lie.'

Kemp remained silent; there was nothing useful to be said. He swayed again, reached out to the rail for support. As he did so he felt the blow, the sting of Cramm's hand, the bony back of it,

167

taking him across the face, twice, once each side. His head rang like a bell. He wasn't aware of Cutler coming across from the wheelhouse and taking Cramm by the scruff of the neck. He wasn't aware of Cramm turning, and squirming free; but he heard the crack of the Nazi's revolver and then he saw Cutler lying on the deck of the bridge, in a spreading pool of blood. Words came to him, blistering words of condemnation for Nazi barbarism. Cramm sneered, and his bunched fist took Kemp full in the mouth. Dempsey, he saw, was being crowded back into the wheelhouse under the guns of the German petty officer and two seamen.

Seventeen

Also under threat of a Nazi gun the *Coverdale*'s radio officer was brought from imprisonment in his cabin to send out the signal as dictated by Cramm, who reminded him that he spoke good English and could read Morse. Like any Mayday signal, it went out in plain language, not code or cypher: Cramm could monitor it. The drama was precisely played: when the essential words had been transmitted, the butt of Cramm's revolver came down on the radio officer's skull and the transmission ceased abruptly – and, to those who picked it up, no doubt convincingly. There would be no more: the radio officer was lifted and carried back to his cabin and once again locked in. From now on there would be the silence of a blown-up oiler, gone with all hands. Soon after this, the course was altered to the north-east.

Sub-Lieutenant Cutler, US citizen in the RCNVR, was a hero now: the only one who'd had the guts to hit back, according to some. According to others, foolish: he'd never had a hope and had probably made things worse for everyone thereafter – but there was general agreement as to guts. Cutler was currently in a bad way, said Chief Steward Lugg who had the responsibility of seeing to him in his cabin, under guard by a German rating. The bullet had entered his body on the right-hand side of the stomach and appeared to have lodged somewhere – there was no exit hole, anyway. The bleeding had been profuse. Blood-stained towels littered the cabin. Cutler was white and unconscious, probably, Lugg thought, from the loss of blood.

Lugg soothed his brow with a wet cloth and some ice from the ship's freezer. Lugg was no nurse, but he did his best, knowing that Cutler was due to kick the bucket if they couldn't get a proper quack to him pronto.

A fat chance of that!

There was some disturbance at the cabin door, an argument. Lugg went for a look-see: Porter, yacking at the Nazi sentry, who let him in but stood there at the open door with his gun aimed through.

'How is he, Chief?'

'Poorly.'

'What can you do?'

Lugg shrugged. 'Blowed if I know, lad. Where's the Old Man?'

'Still on the bridge. That Cramm, he's let Kemp go below to his bunk. The Old Man'll be next.'

'Generous!'

Porter said, 'Cramm knows they'll be bloody useless as they are now. And they're going to be needed.'

Lugg nodded, understanding the German need. He said, 'I reckon that bullet ought to come out – obvious, really.'

'Can you do it?'

Lugg said, 'I can *do* it, yes. There's a scalpel in the medical kit. But can I do it proper? Answer: no, I bloody can't. How do I know what I might cut through on the way? Gut, gristle, veins and arteries. Appendix. There's a long bowel, bloody feet of it so I've read. Chances are, I'll kill him.'

'He'll die if nothing's done, won't he?'

'Yes,' Lugg said simply.

'Well, then. I reckon that's your answer, Chief.'

'Not really my job nor my decision, lad. Skipper's the *official* MO aboard a quackless ship, you know that.'

Porter said, 'The Old Man's too dead tired to operate on a boiled egg, right now. And time's short by the look of him,' he added, indicating Cutler. 'I'll give you a hand, Chief.'

Lugg shook his head: there was an obvious and strong reluctance. He dithered, under the stare of the German sentry, under the sub-machine gun. He said, 'Well, maybe. But I'll need authority. Mr Cutler, he's Navy.'

'The skipper –'

'Not from what you say – he's probably not co-ordinating. And it'd be another worry. Same with Kemp. I'll take the authority of the senior naval bloke left on his feet.'

170

'Rattray?'

'Yes. Get him along, lad, all right?'

Rattray felt flattered to have his opinion asked, his approval sought in regard to a medical, or anyway surgical, matter. He looked very official and knowledgeable, and stroked his chin like a specialist considering his verdict. After a moment he gave it. 'Not my job. Ask the Commodore. Or the skipper.'

Lugg explained. 'Dead beat the both of 'em –'

'Commodore won't thank you if Mr Cutler pegs out. Tell you what. I'll take a look for myself. Know better then, won't I?'

Porter started off for Cutler's cabin, expecting Rattray to follow, but the PO put out a restraining hand, having just been struck by an idea: the bridge still had to be told about Sinker's bag, and he himself might never get the chance to tell Kemp – the Jerry guard would be too much present. He said, 'Just a minute. You got access to the Commodore and Dempsey still, have you?'

Porter said he had. Rattray said, 'Get a message through, can you? Just in case I can't.'

'I should think so, yes –'

'Right. Don't get over'eard by the Jerries. Tell one of 'em, Leading Seaman Sinker's found a bag with 'oles in it – they'll know what you mean. Tell 'em it's safe for now, but I'm awaiting orders from the Commodore soon as he can be told. All right? Don't make a muck of it. It's important.'

Porter nodded and with Rattray headed for Cutler's cabin. The Nazis seemed to proliferate, as though by some sort of automatic breeding process: they were always watching yet enough freedom was allowed for movement about the ship. After all, there wasn't anything the British could do: too many German guns, and the sea's isolation. Rattray was allowed by the sentry to look at Cutler from the doorway and he didn't go much on what he saw. He sucked in his cheeks, looking shocked, then blew out his breath. 'Curtains, I reckon,' he said. 'I'll go and wake Kemp.' Maybe, he thought, he'd get that chance of reporting the bag after all.

He went to the Commodore's cabin. He was stopped by the

guard. 'Look,' Rattray said truculently. 'I want a word with the Commodore –'

'*Nein.*'

'Bloody Hun –'

There was another *nein*. The snout of the sub-machine gun butted Rattray in the stomach and he stepped back, flinching. 'Bloody, sodding Nazi. Look, I –'

'Fuck off.'

'So you do bloody speak a proper language. Now listen, I –'

Rattray found himself taken from behind, another gun muzzle. He turned to face Lieutenant Cramm. He explained; Cramm listened, then said, 'I shall not permit speech with Commodore Kemp. I shall take the responsibility. We are merciful people. The operation will be done.'

'Right,' Rattray said, and went below one deck to Cutler's cabin. He felt relief that the decision had become a German one, almost might be considered an order. He gave the thumbs up to Lugg. 'How about an anaesthetic?' he asked.

'Haven't any. Bottle of rum with the cork lifted, like they did in the windjammers.' His own face pale and his hands already shaking, Lugg ferreted about in the ship's medical kit for the scalpel. He had no idea in all the world what to do. Just plunge in and hope for the best, hope to find the bullet and pull it out, and then plenty of bandaging to stop the flow of blood. He felt like a murderer, just thinking about it.

iii

When the dawn was well up, still in the freshness of the early morning before the sun bit, the body of Fireman Passmore, dead by the desperate hand of Stripey Sinker, was at last committed to the deep, sliding from the plank rigged on the tank deck guardrail aft, sliding from beneath the Blue Ensign as the ship lay briefly with her engines stopped. From a distance Stripey Sinker watched, the sealed bag still between his legs and getting in the way of things: peeing was potentially extremely dangerous, because a Nazi guard was always watching, but Stripey's turned back was a shield. To him, the bag had become a very personal bomb. The bloody Germans would go mad.

172

Dempsey watched from the bridge: he was not permitted to go down to the tank deck. It was Cramm who read the service, in English, demonstrating more of the Nazi mercy and good fellowship . . . they were a weird lot, Dempsey thought. They saw no inconsistencies in alternating phoney mercy with brutality. Like Adolf Hitler himself, who authorized the concentration camps and so on at the same time as patting babies' heads all over the Fatherland, the kindly despot – they just didn't see themselves as others saw them. Dempsey, motionless at the salute as the body hit the sea, caught sight of Leading Seaman Sinker standing on the flying bridge, gawping and with his legs a little apart. He recalled some earlier words from Cramm, when he'd asked permission – asked permission, aboard his own ship! – for the committal ceremony to be held. He'd been forced to explain.

'So, a murder. Who did this, Captain Dempsey?'

'No idea,' Dempsey said.

Cramm said, 'I shall find out. We in Germany do not condone murder. When we reach port, the man responsible will die.' Then, for no particular reason that Dempsey could see, he shot out his arm in the Nazi salute. 'Heil, Hitler!'

As Passmore's body, sewn into its canvas shroud, lead weighted for fast sinking, began to disappear, Cramm heiled again. Then he turned about and went into a huddle with his petty officer, who hurried below.

Cramm spoke loudly, in English. 'All British men are to remain precisely where they now are. Any who move will be shot. You will be joined shortly by the rest of the crew.'

Stripey Sinker gave a strangled bleat and looked around for Petty Officer Rattray: He knew what was coming: the personal search. He reckoned he'd had it. There was no way out. He couldn't disconnect the bag from Rattray's lanyard and throw it over the side in full view of the Jerries. Panic set in. He started running along the flying bridge, making further aft, away from Cramm, straight towards the armed Nazis, his mind a mere pool of unthinking terror. He heard the crack of bullets as he reached the deck above the engineers' accommodation, heard a lot of shouting, felt the wind of the bullets as they zinged past him. There was a stinging sensation, and the sudden dampness of running blood as he was hit, or anyway grazed, nothing too

173

serious, but something had happened to the bag, which was dropping. That bullet had parted the lanyard round his waist, a very near thing. He stopped, breath rasping in his throat like an organ, chest heaving, eyes wide now and staring back at his tormentors. He put his feet together in order to clamp the bag tight: it impeded him. It was no good now; he'd had it. He raised his hands in surrender. The Nazis got the message: Cramm gave the cease fire order and at that moment Stripey, starting to move for the ladder down to the flying bridge, trembling, put a foot on a patch of oil.

His feet went from under him and he fell sideways, his fat body coming slap across the guardrail of the poop deck with his top half, the heavy half, outboard and hanging over the South Atlantic.

He tried to grab with his feet. He failed. As men ran along the flying bridge, he dropped, straight into the water. The engines had not yet been started up again following the sea burial. Stripey lashed about with his arms and legs, desperately, creating a flurry of foam. He drifted off the ship's side, was aware of a line being thrown, with a lifebuoy. It went wide. Soon he became aware of a boat being lowered from the falls, with Nazis embarked. He kicked out and the bag dislodged. He shoved a hand into his flies and dislodged it further, into the deep ocean water. It sank. Thank God, fucking thing.

Hope returned: they couldn't pin anything on him, not for sure. The seaboat hung poised above the sea and was slipped. It took the water with a splash, came free of the side and was pulled fast towards him. That was when he felt the awful kerfuffle in the water, the dreadful proximity of a powerful body propelled by a lashing tail, then the slicing of a fin followed by the iron-hard clamp of teeth cutting through a leg. He screamed, and the water turned red. The boat wasn't fast enough. The shark did its work.

The boat came up: one of the Nazis was sick over the side. Too late now, the shark was despatched by gunfire. Stripey Sinker's body teetered just beneath the surface. What was left of it was stark naked. The torso was rolled over with a boathook. A Nazi seaman called up to the *Coverdale*'s deck, addressing Cramm. Cramm swore viciously, having put two and two together after Sinker's panic dash. The boat was hoisted to the davits, and Captain Dempsey once again put his engines ahead. Ten minutes

174

later he went below to his cabin: he was not prevented, though an armed Nazi accompanied him as far as the door and then remained on guard. Porter came through from the pantry, teacloth over his arm.

'Breakfast, sir?'

Dempsey shook his head. 'After that? Just coffee, Porter. Strong.' He lit a cigarette, his hand shaking. He'd had a very good view.

Porter said, 'There's a message, sir. From Petty Officer Rattray.'

'Well?'

In a whisper, standing close to Dempsey as he poured the coffee, Porter passed the message. Dempsey said, 'Pass it to the Commodore as fast as you can without being obvious.'

iv

Chief Steward Lugg was bathed in sweat. He wore only a pair of white uniform shorts and sandals, with a towel draped about neck and shoulders to catch the sweat from his face. His body hair was matted, sticking flat to chest and stomach, and he was covered in blood. There was an air of a butcher's shop. Things were not going well. To start off with there had been a lengthy delay: the medical kit contained just the one scalpel and it was as blunt, Lugg found, as a pig's arse, probably been aboard the ship since she was built and used too many times on seamen's corns, callouses and boils and God knew what else – opening tins? The tip had a bit of a twist and it was useless. Finding just the right sort of knife from the galley hadn't been easy, and once selected it had had to be cleaned and sterilized. Also, there had been the order from Cramm for all hands to muster on deck and that had entailed a good deal of argument and never mind mercy; the German PO would excuse no one without express orders from his officer. Cutler could wait. After the boat had returned to the ship, the search was conducted, the personal body search, for Cramm couldn't be sure about Sinker and was taking no chances. At last, after speaking to Captain Dempsey and Commodore Kemp, Porter had gone to Cutler's cabin to act as Lugg's assistant and the chief steward, shutting his eyes, had gingerly placed the

tip of his knife against Cutler's stomach in the region of the point of entry of the bullet.

Summoning up his nerve, he pressed. The knife was sharp and went in fairly easily. Still with his eyes closed, Lugg inserted two fingers and probed around.

'Anything there, Chief?'

'Sod all yet.'

There was plenty of blood. Lugg probed deeper and the flesh tore, but there was still something to be cut away so Lugg cut. He got a hand in, shuddering as he did so, and praying that he wasn't doing too much damage. The sweat went on pouring, the towel around his neck became soaked. Then he felt something hard.

'Got it,' he said. He clamped the object firmly between thumb and forefinger and pulled it out. It was, of course, the bullet. Lugg stared at it, shaking his head. He'd been lucky: the incision had been in the right place. He needed a good, strong drink, some of the rum. Cutler's face, he saw, was a nasty grey colour, bloodless, and the breathing was heavy, but he didn't appear to be feeling any pain, being still deeply unconscious.

Porter said, 'Well done, Chief.'

Lugg didn't hear him. Cutler's breathing changed, became for a moment harsher, then there was a sort of glug and gurgle and it stopped altogether. One of Cutler's arms flopped from the bunk and dangled down towards the deck of the cabin.

'He's a goner,' Lugg said, his voice hoarse, and with a note of disbelief although in all conscience he should have been prepared. 'Cut along and tell Rattray, lad.'

v

Porter met Rattray at the head of the ladder down which the PO had fallen in Simonstown. There were no Germans within earshot. Rattray sucked in his cheeks at the news that Cutler had bought it.

'Dirty bastards.'

'We did our best –'

'Not you, you oaf, the Nazis.' Rattray looked around before going on, 'Get that message across, did you, eh?'

'Yes. Kemp and Dempsey both.'

'And?'

'No orders,' Porter said.

'Uh-huh.' Rattray sucked at his teeth, frowning. 'They won't know the bag was still on Sinker.' He looked quickly at Porter: the steward wouldn't know what was in the bag, shouldn't by rights know anything at all about it, presumably, any more than Rattray himself. He wouldn't be seeing the significance though if he had any wits at all he'd be making accurate guesses. 'Another message, Porter: *Leading Seaman Sinker had the bag* – all right? Just that.'

'I'll see to it,' Porter said. They parted company. Later that morning, word came back to Rattray that Kemp was much relieved, was grateful for Sinker's quick thinking, and that once they were back in UK, Sinker's selfless act would be reported to the Admiralty.

'Died a hero's death, did he?'

'Something like that.'

Rattray scratched at his lifted jaw. 'Don't know so much about hero. Scared out of 'is mind and fell arse over bollocks into the drink, clumsy bugger.'

Porter felt a sense of shock at the insensitivity: Rattray read this in his face, and reached out to lay a hand on the steward's shoulder. He said, 'Face facts, lad. That's what 'appened. But never let it be said elsewhere, all right? Me, I'll go along with the hero lark when we get 'ome. If we do. Better for 'is old lady than a charge o' murder. This way, she'll get a pension out of it.' And what, he wondered to himself, about Fireman Passmore? Case not proven – both dead. Well, somebody always had to suffer in this world.

Rattray climbed the ladders to Cutler's cabin. He got there just as Kemp was leaving it, looking a sick man. Rattray saluted. Kemp returned the salute without speaking: Rattray had the feeling the Commodore couldn't trust himself to speak, not even to give the PO a good-morning, which wasn't like him. Kemp was taking it hard, Rattray thought.

Kemp was: he'd come to like Cutler, a dependable, intelligent officer, a US citizen who'd had no need to join the fight against Hitler's Germany at the time he had. Cutler, Kemp believed, would have gone far, both in the war and after it was over. When the *Coverdale* reached Chesapeake Bay, and Kemp refused to consider the fact that she might not, he would go to Cutler's home and face the parents.

On the bridge he nodded at Dempsey. 'I suggest you get some sleep.' he said.

Dempsey was looking haggard, deep hollows beneath his eyes giving his face an almost skull-like aspect. He said, 'Later.'

'I'm here now. I'll take over.'

'My ship, Commodore.' Dempsey gave a faint grin. 'I've a feeling something's going to happen very soon.'

Kemp lifted an eyebrow. 'Clairvoyant?'

'Perhaps.'

Kemp had an idea Dempsey was waiting for something he already knew was about to happen. Dempsey said nothing further and Kemp refrained from pressing: he was beginning to feel that Dempsey had organized something without reference to Kemp as Commodore. Commodore of what? There was no convoy now so far as he was concerned. In those ships still steaming north-westward for the Virginia Capes, the Vice-Commodore would have taken over and he, Kemp, would have been written off once the false Mayday signal had been picked up. The families at home? Kemp wiped sweat from his face. Nothing would have been said – not yet. No announcement would be made, at any rate while the main convoy was still at sea. Probably not even after the arrival: the Admiralty was never going to admit that an RFA oiler had been cut out from an escorted convoy by a boarding party from a U-boat. In due course it would be announced from Berlin, gloated over by Lord Haw-Haw, but it would be denied, put down to Lord Haw-Haw's usual lying boasts. Of course, in the meantime a story would have been cooked up, the women notified that their menfolk had gone, but for the moment they would all be in happy ignorance, the time for tears not yet come. Kemp thought again, as he'd scarcely stopped thinking, of his son, now apparently in German hands. He found no reason to disbelieve what Cramm had said since Cramm seemed to know his facts. It was a relief, but in the circumstances not much of a one, that Harry was still alive. As things were, whether or not he remained alive might be up to Kemp.

Or Dempsey?

In the wheelhouse, a voice-pipe whined. Neither Kemp nor Dempsey moved, but Kemp noticed a sort of tic in Dempsey's face, a betrayal of nerves. The third officer came out to make a report to the Captain.

'Captain, sir. Engine-room –' The third officer broke off: Cramm had come up the starboard ladder.

'Go on, Mr Peel.'

'Bearings running hot, sir. Mr Evans can't trace the fault. He wants to shut down, sir.'

Dempsey nodded. 'Telegraphs to stop, Mr Peel.'

Eighteen

Cramm went up to Dempsey, sparrow-like against Dempsey's bulk. He demanded, 'What is this for, Captain Dempsey? Why do you stop engines, without permission?'

'Permission?' Dempsey laughed. 'I need no permission aboard my ship –'

'We will not argue,' Cramm interrupted angrily. 'Why is the engine stopped?'

Dempsey repeated what the third officer had reported. 'Hot bearings mean trouble. You should know that, Lieutenant Cramm.'

'Why are the bearings hot?'

'I don't know. No more does my chief engineer, yet. We must be patient.'

Cramm muttered something in his own language: he was tense and growing angrier. 'I shall go to the engine-room,' he said. Dempsey nodded, said he would follow Cramm down himself. As Cramm left the bridge, Dempsey spoke briefly to Kemp.

'You'll take over up here, Commodore?'

'Of course –'

'Leave the rest to me,' Dempsey said. 'It's better that way. You'll see.' Without further explanation he left the bridge and deviated into his day cabin on the way down to the flying bridge aft. Porter was there, moving about with a dusting cloth. As Dempsey went towards his desk and rootled about in a drawer he spoke in a low voice to the steward.

'You're a useful go-between, Porter. Now you're going to

help save the ship. Can you drum up an excuse for a word with Petty Officer Rattray?'

'Yes, sir, I –'

'Good! Tell him I expect the U-boat to close us when the way comes off the ship. Tell him to pass the word around his guns' crews, and round our own hands as well. I want him to try to regain the guns . . . he'll recognize his opportunity when he sees it – tell him that.'

'Very good, sir.'

Dempsey said, 'Good man,' and squeezed Porter's shoulder briefly. He'd been in the cabin less than a minute. He came out carrying his long torch, the powerful one used for looking down to the bottoms of the cargo tanks. He brushed past the German sentry and strode out to the flying bridge. Reaching the after end he dropped down to the tank deck. Watched by the German ratings he stopped short, put a look of puzzlement onto his features, and walked across to one of the clipped-down tank tops, one of those that, now empty and cleaned, had carried aviation spirit, the dangerous high-octane stuff. He paused by the tank, bent as if to sniff the air around it, then shrugged and went back across the tank deck to the entry into the engineer's alleyway, a perhaps useful little charade completed. He hoped – he prayed – that Cramm and his party wouldn't know much about tankers cargoes, the unpredictabilities of high-octane spirit, and the general management of fleet oilers. Just enough to make them appreciative of the possible dangers.

Down along the alleyway he went into the air-lock, closed the door behind him, went through the next one, closed that, and descended the intricate web of steel ladders leading down to the starting platform.

Cramm was haranguing acting Chief Engineer Evans, who was shrugging and looking baffled.

'I see no heat, no red-hot bearings.'

'They don't have to be red hot to be dangerous.'

'Dangerous?'

'Dangerous in the sense that to keep the engines moving would lead to a seizure,' Evans said.

'And then?'

'Then we can't move.' Evans looked around as Dempsey

181

reached the starting platform. 'Sorry about this, sir. I hope it's not making things awkward up top.'

Dempsey grinned and said, 'As you can see, Lieutenant Cramm's not happy. Where's the source, do you know yet?'

'I'm not sure yet, no.' Evans' face was creased with worry, a good act Dempsey thought with satisfaction. The acting chief gestured towards the for'ard bulkhead of the engine-room behind the starting platform itself. 'I believe there's heat coming through there –'

'The cofferdam?' Dempsey put alarm into his tone.

'Yes, sir. I was just going to call the bridge for permission to open up for inspection –'

'One moment.' Cramm intervened, frowning. 'At first it was a heated bearing. Now it is a cofferdam. I see no connection between bearings and cofferdams.'

'No connection, no. This is something else. If the cofferdam's heating, and God knows why it –'

'What is this cofferdam?'

Dempsey caught Evans' eye and took over. 'The cofferdam seals the cargo tanks off from the rest of the ship fore and aft – two cofferdams, two pumping stations –'

'You are saying there is danger, Captain Dempsey?'

'The cofferdam is hard alongside an empty tank that recently carried high-octane aviation spirit. And we've had trouble already. I think I detected gas a few minutes ago – and now my chief engineer suspects heat in the cofferdam. There's nothing aboard a tanker more dangerous than an empty tank that may not have been properly cleaned. Hydro-carbon gases from oil residue . . . it's best described as a bomb, one that's liable to go up at any moment.' Dempsey turned his back on Cramm and spoke urgently to Evans. 'Open up the cofferdam at once, Mr Evans. In the meantime, clear the engine-room of all hands.'

He turned back to Cramm: the Nazi was wide-eyed, clearly scared, clearly out of his depth. He said, 'You think –'

'I think we're liable to go sky high at any moment, Lieutenant Cramm.'

Cramm was first up the ladders, his skinny body moving like a streak of lightning. He was followed by the two Germans on engine-room watch. Dempsey grinned again and gave Evans a thumbs-up. Maintaining the charade they climbed the ladders

182

fast behind the greasers and firemen. As Dempsey emerged onto the tank deck from the alleyway he saw Cramm making his way for'ard with his petty officer, who was shouting orders in German to the ratings of the boarding party, one of whom was making fast up the ladders to the bridge. Soon after the man reached the bridge Dempsey saw the signalling projector in action, saw the answering flash from the U-boat. By this time the hatch into the cofferdam was being opened up: none of the Germans noticed that the overall pockets of the fourth engineer, who was going down for the inspection, were filled with cotton-waste.

Dempsey lifted an arm to Rattray, who was on the port-side flying bridge.

Rattray gave a nod, and waited, feeling excitement mount.

Dempsey, also, waited: the U-boat was already starting to close the *Coverdale*, coming up towards the oiler's starboard side. Cramm was right for'ard in the eyes of the ship. The Germans who had taken over the after 3-inch were still at their station but their attention was on the U-boat. To Dempsey they had the appearance of dogs straining at the leash.

Three minutes later, Evans appeared on deck, moving fast, shouting. 'Smoke from the after cofferdam, sir!' As he spoke, a rising trail was seen, spiralling out from the engineer's alleyway to waft for'ard over the tank tops.

Dempsey looked towards the U-boat. It was now within six cables' lengths, moving up fast, still to starboard, a nice clear surface target. Dempsey lifted his voice in a carrying shout.

'Mr Peel, there is fire in the after cofferdam. Swing out the boats – prepare to abandon ship!'

From the corner of his eye he saw the Nazis, the after gun's crew, drop down fast to the flying bridge and go for'ard at the double; and saw Rattray and some of his gunnery rates move the other way. Within thirty seconds Rattray had his gun in action.

ii

Evans had already had his orders from Captain Dempsey: as soon as he had made his report of fire in the cofferdam he had gone back into the alleyway and collected his engine-room hands,

183

waiting by the air-lock. He gestured them to get below, going down after them and putting the engines to full ahead after he'd called the bridge. Once again the *Coverdale* began her movement through the water. Petty Officer Rattray, eyes blazing, lips moving in a succession of oaths, had his gun well and truly laid on the approaching U-boat: point of aim, the base of the conning tower. The range was nicely close. His second shot had taken out the U-boat's casing-mounted gun; two minutes later a shell sped over the conning tower itself, smashing through the machine gun and the man behind it. Rattray grinned savagely as his loading number rammed home the next shell and the breech closed. In the water between the oiler and the U-boat were bobbing heads, making it as fast as possible for security: many of the Nazis had jumped the gun as it were, not waiting either for Cramm's order or for the *Coverdale*'s boats to be got away. Dempsey was now at the seaboat's davits, passing his own orders to his crew. The word hadn't got round them all, and to those not in the know the fire was real. By this time Cramm had ticked over and the remainder of his men, clustered by the bows, were firing towards the seamen on the master's deck where the seaboat was being lowered for embarkation. Dodging bullets, Dempsey got his men into cover aft of the bulkhead outside the officers' quarters. On the bridge Kemp, at first bewildered but getting the point fast, also dodged bullets as he gave the helm orders to close the U-boat.

Peel asked, 'D'you intend to ram, sir?'

'I'll try it. But the first thing is to present as small a target as possible – don't forget the torpedoes.'

As the ship's head came round Rattray fired once again before shifting his bearing. He'd been close before, very close: he was a first-class gunners' mate. This time he was right on target. The shell exploded slap on the base of the conning tower, there was a brilliant flash, the conning tower sagged and toppled, and a large hole opened in the fore casing. Kemp, watching through his binoculars, saw that the shell had split the casing down the port side. The U-boat was taking water fast and developing a pronounced list to port. It was just a matter of time. As Rattray scored another hit Kemp took a deep breath and spoke to the third officer.

'Telegraphs to slow ahead, Mr Peel. Wheel amidships.'

'Slow ahead, sir, wheel amidships.' The orders went to the helmsman and the starting platform. Kemp moved to the voicepipe and called the acting chief engineer.

'All over, Mr Evans. I'm moving in for survivors – that's all.' Then he remembered Cramm and his armed Nazis in the fore part of the ship. As he did so he saw movement by his side: Leading Signalman Goodenough was making for the ladder to monkey's island, where the close range weapons stood idle. A moment later Kemp heard Goodenough's shout.

'All right, you bastards. Guns over the side – or else!'

iii

It had been something of a miracle, Kemp thought two weeks later as the masthead lookout reported the landfall off the Virginia Capes. Full speed all the way, no more alarms or excursions, no escort until after some days the *Coverdale*'s speed had enabled her to overtake the convoy. There had been astonishment in the Rear-Admiral's welcoming signal: a ship and her company had returned from the dead. There had been no more enemy attacks; but the *Coverdale* had her wounds to lick nevertheless, the wounds of the closing stages of the shipboard battle for final control, for the Nazis had not given up easily. Third Officer Peel had died in the sub-machine-gun fire; so had Dempsey, down by the seaboat's falls, a sad reward for his initiative. Light enough casualties, perhaps, for the recapture of a ship, the sinking of one of Hitler's U-boats and the taking prisoner of Cramm and a number of German seamen, now under lock and key and one of their own guns held by a British naval sentry. Light enough in number, but each man a human loss, someone who would go home no more. . . .

The convoy moved towards the outer approaches to Chesapeake Bay: the pilot boats came out, signals were exchanged with them and, as the ship came closer in, with the US Naval Operating Base of Norfolk, Virginia. There were unanswered questions: had that prickly Australian in the High Commission at Cape Town been a traitor, a spy for Hitler – or merely an enemy of Brigadier Hennessy and his ideas of keeping the Australian troops back for the defence of the homeland? And what about Hennessy himself, what about that bag now gone for ever beneath the waters of the South Atlantic? Kemp had a feeling he might not have heard the last of that.

And Dempsey? Why had Dempsey not taken him into his confidence in regard to his plans for re-taking his ship? Kemp had worried a good deal over that. He saw two possible answers: one, Dempsey had had some sort of idea, a misconceived one in fact, that if Kemp was seen by the Nazis not to be taking an active role himself, then things might go easier for Kemp's son in German hands. Two – and the more likely – Dempsey had believed that when it came to the crunch Kemp might not have jeopardized his own son, might have played for safety. If he'd thought that, then he'd been wrong. But Kemp could see the point: Dempsey wouldn't have wanted to risk any personal reservations leading to an abort.

In any case, the truth would never be known now.

Kemp breathed deeply of the land: it was a bright, fresh day, with clouds moving before an offshore breeze, and America could be smelled, a welcome smell of journey's end as the convoy came between the arms of the land, between Cape Henry and Cape Charles. Away ahead an old stern-wheeler moved across Chesapeake Bay from Norfolk to Newport News. Had it not been for the big troopships, the warships and the guns, it could almost have been the Mississippi in the eighties or nineties.

Porter was at his side. 'Coffee, sir? Before the pilot, sir. Captain Dempsey, he always liked coffee before the pilot come aboard.' There was something like an appeal in his voice: he wanted things to be the same, as if Dempsey was there still.

'Captain Dempsey said he often did his own pilotage, Porter.'

'Yes, sir. But not in a strange port. Didn't take *foolish* risks, sir. Not Captain Dempsey.'

Kemp felt himself rebuked. He said, 'All right, Porter. Thank you.' The steward had already brought the coffee on a tray; it would have been churlish to refuse. Kemp drank; Porter went below.

Chief Steward Lugg was on deck, watching the land as it slid past. He said, 'Mail should be aboard soon. Maybe a photo of my grand-daughter. Never thought I'd ever see that, not till the war was over anyway. There's a lot to thank Kemp and the Old Man for.'

186

'That's right,' Porter agreed. He was thinking of Beryl, who would no longer be alone in her pregnancy. Funny, the way things turned out in war, the way things could change. There ought to be a letter for him as well. Rattray, also looking out at the land, knew there would be at least one for him, the almost daily moan from home with Ma Bates' illnesses in detail. There were some things that didn't change no matter what, not until death intervened. Sometimes Rattray felt he would peg out before Ma Bates and that wouldn't be fair. . . .

Below on the starting platform acting Chief Engineer Evans followed the pointers of the telegraphs as the bridge signalled slow ahead: the ship would be beginning her approach to the berth now. Journey's end . . . Evans gave a sigh of relief and mopped at his face with his handful of cotton-waste: he believed he'd acquitted himself all right and next time the telegraphs were rung to stand by for the outward passage he would no longer be doing his first trip as chief and things would be that much easier. He hoped he'd have earned his father-in-law's approval at last, that now he would be regarded as a professional ship's engineer.

Kemp, on the bridge as the *Coverdale* moved alongside, braced himself mentally for the rush of shore officials, both naval and civilian, who would inundate the Commodore's ship the moment the lines were secured and the gangways rigged. Perhaps there would be official news of his son, perhaps Cramm had lied . . . not, if you looked at it one way, a happy thought. Now he couldn't wait to get home; but there was still the North Atlantic in between.

One more convoy, less its losses, safely in. One more of life's chapters over and done with, never to be exactly repeated no matter how many more convoys. Kemp was dog tired but many people would be claiming his attention before he could find sleep. There would be reports to write, one of them being a commendation for Petty Officer Rattray; others for Captain Dempsey and young Cutler and Leading Seaman Sinker, posthumously. Uselessly, really; it wouldn't bring any of them back. Somewhere, somebody would be missing them. And God damn this war.